*Back then I thought
that if it weren't for
that cliff, our cities
would be one and there
would be no need for
all this fierceness towards
each other. But then
I learned about pride
and tradition and
prophecy, and those
things are even
harder than rock.*

ARIADNIS

JOSH MARTIN

Quercus

QUERCUS CHILDREN'S BOOKS

First published in Great Britain in 2017 by Hodder and Stoughton

1 3 5 7 9 10 8 6 4 2

A CIP catalogue record for this book is available
from the British Library.

ISBN 978 1 78429 821 0

Printed and bound in Great Britain by Clays

MIX
Paper from
responsible sources
FSC® C104740

Quercus Children's Books
An imprint of Hachette Children's Group
Part of Hodder and Stoughton
Carmelite House
50 Victoria Embankment
London EC4Y 0DZ

An Hachette UK Company
www.hachette.co.uk
www.hachettechildrens.co.uk

For Mum and Dad. Of course.
Also, for anyone who has ever told me a story.
This one's for you.

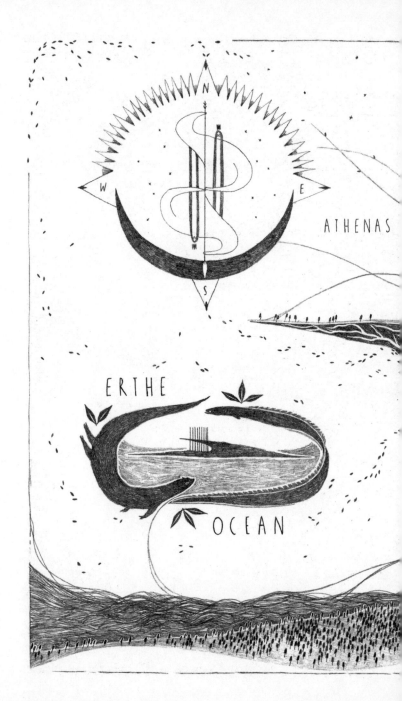

ATHENAS

ERTHE

OCEAN

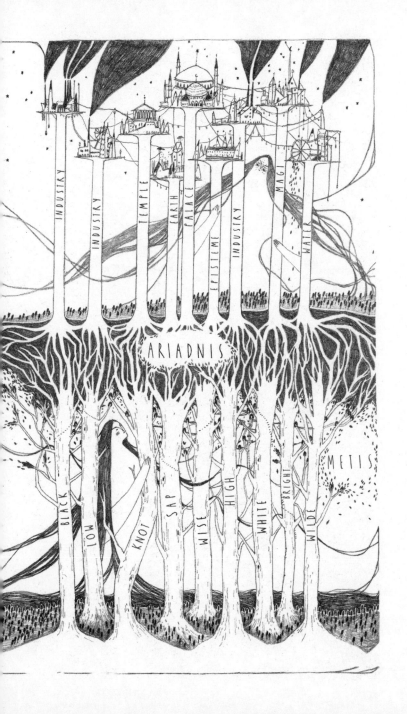

The Chosen

We are the ones who came after the comet.

We are the ones who survived the Great Wave.

We were Chosen Ones, once, and we had many voices.

But the people we were have bled into one another, like water droplets gathering on a leaf.

So we no longer remember . . .

Who . . .

Was who.

But we remain; we are here, waiting. We are in-between, in the home of the Wise One: Ariadnis – carved inside the cliff shelf that stretches out between the last two cities on the last island.

It is an improbable setup: the rock should not be able to reach so far without crumbling. The metal city above should collapse onto the city beneath, the city of trees. But it doesn't. It should not be possible, but it is.

There is but a single path that joins the cities and it begins there on that topmost ladder rung through the trapdoor in the owlery. It spirals down the tallest pillar of Athenas and continues into the cliff. It winds past the entrance of Ariadnis and descends to that hollow passage accessible from the topmost branches of Metis.

The path is like a nerve: a feeling, a promise of unity, however reluctant, and that feeling has never been stronger than now.

We know the moment that the newest Chosen Ones come into the passage because the nerve is, all of a sudden, ablaze.

365 Days

Athenas, City of the Nine Pillars

Aula

Cos today is my birthday, seventeen owls are culled outside my window at dawn.

I can hear each bird screeching before its neck is wrung. Then there's the murmur of the priestess giving the blessing: 'Let the knowledge of the Wise One pass to the Chosen One on this, her seventeenth birthday, that she may better know how to serve Him. That she may better know how to serve her city. That she may better know how to serve herself.'

I blink myself awake, wincing at the smell of incense over the top of oil and spice and hard, thick heat, which means the people in the kitchens are already hard at it.

'Aula.'

I look up and see Nadrik is in the doorway.

'What?' I groan.

His eyes bore into me. You've gotta wonder if he was born with that brooding put-upon-but-don't-worry-I'm-a-martyr look or if he's been cultivating it since they made him Anax – that's the leader of our government – back when I was nine. I guess the government are probably regretting that now cos they don't seem to get to do much. Nadrik would probably say they never did much in the first place anyway, and I'd just agree, cos like hell I know more about politics than he does and anyway, his people love him and no one's trying to throw him off the throne so . . .

He says, 'I'll meet you in the courtyard in five minutes.' Then he's gone.

'Oh, and by the way, *happy birthday*, Aula,' I mutter.

I crawl outta bed and find a tunic that might've been white once buried under all the crap on my floor.

'And can I just say what an excellent Chosen One you're turning out to be. Everyone in the city thinks so. I certainly do. You're brilliant. Actually, now I think about it, why don't you stay in bed.'

I root around for a headscarf and stuff every straggly bit of my too-long ginger hair up under it. The warped, black-edged mirror Nadrik gave me last year fell off its bracket a few days ago and I'd have to relieve it of some underwear and a few dirty plates if I wanted to stand it up. Judging by how puffy my eyes feel, I'm guessing looking into a mirror en't gonna be the most morale-boosting experience so I just rub my face with water and thank the Wise One that being Athenas's Chosen One en't any kind of beauty contest.

My best friend Etain ambushes me in the courtyard, outside the palace tower where I live. She throws a necklace she made in her workshop over my head as a present and hands me a book from her mother.

'Ma wanted to come down but no one was there to take over her shift in the prophet house,' she says.

'Perils of being Head Prophet,' I say, wondering if my smile is enough to convince her it doesn't bother me that Etain's ma, Ashir, en't wishing me a happy birthday herself.

Clearly it en't, cos she hugs me. She smells of metal and scorched hair and there's a burn going black on her smooth brown shoulder. She says, 'Party later,' all quiet so we en't overheard and, 'Meet in your room at ten.'

I say, 'Can't wait,' and we do this dumb fingerlock thing that we started when we were, like, five, and never grew out of. Then Nadrik does his creepy magi trick, appearing right next to us, and Etain bows, 1) cos he's Anax, and 2) cos she's the Anax's scribe, which basically means his assistant and involves a whole bunch of thankless jobs I wouldn't want to do.

'Sire,' she says.

'Lady Etain,' he says.

'I hope the day is good for you,' she says, and her voice switches instantly from the lazy, shortened sounds that we use with each other to clean, round syllables that make you sound like you're chewing on them.

'And for you,' he says. 'Come, Aula.'

'I en't a dog,' I mutter, but he's already walking away.

It's so hot my skin feels like an apple's shrinking tight in an oven. I swear Nadrik's taking us on the route with the least shade, but at least we get to go past the viewing point, where you can see the rest of the city sprawled out below.

It *is* sort of amazing, my city.

I've been told that, originally, the nine pillars that keep us in the sky were made out of nine trees. The trees are still alive, somehow, but they don't look like trees any more.

They're cased in metal, and hollowed to house the steam machines that power our buildings and water systems and all that. Each pillar supports a wide plateau – the same shape as a dinner plate, but half a mile across; and each has the same concentric-circle pattern of simple whitewashed houses and cobbled streets. Add watch towers, chimneys and pillars; connect each plateau with bridges and platforms and interlocking stairwells and there you have it: Athenas.

As we pass the view, I have the brief fantasy of taking the ladders down to another plateau for some nice birthday shopping like a normal person, but the dream wilts pretty quick as we turn away towards the owlery, and the breeze coming from that direction tells us about all the dead rodents the city owls have eaten.

It smells worse up close. I crane my head nervously as I follow Nadrik in through the arched door, wondering if any of the bright-eyed faces up there are pissed at me for those of them that got murdered just now in my name. I look into their yellow-eyed, I-will-kill-you-if-you-move faces and try and stare them out. *Look*, I wanna say, *it en't like I ever said, What I really want this year is a dead owl for every year my heart's been thumping, and while you're there do you mind hanging their corpses outside the palace temple.* The owls don't move. Maybe they're biding their time. Waiting to avenge themselves at my funeral when they get my head to chew on while everyone meditates on how all the wisdom in my brain is being passed to them, and through them, to the Wise One.

Nadrik clears his throat, which is what he does sometimes

to get my attention, and I know he wishes he didn't have to do it cos it ruins his air of mysticism. He's holding open the trapdoor that's in the floor of the owlery, which no one ever seems to discover (and judging by the owl shit caked on it, no one ever will).

'Yeah, yeah,' I say, like I en't in the least bit bothered about treading on all the mouse bones.

I approach. Below us is a ladder and then a platform, and below that, another ladder, another platform. It goes on for ever. And every year I struggle to get my head around it: we're going down into the hollowed-out trunk that holds this plateau over a mile up in the sky.

Nadrik clears his throat again and I snap, 'Yeah, OK, I'm going.'

Metis, City of the Nine Trees

Joomia

I wake up and remember what day it is. The air tastes of heat and warning, but it's still early. No one else is awake. My hands shake as I fold my blankets. I go to wash. I brush my hair.

'Happy Birthday,' says a voice.

I jump and Taurus laughs his rich laugh. He has a basket in his hand.

'Tea,' he says, putting down his basket in order to knot his dreadlocks high on his head. 'Brightbird eggs. Eros's flatbread,' he continues. 'I'm even going to cook for you.'

I smile sadly and shake my head.

'Why not? We've got plenty of time before Mathilde comes to get you.'

I shake my head again, and point.

He turns, and there is Mathilde, Elder of Metis and my mentor, standing at the end of the branch that leads to my hut. 'Can't it wait till after breakfast?' Taurus asks as she nears us.

'I dunno,' Mathilde snaps. 'Can we wait another *three hundred years* for a Chosen One?'

'Ah, come on, Mathilde. It'll take twenty minutes.'

'Twenty minutes worth risking the lives of all your people, Master Taurus?'

'She needs breakfast,' Taurus says, looking mutinous. 'It's her *birthday*.'

'But she remembers what is expected of her!' Mathilde snarls. 'More than I can say for you.'

Taurus gives me a furious look that says, *Go on, tell her*.

For a moment, I feel hot and frustrated and on the verge of the kind of tears that only appear when you're hot and frustrated. Because I've dreamed of having a voice – a real voice that I could surprise them with at a moment like this. Instead, I have only the voice I can pitch from my mind at a tiny handful of people – these two included.

Let's go, Mathilde, I say.

'Come on then,' she grunts.

Taurus clutches his basket like I've wounded him. I touch his arm.

Sorry, I say, but he doesn't answer.

I used to have this dream where I was flying along the shore of our island, looking towards the land.

The last two cities in the world: the nine trees of my city, whose branches tickle the underside of the cliff shelf that yawns out over us. On top of the cliff, Athenas, the *other* city, whose nine trees barely justify the name, devoid of branches and covered in hard steel casings. If it weren't for the fact that the roots of these trees grow thick and healthy through the cliff shelf to tangle in the branches of our own, you would have thought them dead.

Back then, I thought that if it weren't for that cliff shelf, our cities would be one and there would be no need for all this fierceness towards each other. But then I learned about pride and tradition and prophecy, and those things are even harder than rock.

I think of this as Mathilde leads me away from my hut, up through the hollow passages of the cliff rising up out of the forest – the tallest trees you've ever seen, sprawled out before us in a lattice of branches so thick you can't see how far the trunks go down. This is my city. This is Metis.

If I squint, I can make out Taurus's thin figure watching us leave from between some of the outermost branches. But then we have to turn up through the tunnel in the cliff and the space around me draws in, and there is only dank stone and darkness.

'Exciting day,' Mathilde says, and I hear the clank of her bracelets as she claps. Light appears between her long, pickled-looking hands and spreads out around us in dingy clouds. She shakes her three long braids down her back and smiles at me out of her strange old face. She seems to be waiting for me to say something – perhaps to agree: *yes, it's an exciting day, isn't it?*

I nod, to please her and she gives me a knowing look.

I'm fine, I say. But I'm not. My throat feels small. My insides are vinegar.

We walk. The tunnel ascends gradually, in a tight spiral that has tighter consequences on the muscles in my legs. We're many turns up when I feel it: that tug in my solar plexus. I stop, gritting my teeth.

Mathilde looks back. 'Joomia?' she says.

It's nothing, I say. **She's coming. The other Chosen One.**

12

'You can sense her,' Mathilde says.

I shake my head, because she's looking at me like I might suddenly have an explanation for the phenomenon I've felt every year on this day.

She is . . . stronger this year, I say.

Mathilde presses her lips together. 'Come on,' she says. 'Let's keep going.'

The ascent takes ages, but we Metisians are no strangers to climbing. Eventually, we reach the strange place in the tunnel. Ahead of us, it spirals upwards out of sight. Off to our right, it widens into a circular cavern.

'He's late again,' Mathilde says, and she makes a kind of *humph* noise as she settles herself against the wall of the tunnel.

I glance into the cave, where the door to Ariadnis is. There is the archway – the entry to the Wise One's home, outlined by pale orbs of mineral which are stuck fast into the rock. I take a step towards it, and the markings in the doorway shimmer, as if I've passed a beam of light over them.

'Might be wise to have a look, kid,' Mathilde says.

But I'm afraid to leave the pool of light she's created. All I want to do is go back. I want the heat of real air around me, and Taurus making me laugh, and the smell of the soap bar that Ade makes for me every year.

'Don't be nervous,' she says. 'You've done your best this year.'

But I *am* nervous. If the past Chosen Ones don't approve of me, of how much I've learned, it's the end. Athenas will win the Wise One's book and the island will be theirs. After nine generations, I will be Metis's downfall.

Mathilde glances up the passage, as if she's heard something. But when nothing appears, she says, 'Tell me what you know about how the Chosen Ones came to be, Joomia.'

Aula

'Tell me what you know about Ariadnis and its guardians, Aula,' Nadrik says as we climb down, deeper into the cliff.

'Why?' I say.

'Because I am asking you to.'

'But you *know* what I know about being one of the Chosen Ones,' I snap. '*You* taught it to me.'

Joomia

I shift irritably. *Mathilde*.

'Why not? Good to remind yourself of why you are here.'

I suppose at least this will distract me from my nerves. I close my eyes and think of everything I've learned by rote: **There have been nine recorded Chosen Ones in our time. Since the Great Wave that covered the world, since our ancestors came here – to the last island on Erthe – there has been a Chosen One for every generation. When the ancestors first arrived, they warred over how to build a new world: should**

14

they keep the industry that had once dominated the planet, or should they start anew, embrace a natural life?

Aula

'And everyone got pissy with each other for a long time—'

'*Aula*,' Nadrik says, and I roll my eyes but carry on.

'Until they decided that their issues couldn't be resolved and they had to go and build their cities separately. Then they found this cliff with nine vishaal trees growing underneath it and nine growing on top of it. Which sounds a bit convenient to me, but there you go.'

'*Aula*.'

'One half of the ancestors went to the top of the cliff and made Athenas. They hollowed out the trees and filled them with machines that would be powered by steam. The other half went to live below the cliff in the other nine trees and called it Metis.'

Joomia

But this didn't stop their disagreements, especially when Athenas began to build more and more ostentatious things and use the island's resources wastefully. Soon, the two cities were at war again.

Aula

'. . . And the war went on for years and years, which is pretty surprising cos of how Metis is made of *wood* so I dunno why someone didn't think of just burning it down.'

Nadrik makes an impatient noise. 'Aula, you know very well the pillars of Athenas are *also* made of wood. And I have no doubt you also recall that vishaal trees are naturally fortified. How else did they become the tallest trees in *this* climate? They cannot be burned.'

I pause to think about that. Possibly someone did tell me that in a lesson once. The question is whether I was listening.

'Carry on,' Nadrik says.

'So the war went on and on. And the people reduced their populations even more, which I'm sure is *exactly* what they wanted to happen.'

'*Aula.*'

'Yeah, yeah. Anyway. Their war woke the Wise One.'

Joomia

She had slept in the cliff for a long time, but they had disturbed Her.

I am the God of this island, She said. *What do you mean by this fighting? How dare you disturb the balance here!*

Wise One, the ancestors said. *If you are truly the God of this island then tell us who is more worthy of it.*

You must prove yourselves, She answered. *The thing I prize above all things is wisdom.*

16

Aula

'And so He decreed that for the next nine generations, the ancestors would choose a Chosen One who would dedicate their life to proving their worth. The Chosen One – boy or girl – would be born with the shape of a vishaal cone upon them, to symbolise the trees from which each city took shape.' My hand moves unconsciously to the splattered birthmark on the back of my neck and I shiver.

'Go on,' Nadrik says.

'On their eighteenth birthday, each Chosen One would travel into the cliff where the Wise One lived and enter His home – Ariadnis. There, they would complete a task for Him, and there they would die.

'None but the Chosen One could do this, and woe betide any person foolish enough to try to enter Ariadnis without the mark of the Chosen upon them. The first city to produce a Chosen One would be Metis, and then it would be Athenas, and so it would go on, until the time came when eight generations had completed the Wise One's tasks. When that happened, the cities would *both* produce a Chosen One at the same time – someone to represent each city in a competition for the Wise One's favour.'

Joomia

The winner, She said, *shall have my book.*

'And what book was that, Joomia?' Mathilde asks, as if she doesn't already know.

17

It was the Book of Omniscience, I say. A book that would grant the one who read it all the knowledge in the world. Whichever Chosen One won the book would win the war. It would be hard – these Chosen Ones would have to be trained and honed, and for this reason the Wise One would only allow them access to Ariadnis on the day of their eighteenth birthday. *I will bless these Chosen Ones with certain powers, so that their opportunities are equal*, the Wise One promised, then She said: *Since you cannot be trusted with my lands, you are no longer permitted to roam them. You will be trapped in your cities from this day until the day the last Chosen Ones complete their tasks.*

Aula

We've reached what seems to be the end of the ladders and we now stand in a cold, dark stone passage that smells of damp and silence. On the whole, I reckon I'll take the owlery. To my left, I can see the passage that leads out of the cliff, out of the cities, to the rest of the island – the great forest I can see from Athenas, and the sea.

I've heard what happens to people who do try to leave. Nine days after they've gone, they end up back here, moaning in hunger and apparently without any memory of what happened to them while they were away. It doesn't matter if you try and leave the cities on rope ladders or gliders or whatever else you can think up. Nine days later, you'll end up here, in this passage, with piss all to tell about what you saw out there or what you did. It makes me want to try it for myself. See if there really is no escape from either of our cities.

I could. But I know in my stomach there's only one way out of this. I've gotta win that book. And the only way to do that is to prove I'm better than the Chosen One from Metis. Prove my city's more worthy than hers; more deserving of the chance to shape this island the way it should be shaped. It's up to me. Wise One, help us all.

Joomia

And that's why we come, every year, every birthday, since the year we turned nine, to prove to the Chosen Ones who came before us that we are still worthy, still true competitors, still learning.

There's the sound of footsteps from the curve of the tunnel. Mathilde gets to her feet so fast I imagine that her old limbs must creak, and I swear even her bracelets are bristling.

And then a man appears. He is wearing robes that I know from occasional messengers to be the clothes of Athenas. A dark grey tunic, belted at the waist, and a long cloak draped over one shoulder. His fading black hair knotted elegantly at the back of his head. Nadrik, Anax of Athenas.

I have only enough time to take him in when *she* appears behind him.

And I take the first true breath I've taken all year.

Aula

She's me.

Long face, small chest, wide hips, strong legs. Hair like a whip of frayed rope. Freckled like a sheet spattered with mud.

It's me. But it en't.

Like someone held a picture of me and painted over it in different colours, and what pisses me off about that is that she clearly got the better deal. Her hair is a nice sort of ebony brown next to my eye-watering ginger, which wouldn't be so bad except for the fact that it's cheated me out of having eyebrows that show up unless you're close enough to squint. Her skin also has the decency to come in the mid-tone range of almond-brown, which sums up most everyone left on Erthe. I mean, OK, I en't *white* like an Old World ginger, but putting my yellow-olive tone against her en't exactly a brush with self-confidence-I-never-knew-I-had.

I wonder what she makes of me. It's hard to tell cos her expression reminds me of a door without a handle.

Right at the bottom of it, though, is this sense of all my tensions dribbling out of me one by one. When I see her, the ache that I have all year just . . . goes away. Is it cos we're both Chosen? Is it cos we're in the presence of Ariadnis? I dunno. It's occurred to me to ask whether we're twins or whatever, but then I realised it doesn't matter: I'm still gonna have to beat her.

We stare at each other for a long time, but she drops my gaze first. I look at Nadrik quickly, to see if he noticed me winning, but he's got his own staring contest going on with Mathilde.

'Mathilde,' he says, all courteous.

'Hmm,' she says back. 'You came.'

She's taller than him, which is impressive, and holds herself straighter than Ashir, which is even more impressive.

'Of course,' says Nadrik. He's pinned the other Chosen One with his eyes, and right there and then she looks nothing like me, cos her face goes all mousy and frightened. I suppose that I ought to give her credit cos even I get nervous under his gaze sometimes, but just now I'm glad cos at least in comparison to her I'll look better to him.

'Ayla,' says Mathilde, nodding at me and getting my name wrong for the seventh year running.

'It's *Aula*. Like OR-LA,' I say back, giving her a glare for good measure.

Her mouth quivers and I think, for a second, she was about to smile.

Joomia

Nadrik says, 'You know that as the last Chosen Ones, your responsibilities are to your people. To protect them when danger occurs. To guide them when their resolve wavers. To help them in times of need. They are yours, and you are theirs. You are their beacon, their symbol.'

Even though he speaks the lines as word-for-word from the scriptures – just like me retelling the story of the Chosen Ones – I sense purpose in them. Wise One, let me be that. Their beacon, their symbol. Let me find that strength. I try to hold fast to what shredded nerves I have left.

Mathilde says, 'We have guided you in what ways we know how, through the instructions left to us by the Wise One.'

Nadrik bristles, presumably because of the subtext: Athenas and Metis have very different ideas about the Wise One, the foremost of which is that they believe in a God. We believe in a Goddess. I've never been sure that it makes much difference what *gender* the Wise One is, but—

'This year, as with every year you have gone to Ariadnis, you will be required to present your learning to the Guardians. You know what it will mean if you have not reached an acceptable level of wisdom and strength.'

Aula draws herself up, and for a second I really get a look at how similar she is to me: how she too has a small mole that bleeds into her top lip, how her fingers are just as long and just as bulbous at the knuckles, how her leg jiggles when she's nervous.

For a strange, dizzy second, I want to take her hand, to share strength. But then she moves towards the archway, so I hasten to follow.

I won't be the weak one. *I won't be the weak one.*

You wouldn't know it was a door, to look at it. It's just the outline of an archway in the rock, headed by nine pearly bulbs of some kind of mineral.

Aula puts her left hand on the last bulb of mineral nearest to her. I force the shakes out of my shoulders and put my right hand on the opposite bulb.

All nine bulbs brighten and seem to come alive, like leaves turning towards the sun.

And then my senses close in on themselves. Sound falls away, sight smudges into darkness, smell evaporates.

The Chosen

Blinded, senseless, Aula and Joomia wander towards us. Their fear tastes sour.

'Hello?' calls Aula.

WHAT HAVE YOU LEARNED THIS YEAR? we ask.

Joomia says nothing, but both girls flinch, and the details of their year hum from them, like the vibrating skin of a drum.

We listen. For nine years, they have done this, brought to us the fruit of their lessons. It is not, as their teachers presume, as simple as question and answer, learning by rote.

It is Joomia learning to speak to the vines that make up the living bridges of her home. Errors. Snapping twigs in frustration. Trying again. It is Aula learning to fight and fall in love. It is embarrassment and shame and jealousy; laughter and doubt, loneliness and parental disapproval. It is new rhythms, new perspectives. And more strongly this year than any other, it is the suffocating experience of embodying so many people's hopes and dreams and expectations.

YOU HAVE BOTH LEARNED WELL. WE SHALL GIVE YOU THE MARK.

We lean forward, forming a physical shape. We nick their wrists, where eight lines already tell of their years of learning.

THIS IS THE LAST YEAR, we say. NEXT YEAR, YOU WILL RETURN TO US. YOU WILL COMPETE IN ARIADNIS FOR THE BOOK OF YOUR GOD.

Joomia nods.

'Yeah,' Aula shrugs.

And so, now. The advice. YOUR CITIES HAVE BECOME CORRUPTED. YOUR CITIES DO NOT LEARN FROM THEIR CHOSEN ONES AS THEY SHOULD. THEY HAVE FLOUTED WISDOM AND TRUSTED

23

POWER. YOU MUST DO YOUR BEST TO CHANGE THIS.

Both girls look appalled. We almost want to laugh. Seventeen, and so much unwanted responsibility.

YOU MUST UNDERSTAND: BALANCE IS THE KEY. BALANCE. IF YOU TWO DO NOT UNITE BEFORE YOUR EIGHTEENTH BIRTHDAY, BEFORE THE DAY OF THE NINTH TASK, THERE WILL BE NOTHING LEFT FOR YOU TO SAVE.

'What?' Aula snaps. 'Nothing left? What do you mean?'

YOU MUST CONTROL THE DIRECTION OF WISDOM.

'Control? How?' asks Aula.

But this is the question for them.

REMEMBER, YOU ARE STRONGER TOGETHER.

We draw ourselves up.

We push them out into the world.

Outside, we watch them stumble, recuperate, look at each other. Their mentors are stunned. Never have they seen their pupils pulled *into* Ariadnis before. Before, we simply allowed our voices to be heard.

We turn inside ourselves. Was it enough? Will it help? Will they remember? The last bit of humanity left in the world . . . it is so delicate.

STRONGER TOGETHER, we whisper to them.

Will the idea take root? Will they learn?

They are strong Chosen Ones. But the Chosen Ones have always been strong.

That was never the problem.

274 Days

Aula

I call it the ache, cos that's what it's like – an emptiness. Needing something you don't have. It starts like a sort of itch in my side, and it's uncomfortable, but you know, fine. Then it gets worse. Till it's like a flap of skin coming loose and letting dirt and grime and stinging fresh air in and that's when I have to run.

Today is like that.

I can't be on the Palace plateau where I live. Everyone knows me here. So I run all over. I use the ladders between the plateaus to go as far as I can.

Here is the Earth plateau, where I weave in between the sowers and their plant beds. I run past the tomato vines and snag the smallest ones so I can stuff them, still warm from the sun, into my mouth. Then through the Episteme plateau, with its hulking white pillars and archways and dodders like Nadrik who are all obsessed with wisdom. They hiss at me as I fly past them, clutching books to their chests.

There are three Industry plateaus, so hot from the engines that it's almost unbearable on top of the already-sticky heat. Over the mess of noise – hammering, screeching mechanisms, high-pressured steam – I hear laughter and

27

cursing. If Etain weren't the Anax's scribe, she'd want to be working down here. She should be working down here, really. She's better than any of these idiots.

On. Sometimes, if I wanna ruffle some feathers, I'll run through the Magi plateau and interrupt them while they're studying, or I'll do a lap of the Temple plateau and yell something that'll make the priests and priestesses come out of their cloisters.

And sometimes . . . sometimes, I'll go and see Sander at his house on the Water plateau. I skid to a halt as I come to his street. If yesterday hadn't happened that's exactly where I'd be going. But not today . . .

But I need something now to distract me from the ache. When I was a kid, I could do it by letting Nadrik lecture me about what I was doing wrong in training and everything I need to work on and why I was talking like a street kid when I was brought up to speak proper. If we got time, we'd eat in between the scolding.

But Nadrik doesn't show up for meals in the banquet hall any more. Maybe it's cos all the rooms in the palace are the same: wide and grand and stuffy with too much floor and not enough windows. Nadrik always did like his rooms poky and his tables covered with books and notes rather than food. I eat with Etain in the prophet house these days anyway, so it's not like I care.

The difference with the prophets' rooms and the palace rooms is that all of theirs are full. There are twenty different seers and another thirty helpers living here in the prophet house – they've got a fancy collective name, the Cassandrae – but none of them know how to tidy. No one

28

really knows what the furniture looks like cos it's been buried under all their crap. Walk into any room and you'll see rickety shelves of oils for improving a prophet's vision; tinctures for dulling it when they See too much and can't sleep. There are huge ceramic bowls and stacks of warped mirrors for casting visions; massive reams of paper with sketches and notes from dreams or foresights. Olive pits and apple cores from prophets caught up in visions and having no time to eat properly.

I dunno how to tidy either so it suits me just fine, especially cos when the ache gets really bad and I don't feel like running, nothing fills the emptiness like inane chatter and watching prophets trying to sort through the chaos to find their scrying bowl.

When I slouch into the kitchen there for breakfast, I'm hoping it will be the usual thing where they all talk over my head and leave me alone, but then I catch sight of Etain just across the room and the warning look she gives me lets me know that I'm gonna be disappointed. Sure enough, I'm about to go and sit next to her when a voice says, 'Plates, Etain,' and I look round and see that Ashir is behind me and wearing a look that'd put a dog's tail between his legs. I can tell by the expression she's got on that she knows exactly what happened last night with me and Sander.

I try to put her off by smiling at some of the other prophets round the table – there's never all fifty of them there cos someone's always off trying to decode a prophecy or make a weather prediction (which frankly, I could do in my sleep. In the summer: hot. Wear as little as you can get away with. In the winter: warm. Maybe try a shawl if you're a reptile). Today there are only twenty or so of them. I get a couple of nods and a hello but you can practically see Ashir's anger gathering darkness and sulphur and no one wants to risk taking the heat off me when she's clearly in a pissy mood.

'Plates, Etain,' Ashir says again, and Etain goes to get them. As she passes, she mouths, *are you OK?* and I just shake my head and mouth back, *later*.

'So,' Ashir says as I sit down next to a knobbly old woman called Igra. She's our Deputy Head Prophet.

My shoulders come up.

'So, Aula,' Ashir goes on. 'How is Sander?'

Ashir thinks cos she brought me up she gets to prod all my sore spots with her twiggy fingers.

I bite my tongue.

'Aula. I asked you a question.'

By now my shoulders are somewhere around my ears.

I am *not* gonna talk to her about what happened with Sander. Not about what I saw him doing in the bathhouses. Not about following to him to his house and knocking on the door. *Definitely* not about accidentally knocking too hard and watching the door cave in around my fist.

'*Aula.*'

I'd sworn and pulled my hand out, looking at the ruin of wood fragments and metal hinges. Oh well. What's done is done. Instead of leaving, I had stood back and roared, 'SANDER! GET OUT HERE!'

But it was his pa who came out. We have this history of hating each other which wasn't improved by the sight of what I'd done to the door. We had a brief yelling match which ended when Sander appeared behind him.

'What do you want, Aula?' he asked.

Oof. All my rage rose to a hacking laugh. 'What do I want? How about an explanation? You haven't been to see me in days and now . . . You and Elea?'

He blushed, but his jaw hardened, all defiant. 'I never said we were a thing.'

'Not a thing!'

'Come on, Aula. It's been nice but I just can't handle—'

'What?'

He stared at me. Didn't say anything.

'What? *What* can't you handle?'

'You!' he shouted. 'I can't handle *you*.' He stopped, and looked up and down the street, I guess to see if anyone was listening. 'It en't . . . natural. You being stronger than me,' he went on. 'It en't right. A man's gotta feel like a man. And I en't even gonna mention your temper.'

'Well, gather round – look at Sander being manly!'

He sighed, came out into the street. 'What do you want, Aula? Besides a fight?'

'I came to tell you I won't be made a fool of!'

He gave me a sad look. 'I reckon you're doing a better job of that than I ever could. Look at you. You wanna put your head in an ice bucket.' He turned to go.

'I en't finished!' I said.

'I am,' he said. He closed the door.

I ran forward and ripped it open. It tore clean off its hinges with a shriek. I was still holding it aloft by the handle when Sander's pa had started yelling again . . .

'Aula,' Ashir says now.

31

'Why do you care?' I snap. 'You en't his mother.'

Next to me, Igra flinches out of her doze.

'I am not his mother, no.'

'You en't mine either,' I say, which is a lie cos she might as well be. She looks like I've slapped her, and I feel my stomach turn guiltily.

'I am not your mother either, no,' she says. 'But I do care about the people the Chosen One turns her temper on, especially if she uses her powers in front of them just because she can.'

'Ma,' Etain says quietly, putting the terracotta dishes down in front of her.

Ashir ignores her. 'You have your gifts for a reason,' she says to me.

Oh, here we go.

'You have an obligation to use them wisely.'

'It en't a gift,' I say. 'You get *given* a gift. I was *born* with it. It's part of me. I can't help it.'

'Just as I was born with prophecy. But I learned to control it, and so will you. And don't be pedantic.'

'It's not my fault his door's full of woodworm. And I en't pedantic.'

'But it is your fault that his door is no longer there. Someone will have to pay for a replacement.'

'Fine! They can take it out of the treasury!'

'That's not the point, Aula—'

'Then what is?'

'You can't go interfering in other people's lives just because they've chosen to exclude you from theirs. Sander . . . Sander has decided not to be with you. Don't you

32

think you should have respected his decision?'

I don't say anything.

'I know that it's hard, Aula,' she says. 'But you have a responsibility to control yourself, just like we all do. More so, because you are the Chosen One. It is the city, not just the Cassandrae, that will be watching you.'

Etain returns and puts down an antipasti board in the middle of the table. I look miserably from the crumbly white cheese to the olive bowl and the stack of floury bread, but I don't want to be here any more. I reach for a handful of tomatoes and the end of a spiced sausage and get up.

'See you later,' I mutter to Etain.

'Where are you going?' she says.

'Back to my rooms,' I say.

'Don't forget to tell the treasury about the door,' Ashir says smartly as I pass her.

I'd looked at Sander desperately. 'Please, don't leave me,' I whispered. 'People always leave me.'

But he was staring from me to the door and shaking his head. Like I was the scariest thing he'd ever seen in his life.

'Aula,' he said. 'Don't you ever wonder why?'

Joomia

I call it the emptiness, because that's what it's like – the strangest, hardest feeling of *not quite*, *not enough*, *never there*.

It is a void that doesn't just swallow, it sucks up. It

vanishes things. I am afraid one day it will take me as well. I am so, so afraid of it.

But this leap?

That is not fear.

That is *sense*.

'Come *on*, Joomia. Just jump.'

We're in the biggest of Metis's nine trees, and I'm standing on a typical Metisian viewing platform – a surface that's woven like a basket, but made with living vines rather than dead ones. There are platforms, bridges and walkways all over Metis like this – but this is the lowest one on this tree. I have genuinely never thought to come down any further than this, but Taurus has.

He stands across from me on the least stable branch I have ever seen. The bough sways warningly under him, though we've climbed places like this more times than I can recall and I've never seen him fall yet. It's uncanny, in fact, the way he keeps himself upright, as if there were a string attached from his head to the sky. He adjusts the tilt of his head, shifts the bend in his knees – all to the right degree, all keeping him in one place. Taurus is a typical Metisian – generally only half-dressed in the heat; arms and legs ropy and sinewy from all the climbing we do; skin deep brown from the various ethnicities of our ancestors and the ever-present sun. The Old World used to have far more diversity – people with hair and skin like milk, different bodies, different languages; not to mention a plethora of religions and cultures, all of which were fair game for war and oppression. But there's only us now: brown-skinned and dark-haired – with one or two exceptions. And the cultures

34

and wars of that world have dwindled down to just us – just Metis and Athenas, at loggerheads over a book of wisdom.

Are we different from them? Probably not. Will we be better? I suppose that's what everyone's hoping me and Aula will solve for them.

I shake my head to clear these thoughts out and look at my present predicament: this jump.

Like I said, it's not that I'm afraid. I've spent my life climbing through the living wood pathways of Metis. I know how to shimmy my way up trunks and scale branches. But I also know when something's not possible.

'Come on. You won't fall,' Taurus says.

I shake out my leg in nervousness. **My lesson with Mathilde. If I miss it . . .**

'She'll get over it.'

You have _met_ Mathilde?

He lets out a sigh, which is how I know I'm boring him. I tap my foot. Oh hell. I close my eyes. **Catch me.**

And I leap.

He snags my arm – nearly yanking it out of its socket – and hauls me steady against him and I gasp as the branch creaks and jostles beneath our weight.

'Got you,' he breathes.

What now?

The grin he's giving me means trouble. 'Listen.'

I hear water. It's loud and clear as a drum, which is strange because on the platform I heard nothing. I squint down and up, but there are so many vines hanging here I can't see a thing.

'Look down,' he says. 'Right down.'

I hold his arms tightly, and lean away from the branch. Then I see what is unmistakeably a pool beneath us.

I turn back to him with surprise on my face and his grin gets wider.

'Now for the fun part,' he says.

He lets go of me and throws himself against the vines. He reaches, catches hold, then slides. And just as I think, *Good thing he never falls*, he does. He drops out of my sight.

I let out a shriek, but he's gone, I can see white spray in the surface of the water, but the vines are swinging wildly, and I can't tell if he's come up. I wait, but there's only the sound of the water.

What do I do? What do I do?

I open my mouth to scream. Someone should hear me.

But his voice comes then, faint as a breeze.

What is he saying?

'JUMP!'

As my heart tries to reassert normal beating patterns, I vow to exact a painful revenge on him. I bend my knees and close my eyes. I'll never live it down if I don't follow him.

I don't so much throw myself forward as slip and fall.

Aula

I don't go back to my rooms. I go and climb the Spindle. It's an old watch tower on the edge of the Palace plateau and the tallest point of the city. Cos it en't been used for lookout in years, it's technically illegal to climb it, but no one ever sees and I'd like to see them stop me if they did.

The rungs along the inside of the tower are rusted and broken and I always manage to cut myself on one of the jagged points, but the bit of peace I get when I'm at the top is worth the scrapes and the rust stains on my clothes.

This morning the air smells of engine oil and frying food. I close my eyes. There's the loud, rhythmic *clank-crrrr-clank-crrrr* of the mechanisms down in the trunks that hold us all in the sky. The machines are powered by fuel from the hot springs, far down in the earth. Sometimes I wonder who keeps all them cogs oiled and that, but I guess they have a magi for it or something. Closer, I can hear the far-off rumble of music from the drink houses in the Earth plateau. The sound of kids screeching as they run up and down the streets, heading to school. The dull roar of the massive mill that feeds water from the trees to everywhere else.

I gaze across to the Water plateau, picking out the familiar rooftops to Sander's house even though I'm telling myself not to look. The last time I was up here, it was with him. I pointed out his chimney. He pretended to see it.

I aim a spit ball at the gutter running down below me.

And then I look down. Right down, past the edges of the city, to the ground. If you look close, you can see the roots of the trees that Athenas is made out of. And under the roots, *inside* the rock we rest on, is Ariadnis. Below that, the city of Metis, the city of trees. And somewhere in there is Joomia.

I think about my little doppelgänger almost every day. I wonder if she's thinking about the fact that we've ignored what the Wise One told us to do. Unite before our eighteenth birthday? Back there in Ariadnis I almost believed it. But it just en't gonna happen. How the hell are we supposed to unite two cities whose only joy is the fact that one day soon, their chance to settle the dispute of long ago will finally be over? That it's gonna be me, or it's gonna be her – but only one of us coming out with that book.

There's the creak of someone on the ladder.

I turn.

Etain's pulling herself up through the gap in the roof beside me. I watch her steady herself on the tiles. Even doing that she looks like some sort of demi-goddess with her neatly teased afro and her skin like clay after it's been fired and smoothed. I look down at my arms and chest – at the angry splatters of freckles against my burned red skin. If I avoid going out in the sun (I don't) it'll go back to its usual yellowish-olive colour, but nothing like Etain's smooth, dark hue.

'If you're coming up can you sit far away so I don't have to feel ugly?'

Etain rolls her eyes. 'If you're so ugly how come every girl in Athenas is racing to grow their hair as long as yours and buying shani root to dye it red?' she says. 'And what about at the last Wise One festival? Who was that boy who snuck us in? Emyll?' Etain says. 'And then all those boys you danced with . . . ? Gideon, Martik, Ilan . . .'

'They were idiots. They were sweet on anyone with a pair of tits.'

'Well, not in your case,' Etain says, nudging me. 'Tit-ettes. That's what you've got.'

I snort but it catches in my throat.

She says, 'You OK?'

'Yeah.'

She knocks her head against my shoulder. 'What happened?'

I tell her about yesterday, about Sander, and afterwards I say the thing that's been eating at me like acid. 'Etain, what's wrong with me?'

One of my favourite things about her is that she knows I en't really looking for an answer, so she doesn't say a word, she just lets me barrel on.

Etain is my sister in every way but blood cos neither of us have much family left. Her pa was one of the only male prophets to exist in the last century, but he died when a strong vision overcame him not long after she was born. My parents were too old to be having babies – my ma died in childbirth and my pa died of old age not long after they found the mark of the Chosen One on my neck.

I know it en't important who they were – especially not when blind luck's given me Etain – but it's hard to remember in moments like this.

I sigh. 'He – Sander – said I'm too strong.'

'That idiot.'

'Well, I am.'

'If you weren't so strong, I'd wanna know who else could've got everyone out of the magi's quarters when someone's spell went supernova,' she says. 'And who else could have bashed that teacher at school for creeping on the kids? Who else could have stopped that rebel running Ma through with a knife that time during one of Nadrik's speeches?' She pats my shoulder lightly cos she knows I'm not big on hugging. 'You're OK, Aula.'

I nod, and sit up straighter. 'You should've been the

Chosen One,' I say. 'You're a better person.'

She grimaces. 'If I was, I dunno if I'd be doing any better than you. What's brought this on, anyway? And don't say Sander. It's not just that, I can tell.'

I shake my head to try and clear it. The sun is high now and it beats down relentlessly.

'I just . . . there's something, er . . . not right . . . inside me. I'm . . . I dunno. It's like I'm missing something. Does that make sense?'

'No,' she says. 'But I dunno why it should.'

'I'm so tired.'

She nods. Then her eyes take on a sly gleam. 'I know what you need.'

'What?'

She mimes a bottle. 'No one will be in the cellars,' she says, downing her imaginary drink.

I laugh, cos it amazes me that she can be like this with me, and tomorrow she'll get up and be Nadrik's straight-backed, intent assistant, and then if she's got time she'll go to the forge and be this expert metal worker, transfixed by her latest project.

I'm lucky if I can just keep track of being *me*.

She beckons to me, and I get up off my misery and follow her.

Joomia

There are those terrifying untethered moments of falling, and then I'm crashing into cold water, and going deep, deep

40

down. I come up spluttering, scraping all my wet hair out of my face. And then I open my eyes.

I'm in the centre of a pool into which a waterfall is splattering.

I suppose in ordinary trees, like the ones that grow on the rest of the island, I would be asking how in the Wise One's name a waterfall got to be there, but the nine trees that make up Metis are different from normal trees because they have *veins*. The branches of our trees feed into the cliff above us, so some of the older veins have taken to channelling spring water from somewhere in the forest above and consequently there are rivers and pools almost anywhere you go in Metis. That being said, I've never seen *anything* like this.

Taurus is sitting on the lip of the pool a few feet away, wringing out his dreadlocks. Behind him, the vishaal tree has been carved out into a long, wide passage which goes back farther than I can see. He's grinning at the look on my face.

I give him a scathing look and crane my head up to gauge how far we might have fallen but it's hard to say. **Do you think anyone would guess there's something here?**

'Everyone knows about the pool,' he says. 'Just not many brave enough to jump.'

How did *I* not know about it then?

He shrugs. 'If you'd made a few more friends other than me, maybe you would.'

Thanks, I say, stung, before swimming towards him; I'm not a great swimmer but the tree rivers have given me enough of an education. **Let's go back**, I say. **Mathilde**

**will be waiting for me and apparently I don't have enough friends
to be here.**

He rolls his eyes. 'The pool isn't why I brought you here.'
Then what *was*?

In answer, he takes hold of my hand and guides me
towards the passage. Inside, the walls are damp and wrinkled
as paper. It smells musty, like stagnant water and old
herbs. Taurus pulls me along, and eventually the lumps
in the floor even out and we lose sight of the pool. There's
still illumination though – a faint bluish glow that almost
seems to be coming from the walls, though I can't tell
where exactly.

As the light gets brighter, I realise what the source is.
Bright veins of what looks like some kind of mineral are
peering through gaps in the wood around us like iridescent
scars – just like the ones in the rock around the door
of Ariadnis.

The veins glint and blur as we move past them until they
seem to blend into a single colour, and I lose a sense of how
far we've gone until Taurus throws out an arm.

The smell is stronger here: the earthy aroma of rotting
wood. Here, the passage comes to an abrupt stop. What
we're met with is a room, carved out like a cave. It's lit by
more of the strange mineral, and though the recesses of it are
still shadowy I can see that every wall is lined with shelf
upon shelf of books. There are chests stacked in every
corner and right in the centre is an altar, covered with a
faded cloth.

I look at Taurus.

He smiles. 'It wasn't here before. I know that sounds

42

weird but I was just lying out by the pool this morning when I heard something give way back here, and when I came to look . . .'

He gestures, and I look down to see fragments of wood, dark and porous. Well, that explains the smell.

If the tree has rot, we need to tell someone, Taurus.

'I don't think it was the tree. I think it was just an old door, made to look like the rest of the passage. Come on, I'm dying to have a nose around. I came back for you straight away.'

I roll my eyes and push him ahead of me, but I'm touched.

I don't know where to look first. The smell of old paper is so delicious, and I want to pull every book down and read them right here and now. I'm already distracted by the titles on the spines. We have a library in the upper levels of Metis, but none of the spines are like this. These are soft, with flimsy paper covers and bent corners. I mouth some of the titles and hold them in my mouth like prayers. It might be the first time someone's seen these names in many hundreds of years, and it fills me with wonder – not least because surely they shouldn't be intact in a place so close to the damp. But closer inspection reveals a strange static against the shelves, and I assume I'm feeling the last gasp of a spell designed to repel dirt and mould.

'Wow! Look at all these amulets!' Taurus says. Typically, he has gone straight for the stacked wooden trunks.

I peer over his shoulder but it doesn't take me long to get bored of the trinkets so I go back to the bookshelves and pull several down, marvelling at the delicacy of the pages, trying to memorise some of the lines.

Some of them are beautiful, others sad, and all of them open like windows to other worlds and I have to put them down before I am drawn in.

'What's a "hobbit"?' Taurus asks, picking up the nearest book to him and squinting at the title.

I shrug. **It's all Old World things.**

'This one's handwritten,' Taurus is saying.

Taurus, don't bend them like that – they're old! You've got to be careful with them.

But his face has gone still.

What? I kneel down next to him. He's holding a book that looks different from the others. It looks much more like the books I'm used to – with a bark cover and stiff brown pages. He holds it out to me, open at the place he was reading. It's just the front page, but the first line stands out, livid as a scar.

The first line of text isn't in a language I can read, except for the symbol for 'Year' that we use on The Great Calendar carved into High Tree and then the numeral I.

My skin pinches tight all round me. Because the next words I can read quite easily:

Lore Sumati, Year One.

'Yes.'

Lore Sumati. The woman who brought our ancestors here after the Comet and the Great Wave hundreds of years ago. The woman who made our home, and separated us from the savage city of Athenas. The most powerful magi anyone's ever heard of and the most intelligent woman in our history. The mother of the first Chosen One.

Lore, who spoke with the Wise One.

I am holding her journal.

And unless I'm much mistaken, we are sitting in her study.

It can't be possible, I say, but Taurus rubs his mouth and gives me a look.

'Should we read it?' he asks.

I don't know. Maybe we shouldn't. But my hands are already flicking the pages. **It's not written in Babel**, I say, surprised. Babel is what we speak now – an amalgamation of the languages our refugee ancestors brought to the island.

'Didn't Mathilde teach you all the dead languages?' Taurus asks. 'Don't you recognise it?'

I pretend to look annoyed and he pretends to look chastened.

I *think* it's Hindi, I say. **Only, I didn't know that was Lore's language. It is what they spoke in a place called India. Perhaps that is where she was from.**

Taurus looks at me with a face that says, *damned if I know*. 'Let's ask Mathilde later,' he says.

I sigh. **My lesson. We should go back.**

Taurus rolls his eyes. 'Ah, come on, Joomia, we can afford another few minutes.'

I stand up. **You can.**

He moans like I've wounded him but gets to his feet.

The only way to get back up is to climb the vines. Children of Metis are practically born climbing *something* but what makes it difficult are the books, and the trinkets from the chest, that Taurus insists we bring with us. He binds the books together with a vine and hangs as many trinkets

45

from his belt as he can.

It feels wrong taking them, I say as we haul ourselves up through the mist and the greenery. **Like we're tomb raiders or something. Did you ever read about Egypt? It was a place in the Old World where men were cursed for ransacking the graves of the ancient monarchs.**

I know Taurus is rolling his eyes at me further up the vines. 'No, Joomia, I didn't know about that. Have you read *every* book in Metis?'

Not *every* book.

'What happened to the grave robbers?'

They died of heart attacks and pestilence.

'Pestilence?'

It's just an old word for disease.

I hear him swear. 'Just a *little* morbid then, the people from Egypt?' But I think he can tell I'm actually scaring myself now because he goes on, 'First of all, it's not a grave, and second of all, I don't know how many times I have to remind you of this, *you're the Chosen One*. The Wise One chose you. And Lore's daughter was the first Chosen One. She's your birthright. You're directly descended from her. These things basically belong to you.'

Oh, don't start all that birthright rubbish with me, I say crossly.

We argue all the way back to the courtyard of High Tree – which is named for obvious reasons. Vishaal trees are the tallest, broadest trees in the forest, but none come as high as the central tree in Metis. The courtyard is one of the oldest marvels we have – our greatest proof of living magic, because it combines magi design with growing patterns of kernel vines and other parasite plants that infest our trees. The result is like the bottom of a reed basket – fifty feet across: a platform that has been woven from plants that continue to live and grow. All our structures are made like this – from our huts, which grow out of the branches like mossy fruit – to our pathways, which stretch vast distances from tree to tree; but none are quite as masterful.

'What has you got there?'

I look up, and see Ade. She is the last of the three people who can inexplicably hear my strange way of speaking, and sometimes I wish I could trade her for someone else. Ade must be about twenty years older than me, but she's got the mind of a child: flitting, erratic, at times completely crazy, at other, rarer times, lucid and determined, almost like anyone else. She is also – though many people seem to have forgotten – the eighth Chosen One. At least she's alive: all other Chosen Ones before her died on their eighteenth birthday, when they completed their task in Ariadnis.

She's looking at the books Taurus is carrying, her head quirked like a bird.

'Just books,' Taurus says.

'Was you studying?' Ade says.

'Something like that,' Taurus says, winking at me.

Ade, of course, doesn't notice. 'I has a song, if you wants to hear it,' she says, but she doesn't wait for either of us to agree before she begins to trill.

Ade is a cautionary tale for what happens when you have prophecy living inside you. Even the first vision you have can damage your mind – one of the reasons that in Metis *and*

Athenas, everyone is checked for prophecy when they're children. According to Mathilde, prophecy came to Ade late. The strength of it was devastating and now her mind is fractured – existing in the past, the present and the future, with nothing to tell her which is reality. Sometimes she has trouble with things that aren't there, or memories that haunt her, and when that happens we need to calm her down.

Prophecy has also stolen her beauty. It's easy to see that she used to have it, but all the visions have carved webs of pearly scar tissue under her permanently bloodshot eyes, and it's given her a strange, wild look that makes people afraid to approach her.

'She was so glorious,' Mathilde said, when I asked her about Ade before her gift of prophecy came. She would know – Ade is Mathilde's daughter.

We wait for Ade to stop singing and thank her for the song and then she scampers away up into the branches, muttering to herself.

Taurus and I have to separate when we get to the courtyard because of all the traders setting up their stalls. We dodge around people moving baskets and crates. I'd forgotten that it's market day today.

I read once that markets used to be about trading, using bits of metal called money, but thankfully that tradition stopped after the ancestors came to the island. Market day is now just a monthly occasion for people to show off what they've been doing for four weeks. They might have been making soap or flavouring cheese or picking fruit or sewing patterns into fabric but everyone likes to show up with something, and once everyone has been thoroughly congratulated on their work they start to trade. For trade, each tree provides their own offering: meat, vegetable, mineral, cloth, cleanliness, spells, guidance, drink and repairs. It rotates every year, so it becomes a different tree's duty to provide a different offering, which helps keep the trees healthy and our makers happy. I don't know if this was Lore's alternative to the money problem, but it does seem to work and it's a nice way of getting people from all over the city together.

I have to haul Taurus away from a lot of the stands as we weave our way across; many of them attempt to hail me over too.

'Mathilde says it's good for them to see the Chosen One,' he argues as I jostle him away from Alys, who harvests sweetberry, towards the higher pathways to where Mathilde lives. Still, their voices follow me:

'Look at this, Chosen One.'

'Blessings upon you, Chosen One.'

'Food for you, Chosen One?'

And I smile. And I nod. But I don't stop. I know the things they say about me:

'I wonder how Elder Mathilde teaches her.'

'Can't be easy, teaching a mute.'

'But, Pa, isn't the Chosen One supposed to have powers?'

'Maybe we got a dud.'

'I heard the Chosen One in Athenas could lift a building up with one finger.'

They sigh wistfully. Because they don't have a Chosen One who can lift a building with one finger. They have me.

Aula

I'm air.

I'm floating.

I'm drunk.

Etain and me found the oldest wines in the cellars. I try and remember why I ever thought it tasted disgusting. It tastes of nectar. It tastes of fruit. It's *delicious*.

'I think this is *it*,' Etain says, tipping the dregs into her glass and looking at the pile of bottles as though someone else drank them.

'They got *mooore*,' I say.

'You're slurring,' she snorts.

'Am not. Yourr the one who's . . . slurrying.'

For no reason, we collapse into giggles.

'Prolly shouldda got drunk in my room,' I say, looking around at the mess we've made on the floor.

Etain glares blearily at the chaos as if it will sort itself into tidiness. She meets my eyes. There is more giggling.

'I wanna see Sander,' I announce. 'Tell him s'OK. You know?'

'Yeah,' Etain says, nodding wisely. 'Shall we go now?'

I take a wobbly step and collapse and she collapses next to me and we nearly piss ourselves laughing.

'Never mind. Didn't like him anyway,' I say.

'Yeah,' Etain says.

'But you know. I'll miss it.'

'Miss what?'

'SEX!' I yell.

We have to bite our fists to stop ourselves laughing.

'How did you even do it?' Etain asks, a little cross-eyed. 'En't you too strong?'

I belch. 'Nah. We had a tap-if-I'm-hurting rule. He didn't think he'd have to use it at first.' Etain's cackle descends into a coughing fit, but suddenly I don't feel like laughing. I see fragments of me and Sander in the dregs of my wine: skin to skin, pulse to pulse, lips to throat. Not having that again en't funny.

Luckily Etain doesn't notice my new-found gloom cos just as she's calming down her eyes pop in warning and I have just enough time to roll out of the way before she's sick all over the floor.

Hours later, I find Nadrik in his study.

He glances up at me as I hover in the doorway. He's poring over a book, as usual.

'That's new,' I say, pointing at the ornate circlet he's wearing over his eyebrows. I didn't think royal jewellery was his thing – he's protested against his government wanting him to wear some kind of crown for ages – but I guess this is his compromise. Ashir told me that when he was younger, Nadrik was the most prestigious magi in Athenas. By the time I was nine, he'd worked his way through government to be elected the youngest Anax we've ever had.

'I am busy, Aula,' he says. He's always busy when I'm around. Before he was Anax, his face used to light up when he saw me. I dunno what changed.

I nod and trace the wood pattern in the frame of the door. After I've shuffled my feet for a minute or two more, he looks up again.

'What is it?' he says.

I shake my head. I dunno what I'm doing here, really. Etain went to bed after she threw up but there was still something gnawing at me. I felt like I had to talk to *someone* about it.

'Do not play games with me, Aula. Either spit it out or leave.'

I glare at him. 'Fine,' I say, and turn to go.

Please call me back, please call me back.

'Aula.'

I turn and find the ground isn't as solid under my feet without the door frame to lean on.

'Have you been drinking?'

'No,' I say, swaying. 'Maybe. A bit.'

His eyes narrow dangerously. 'Do I need to remind you of your responsibilities?'

'Nah,' I say. 'I won't listen anyway.'

I hear the paper in his hand crumple with satisfaction. I want someone to fight with. I want to fight *now*. My blood is raring for it.

But he just says in his flat, toneless voice, 'You have just a little less than nine months to enter Ariadnis. What are you doing to yourself?'

'I'm *doing* what every other kid my age is doing!' I shout.

'But you do not have their liberties.'

'Well, maybe I should! I have no life!'

'You think this is living, Aula? Filling your stomach with alcohol and getting drunk with the prophet's talentless daughter?'

'She en't talentless!'

Nadrik switches tack. 'Fine, and who will protect her if

52

you fumble the Wise One's test? Do you think the magi of Metis have any less ambition for extending their home than ours do for Athenas? You think they are any less ruthless than I am?'

I open my mouth. And close it.

'Mathilde of Metis doesn't seem ruthless,' I say, partly cos it's true, but also cos I don't want to let him have that one.

'She is a liar. She wears the ambitions for her city under a mask. Just because I wear mine proudly doesn't mean hers are any less. A *Chosen One* ought to know that.'

I take a deep breath and tilt my head back so the tears won't run. 'You expect these things from me,' I say, to the ceiling. 'You expect so much I can't even keep track of all of them.'

When I look at him, there's something naked and strange on his face that I can't read. Is it pity?

Looking at the ceiling has made me dizzy. I wobble and have to tread backwards to keep myself upright.

His lip curls slightly in soft disgust. 'Go to bed, Aula,' he says.

Joomia

Mathilde's hut looks like a bright green egg perched on the elbow of the branch it rests on. As we approach I see her in the porch – her rounded back and the feathers in her collar. She is bent over something, with her smoking pipe wedged between her teeth. Every now and then, she mutters to herself, and smoke billows out, curling over her white hair.

We're almost to her when I see her stiffen. She looks round and jumps so violently all her necklaces and bangles and hair beads swing about, clacking against each other.

'Kids, I told you not to sneak up on an old lady!' she crows.

Sorry, I say, but she doesn't mean it. Mathilde's the closest thing I've had to a parent after mine died so soon after I was born. I think she was quite close to them because she doesn't like to talk about it, but in Metis, children are brought up by the citizens more often than their parents anyway.

Taurus is my only other real family – and his origins are even more mysterious than mine. He was found walking the upper pathways of Metis when he was only two years old. He had no family, no voice, no clothing that identified him as belonging to one city or another. Of course, Mathilde took him in too.

I peer past her shoulder and see that she was fretting over a hole in the wall of the hut. Where yesterday the bark was strong and healthy, it seems to have crumbled and yellowed. It makes me think of the rot back in the passage, but before I can say anything Taurus asks if she's been cooking again and she laughs . . . which is to say, she grunts.

'Hush, kid. I'm concentrating.'

She frowns over the hole for a few seconds more – you can just see her magic winking along her brown fingers – but when nothing happens, she sighs and straightens.

'Have to have another look later. Bless my soul, are you *late*, Joomia?'

I'm so sorry, Mathilde, I got distracted by—

But she lets out a laugh that sounds like twigs snapping and waves her hand. 'Only been waiting seventeen years.

Taurus, you got her to be letting loose at last! Long time coming.'

Taurus grins. 'I wouldn't call it letting loose. *Look* at her; she's in a right state.'

I blush, cross and wrong-footed, which is very easy when you're me and stuck between Mathilde and Taurus who like to joke about everything.

I am *not* in a state.

Mathilde hides her smile by taking another puff on her pipe and Taurus snorts. I *hate* it when they gang up on me.

Mathilde. There is something we have to show you.

Taurus carefully unwraps the vines from the pile of books, but his face falls. 'It's not here,' he says, kneeling down and spreading the books across the floor. 'The journal's not here!'

What?

'It's gone!'

'What are you talking about?' Mathilde croaks.

I open my mouth to tell her but a voice cuts across me. 'Elder Mathilde!'

We all turn around to see Oriha, a young weaver about my age, hurrying up the ladders towards us. Automatically, I try to move behind Taurus but she sees me anyway and throws me as scathing a look as she can get away with before Mathilde notices.

'What do *you* want?' Taurus says, the edge of deep-rooted animosity in his voice.

'I'm here to speak to Elder Mathilde,' Oriha replies.

'She's in the middle of something,' he says, blocking her path.

Oriha gives him a warning shove. 'Let me through.'

'Make me.'

Oriha catches my eye over Taurus's shoulder and glares at me as though this is all my fault. She seems to be about to take Taurus up on his challenge when Mathilde says, 'Kids. You quit your fighting.' She squints at Oriha behind him and says, 'What's got you on a hook?'

'You're needed in the marketplace, Elder.'

'Aren't I always? What happened? Someone drop a baby on its head?'

Oriha pauses, seeming to struggle with a desire to say whatever she has to say and at the same time keep me from hearing it.

But just as she opens her mouth I know.

Ade, I say. **Something's wrong with Ade**.

Aula

It's too early to go to bed but I don't have anything else to do. I mean, I *am* tired, but I can't sleep, so I'm lying on my side scowling at the drapes of my four-poster, when Ashir comes in. She's got such a light step it barely sounds like she's there, but I'd know her feet anywhere. I guess she just finished her shift overseeing all the prophecies that went on today. I can hear her tutting as she moves around the room.

My room kind of deserves a tut; but I frown under my duvet and try to keep my breathing even.

'I know you're awake, Aula. Mercy, do you need *all* these lights on? And I thought we prophets were bad at clearing up after ourselves,' she says, and tries to catch my eye for a smile. My head twinges. I en't drunk any more and I'm regretting it. I look around the room instead, and as usual there's stacked plates that I need to take down to the kitchen or give to one of the servants to get rid of cos there's probably stuff growing on them.

It's true I haven't seen my floor in a while. It's given over to hundreds and hundreds of books from the palace library and probably more from the city library too cos their stock is better. I haven't returned them cos the librarians scowl at me when I go in but they're too afraid to ask me for anything back. The final layer on the floor is clothes, which are thrown in whatever place I was standing when I took them off. The empty wardrobe looks kind of lonely without them but I just never get around to putting them back.

'Another atlas,' Ashir says as she picks the nearest book up and smooths her hand over the cover. 'It's good you're so interested in the Old World. Someone needs to be. We haven't had a proper historical geographer in years.'

'Nadrik says it's a dead subject.'

'Well, he would know,' Ashir mutters, flipping the book back on the nearest pile. A bunch of loose pages go flying and she cocks her head, smiling as she catches one.

'You're getting good,' she says, tracing the lines of the map I've redrawn with her finger.

'M'all right,' I say, but I smile a bit.

'Still dreaming of adventures far away, then?'

'You have no idea.'

She looks at me for a long time, as if she's seeing right into me. Holy Wisdoms, does it make my throat ache. We en't been alone like this for longer than I can remember. She's always got some prophet thing going on, and if not that then Nadrik needs her for some prediction or other. She used to come to me every night, back when me and Etain used to sleep in the same room, and we'd stay up till dawn just talking. So much changes.

'Come here,' she says, sitting on the bed, and I let her fold me into her arms. 'I'm sorry about today,' she says. 'I only say these things because—'

'Cos people need protecting from me.'

She sighs. 'Sometimes I think you need protecting from you.'

'That's your job,' I say, and she laughs softly. I sit up and she tucks my hair behind my ear.

'I say these things because if you lost control . . . if you hurt someone . . . it would destroy you.'

I lower my head. 'Is that something you've Seen?'

She squeezes my shoulder. 'It's something I *know*.'

I nod, and tears slide out through my eyelashes even though I never gave them permission.

'And I can't stand the thought of that,' she goes on. 'So sometimes . . . sometimes I don't say everything you need to hear.'

'Like what?'

'Like you deserve someone who can love you for all that you are. But also that you're seventeen and quite frankly, my girl, love is a headache you don't want to be dealing with right now. You've got a hundred other things to spend your tears on.'

I laugh, cos that's a classic Ashir line. For a while she

just sits there with me, and then she kisses my hair and stands up.

'Goodnight, sweetheart.'

'Night.'

There's a thump, and she curses as she stubs her toe on something hard by the foot of the bed.

'You all right?' I say.

She frowns for a moment, and then sways, as if she's gonna faint. She puts her hand out and catches the nearest pillar of the four-poster.

'Ashir?'

She's silent.

'Ashir?'

I swing my legs out, but then she straightens and shakes her head.

'Are you all right?'

'It's nothing . . .'

But she's shaking slightly and the silvery scars around her eyes are gleaming.

'Did you See something?'

'Just give me a moment. Get . . . get back into bed, Aula.'

She moves to sit on the end of the mattress and I steady her shoulder.

'Ashir . . . what is it?'

Her breathing quickens. It's a vision, I'm sure of it. Her eyes are shut tight. Her hands curl to fists in her lap. Her scars become fiercely white in the dim light.

'Ashir?'

'Stronger together,' she says.

I jump like she struck me with lightning.

'What?'

'It's not what you think,' she says, looking straight at me. Her eyes have gone colourless. Her words carry the echoes of many voices; her body writhes and spasms. 'Not what you think.'

I only have a millisecond to catch her before she falls off the bed.

Joomia

The marketplace is a mess. Stalls have been overturned. Banners have been ripped. Fruit is lying everywhere, mashed and bruised, the baskets that held them ripped apart. Clay pots lie in scattered fragments.

The crowd have drawn to the sides with Ade at their centre. She's panting, arms whipping around her like a flustered bird. She stops abruptly, head questing, and then she's screaming again – rushing at the crowd. They do their best to skitter back from her, but she grabs their clothes and shakes them, trampling over the mess from the stalls she's already made.

Everyone's relief at seeing Mathilde is palpable; they move aside for her wordlessly. I catch a few dark looks and murmurs as I follow behind, but by that point I can hear what Ade is shrieking, so I forget to worry about it.

'Gone! Gone! Gone!'

She turns on me and the full force of her anguish hits me like a high wind. I can hear screaming in her head – a white, fuzzy confusion and a thousand blank figures which seem both familiar and not as they turn against one another and begin to fight. I lose my feet but Taurus steadies me. Oriha stiffens next to us.

'Well, bless me, Ade. What is it you lost?' Mathilde says. She attempts to touch her daughter's shoulder, but Ade shrieks and slaps her hand away. 'Don't be like that, Ade,' Mathilde croons. 'Come on now, my darling. Calm yourself.' She chances another step forward and is rewarded with a wild slap to the face. She staggers back, her lip bloody.

Taurus grabs my shoulder as I move. 'Joomia, don't—'

I brush him off and run forward. All Ade sees is my movement and she lashes out, pure animal. I duck the first fist she swings at me, but the second catches me across the jaw. Blood wells in my mouth.

Ade, I say. **Ade, you're safe.**

But she stumbles back, still panting, her eyes fluttering like wings.

'Gone!' she moans.

I risk another step towards her. She hisses and tries to strike me again – but then Taurus is there, blocking her, taking a few hits himself before folding Ade's arms firmly against her sides. She screams in his ear, tries to kick him – and that's when I run forward and press my head against hers.

You're safe, I say, trying to cut through her fear and confusion.

Images rush at me, like thousands of flies trapped in a room, all warring to be heard. My mind staggers under the weight of them.

I see a line of people taking the road I walk every year up to Ariadnis. I recognise some of their faces, but the people

61

I know from my city are not themselves. Their expressions are dark and completely blank, anonymous as silhouettes.

I see people fighting – blades twisting spines out of place, magi casting spells that blind, gesturing for branches to shield them from an onslaught of arrow fire.

I see owls taking flight – so many of them it must be every single bird on the island, their feathers cutting silently through the night.

I see myself.

I see Aula.

I see the entrance to Ariadnis.

I reach gently for Ade's mind pressed tightly in a far-off corner of herself.

You're safe, I say. **Come back, Ade.**

Gone! she whispers, but I'm not sure she's actually said it aloud. *All gone.*

I see the faces of my people again, and all the people of Athenas cramped tightly in one space, their expressions bovine and listless. Panic tries to close my throat. The emptiness. It's *inside me*. What does it mean?

There is no time for guessing. I concentrate on the image of now, trying to show Ade what's right, what's present. **Here you are. You're here. Come back with me. You're safe.**

Her mind moves hesitantly towards me, only to flinch back. *I have to tell them. It's important.*

I saw what you saw, I say. **I'll remember. I'll tell them. I promise.**

Under my hands, her body stills. Her breath slows.

I open my eyes.

62

273 Days

Aula

I was nine, and standing at the edge of the viewing platform. The very edge.

'Aula?'

Below me, the city was sleeping, and the lights were blinking in windows and doorways – so many you couldn't count them. It was night, but the kind of night where there's a little blue in everything, even the inky sky.

I'd stopped crying, but I was still in shock.

'Aula. Come down now, sweetheart,' Ashir said. I remember her saying it quite calmly.

'Did you hear what I did?' I said.

'Yes.'

'They wouldn't leave me alone.'

'No. But you have to remember you're much stronger than other kids your age.'

'Cos I'm Chosen?'

'Yes, because of that.'

'They were hitting me cos I said it wouldn't hurt. Then they wouldn't stop.'

'I suppose they didn't realise that just because it didn't

hurt your skin that doesn't mean it wouldn't hurt *you*.'

'One of them went and got his pa's knife.'

There was a long pause.

I said, 'I was scared. I only wanted to get the knife out of his hand. I didn't want to—'

I closed my eyes as I remembered the boy's wrist bones snapping. Fear is like anger in the way it gives you strength. I guess none of those kids had counted on just how much strength I had.

Ashir just said. 'Yes, sweetheart, I know.'

'If I fall from here, will it hurt then?' I said.

'Do you want to fall, Aula?'

I backed off the edge a bit. I'd been contemplating it for hours. Not because I thought it would kill me, but not because I thought it would do me any good either. 'No,' I said.

'Come down then, sweetheart.'

I did, and she put her arms around me, and she was shaking so hard but she held on so tight.

'Are you cold?' I asked.

'No, sweetheart, I'm sad.'

'Why?' I asked.

She pulled me so she could look me in the eyes. 'My darling,' she said, 'I am going to tell you something now.' She bit her lip. 'You are going to find that not many people in your life will ever believe that you are scared, because you are so strong. And that might not seem like an important thing to you now, but one day it might be. So promise me you'll always come to me, whenever you are scared, because I will listen. And I will believe you.'

I replayed that memory all last night.

Thank all the Holy Wisdoms for forges. It's so hot, there en't time for any thinking. There's just me pumping hard on the bellows, and Etain saying *now* and *stop* and *more*.

Since her vision yesterday, Ashir's been in the healers' quarters, and she still hasn't woken up. But Etain's metalwork commissions are going well – we're speeding through the list, much quicker than Etain normally would, cos no one loves work like two people trying to distract themselves.

Just then, I notice a draught from the door.

'My Lady Aula.'

I look up. It's a messenger girl but I can't remember her name. Pia? Mia? Something like that. She looks embarrassed.

'Hotter!' Etain yells from behind the forge, not aware of our visitor.

I pump hard – cos God, I en't waiting all day for a messenger to do their job.

I expect her to just come out with it, but she doesn't. I can feel her lingering in the doorway. I suddenly remember the other evening standing in the doorway to Nadrik's office and him getting all bristly at me for exactly the same thing. God, I must've looked pathetic.

Finally I can't bear it any more. 'What? What do you want?'

She flinches. It makes me even more irritated. Why do people flinch when I haven't even done anything?

Etain peers round the forge, sees our mute little visitor

and puts her hammer down, wiping sweat from her forehead with the back of her thick glove.

'The Anax sent me, My Lady,' the girl stammers out.

'Oh, yeah?' I say. 'Wants to talk to me now, does he?'

She gives me this look like, *what the hell are you talking about?* and says, 'My Lady, he wants to remind you of your training.'

'Training?!'

She flinches again.

'Well, I en't going.'

'My Lady, the Anax is waiting.'

I look at her, and she looks right back, knowing she's out of line but determined to test me, apparently. I turn my heel hard into the steps where she stands. There's a cracking sound and she stumbles. She looks scared now. Good.

'W-what should I tell him, My Lady?'

'I'm not training until we get some news about Ashir! Tell him that!'

She bows herself out.

I turn back to the forge. Etain's giving me what I call her square look. 'Nicely done,' she says, meaning *not nicely done at all*.

'Whose side are you on?' I mutter, but I get my sandals cos I think we both know I'm going.

Joomia

When I open the door to Taurus's hut I can see someone lying in his bed, but it isn't him. This isn't unusual. Last week it was Nagesa, the week before it was Peder, the week before that it was Sayid or Alana. Taurus is hardly unique in that area. Metis doesn't place emphasis on exclusive coupling, especially when you're our age.

This one is Lear. I'm pleased – I've seen him looking at Taurus for a while and Nagesa will finally stop pestering me about where Taurus is all the time if she sees him with someone else.

Lear smiles sleepily when I shake his shoulder. He has thin, angular eyes that blink in surprise when they see me and not Taurus. He tries to flatten his straight black hair away from his face and mumbles, 'Morning, Joomia,' as he sits up enough to rest on his elbows.

I crook a finger to pose a question and point to the rest of the bed.

'I think he's gone to get breakfast,' he says, peering blearily around.

'I did,' Taurus says from behind me. He brushes my head with his hand as he puts down a basket with apples and a wheel of cheese in it. He plonks himself on the bed and stretches.

I have to turn away quickly.

I know it's hot, but can't you at least wear something under your sarong if you go out?

'Don't *look*, then,' he says.

I throw an apple at him, and he catches it, pretending to hand it to Lear which (predictably, if you know Taurus at all) turns into a wrestling match. I move away to avoid being hit by a stray elbow or leg and keep my eyes on the door to avoid seeing more than I'd like to of either of them.

Taurus . . .

Something soft hits me on the head and I pull it off, eye it. One of their loose-fitting undershorts. I drop it like it's flaming and quickly go to stand by the door.

Taurus.

'Did you find the journal?' Taurus says, possibly from around Lear's arm.

I shake my head. **I looked everywhere. I even asked Ade.**

'What's this?' Lear says.

I hear a brief break in the wrestling as Taurus changes the subject. Then the scuffle resumes.

'I'm trying to get Taurus to come for a walk with me later,' Lear says, as Taurus calls for mercy from some hold or other he's got him in.

'I told you I can't,' Taurus says. Judging by a hissing noise, I'd say he has Lear in a head lock.

'Yeah, but you didn't say *why*,' Lear grunts.

'Mind your own tree sap,' Taurus laughs. Lear lets out a yell which I think means Taurus has won that round. I sneak a look at them, and thank the Wise One there are no risks of me having to scrub my inner mind of anything I don't want to see.

'Walk with me, Joomia?' Lear asks.

I smile, but shake my head. **I have a lesson with Mathilde**, I say, trusting Taurus to translate for me – which he does between play shoves and yelps. I wonder vaguely how long the lesson will be before Mathilde goes into the Meet – a council of each of the nine Elders of Metis; and if we'll get time to go into what they'll talk about.

Like he's reading my thoughts, Taurus asks, 'Will she

have time to talk to you before the Elders Meet?'

'About what?' Lear wonders.

I sigh. **Ade had a vision yesterday.**

Taurus relays this to Lear, and the wrestling – finally – stops.

'But the Elders don't *believe* in prophecy,' Lear says.

It's true. Unlike in Athenas, where someone with prophecy is trained to hone their vision, a prophet in Metis has two choices. They can go up to Athenas and become part of the Cassandrae – the twenty-strong group of prophets the Athenasians set their days by – or have their powers extracted here. Metis recognises magic, even tests for it, but doesn't like prophecy. *It corrupts us*, Mathilde says. *It makes people defiant to nature's course. To death, injury – even the weather.*

And yet, I've wondered – why is the prophecy that foretold me, and the other Chosen One, acceptable? I've never gotten a straight answer about that. Deputy Magi Einar says something like, *That prophecy came from Lore's people. And we have evidence for it – look at the birthmark on your neck, the lines on your wrist . . .* (I'll pretend to listen for as long as I can but he often loses me there.)

Mathilde just said, 'Technically, that isn't a prophecy, Joomia. That was the word and wish of the Wise One Herself.'

So you won't listen to any prophecy that didn't come from the Wise One Herself? I'd once asked.

She winced at the question. 'No, it's not that. It's just that any *other* prophecy we hear is still highly mistrusted.'

Whatever that means. Of course, that still leaves the

question of Ade: why is *she* allowed to go around with her visions still intact, and – as evidenced yesterday – visions still destructive to people around her? The answer to that is easier, though no one's ever said it out loud: because Ade is Mathilde's daughter.

Still, it's strange that such a technicality is allowed considering what sticklers the Metisian Elders are for community ties over family ones, but apparently whatever Mathilde has done as Head Elder gives her allowances for her daughter. I have another theory, that maybe they realise that, with a team of prophets nearly a hundred strong, Athenas *do* have a distinct advantage over us in some areas.

I suppose they're feeling a little nervous, this close to the Wise One's task . . . to my birthday, I say.

Taurus catches my eye. 'You wanted to ask me something?' he says.

Yes, I say. My lesson's in the Magi's Grove. I asked Mathilde if you could come this time. She said it was fine with her.

For a moment he doesn't say anything. Not so very long ago, he'd have jumped at the chance. He goes through phases of what he calls *wanting to be useful*, and being a magi was the most recent obsession. For a while, he really seemed like he was going to do it. If he hadn't given it up, he could have been months away from sitting the Ritual of Acquisition – a rite that encourages magic to see your body as a vessel for it as much as the trees around us. But like most of Taurus's obsessions, it seemed to stale. I wish being the Chosen One were as optional.

'I can't,' he says at last.

I frown. What do you mean? What are you doing?

70

He hesitates, but Lear's looking between us, eyes narrowing. 'Are you making plans without me?' he asks. His voice is light-hearted but there's a feather of doubt in it.

Taurus just laughs and stoops to kiss him before going to retrieve his clothes. Lear settles back on the bed looking like he's fighting to keep the corner of his mouth from flicking upwards. His mouth wins.

Taurus, seriously, I say, as if it's not serious at all. **What are you doing?**

He just smiles.

Taurus—

I've got a question for you, he mouths at me.

I frown. **Yes?**

Taurus glances quickly at Lear on the bed and there's a flicker of movement from his eyebrow. It says, *what do you think?*

I sigh. **He's nice. Try not to hurt him, won't you?**

Taurus gives me a mock bow. 'Yes, Chosen One,' he says.

Aula

As always with training, we fight first, so I find Nadrik in the middle of the palace ground. There's a circular courtyard there that mostly gets used by the magi so it's pretty scuffed up, but all the biggest scars and scrapes in the stone were made by me.

I step into the courtyard as quietly as I can, but I see his turned back tense just a hair more. He turns, widening his

71

stance as he faces me. His stupid circlet blinks at me in the sunlight. He's been wearing it more often recently, like everyone needs a reminder of who he is. I think he misses being with the magi, though.

Nadrik's still known for being the most elite of the magi, and when he's got time he'll come here to oversee their training. Sometimes I train with them too, but Chosen One powers en't like normal magic, so it's usually better for me to train one-on-one. Chosen magic almost always has something to do with the vishaal trees we've based our cities around – manifesting in strength, or the ability to grow things, or being able to regenerate really quickly.

I know from Nadrik that magi both in Athenas and Metis have to go through roughly the same training before they sit the Ritual of Acquisition. Once magic has recognised your body you then have to learn how to control it and manipulate it in other things. It takes a hell of a lot of training and discipline, and no one I've ever seen is more skilled than Nadrik.

Fighting him en't exactly a stroll.

I en't said anything, but he knows I'm here. I can see his fingers flexing and the slight blur in the air around him, which means the magic that protects him from my strength has already been cast.

Like he taught me, I move down to brace my knees and crook my wrists.

Then he moves and I gotta say he's fast for someone with that much grey in his hair. The air hums as he comes at me.

But I'm ready, and I throw myself back, fall on my hands and tilt my head to the floor. The surge of energy he's sent at me rustles my hair as it passes, and then it's gone and I'm back on my feet. I lunge for him, but he's already moving, supple as water. I kick out and nearly trip him, but he jumps and manages to haul out my legs from under me with his next blow.

I fall heavily, heaving air back into my lungs. *Shit*. Downed in less than ten seconds. I flip myself on to my feet, ignore the screech of pain in my muscles. There's dust in the air now and he's got me so the sun's in my eyes, but I can still make him out. I spot a paving slab that's come loose and dart for it, heaving it up. I take my aim. Throw.

The slab hurtles directly at him – I pump a fist, but his power roars as it swirls to a crescendo. I dart away, sensing what's gonna happen next, but I'm not fast enough and the slab smacks me hard in the back and sends me tumbling bum over head.

'Get up!' His voice cuts through my pain and the taste of dirt.

I get up.

'Not good enough,' he says. A long strand of grey hair has strayed from the sharp pull of his coil but nothing else about him is ruffled.

I scowl.

'Go again,' he says.

So I do – swiping at him as hard and fast as I can. He dodges the first two hits but I catch him on the jaw with the third. I don't see him take aim for my gut. I double over. We go again. This time I at least keep him on his toes, ducking and weaving his blows before trying a hit to his midriff. He knocks my hand aside and throws me back.

'Come *on*, Aula!' he growls.

The next blow I try and land goes wide and he has my feet from under me in three seconds. I won't lie; this is a very bad day, and I can see it in every livid angle of his face.

'What is *wrong* with you?' he asks with disgust in his voice.

The answer is in my mouth ready to be spat out like embers. *Nothing. Just a boy I thought loved me doesn't want anything to do with me. Just the only person who ever did love me, no questions asked, like a mother, is really sick and I don't know why. Just every time we train or you teach me in the library I never get any credit, or well done, ever.*

But I don't say anything.

Instead, I kick him across the ring as hard as I can, right in the belly.

He doesn't say anything when I go over and find his back embedded in the courtyard, with a paving slab shattered underneath him. He ignores my outstretched hand, rises to his feet and takes a breath. Rock flakes shower off him. The places I've damaged pull together, the paving slab I threw at him settles back into place. His shield drops, the dust settles. All is as it was.

He nods, just once. 'Again.'

Joomia

Supported by a frame of overlapping branches, the Magi's Grove is mostly made from sap string: pale green threads of sap collected from the vishaal trees. They're filtered and

74

refined to form long, flexible fibres, and in the case of the Grove, woven into a bowl shape. Because of the way magic works in Metis – a process of generating energy that uses the slow, pure power of growth in the same way the vines and the trees do – the fibres help to enhance the magic, to speed it along. Sometimes the magi have a special need to focus their magic without the influences of the rest of the city disturbing them, and it was built for that purpose.

Mathilde is kneeling in the centre when I arrive. Her eyes fly open as I let myself down into the Grove. There's a greasy salve covering the cut on her lip, but it doesn't look too bad.

'Good morning, kid,' she says.

When is the Meet? I ask.

'At noon,' she replies, giving me a serious look. 'I gotta convince them that taking Ade's prophecy at least semi-seriously is better than not at all. I may need your assistance with that.'

How can they *not* take it seriously? I wonder.

'You know how,' Mathilde says impatiently. 'Prophecy. It corrupts. En't it corrupting us now just talking about it?'

I frown. **You do believe me, don't you? About what I saw?**

'Course I do,' Mathilde says. 'But, kid, it en't just *my* opinion that counts here. You know what the rest of the Elders are like. I've a hard time telling some of them the sky is blue some days.'

Is Ade all right? I ask.

'Better,' Mathilde says. 'But shaky still. Now, are you done questioning?'

I nod.

75

'Good,' she says.

And we begin.

My hair feels tight against my scalp as Mathilde conjures the shields that will seal the Grove for me. It's a spell that keeps any magic I do here bound against me. I can't hurt anyone.

So I reach for it, reach for my power.

Magic is a kind of excess of energy in the air from the friction between forces like gravity and sunlight. When people train to be magi, they are asking this energy to move inside them as well as around them. In Metis, magi obviously specialise in the energy of the trees, but because their magic requires conscious effort to hold on to, none of them are in danger of losing control as I am.

Just as having blood in your veins is innate to anyone with a heartbeat, having magic in your body is innate to Chosen Ones. I don't need to ask magic to see me as a vessel – I *am* a vessel, and more than that, a source. At least, this is what Mathilde keeps telling me.

The power is always there, always around the edges of my consciousness, but as long as I push it down, I don't have to think too hard about it. Not until moments like this.

I lift my arms, and the stray vines of the grove come to meet me, twining around my wrists and hips, lifting me gently into the air.

Show me, I say to them, in their language. Their voices yawn like windswept boughs, showing me the ways along their branches and out across the nine trees of Metis.

In Black Tree, a magi inspects the work of her apprentice.

In White Tree, a child chases a wild cat out of his hut.

Knot Tree, where lovers are pressed together in secret, the thrill of a morning passion.

The Elder of Wilde Tree passes the plans for the Day of the Wise One celebrations later this year to a committee assembled for the occasion. In Wise Tree, people kneel at the altar of the Wise One, their echoed song lifting the hairs on my arms. In Low Tree, Lear yawns and finally acknowledges it may be time to get up. But I frown as the vines show me the bridge between Sap Tree and High Tree. Taurus is walking swiftly between them, his feet nimble as he catches hold of a climbing net and begins to ascend.

I open my eyes, stop before I get to Bright Tree. *Where are you going, Taurus?*

We are late for the Meet.

The location of the Meet changes every now and then, but mostly, like today, it's in White Tree, near one of the hanging gardens stretched between branches where we grow crops.

Mathilde arrives, murmuring apologies to the other Elders. There's some muttering about the inconvenience, but eventually Mathilde just draws herself up and raises her hand and, whatever the others think of her privately, all eight of them close their mouths.

'As you know, Ade had a vision yesterday. I want you to hear what Joo . . . what the Chosen One has to say.' There are a few scuffs of laughter here, and quick glances in my direction, but Mathilde carries on as if she hasn't heard or noticed. 'And then the Meet will commence. I expect *everyone* to give the topic its due. I en't heard of a vision like this in some time and if we ignore it . . .' She leaves silence to imply what her words can't.

'We are all concerned, Elder Mathilde,' says Einar of Sap Tree in his smooth voice. 'Let the Chosen One come up and, ah – speak.'

My face fills with heat. I go to stand by Mathilde so she can relay what I saw in Ade's vision. They listen to Mathilde carefully as she describes the people and the fighting, their expressions schooled to cool interest. When we're finished, there are several pursed lips and it's clear they want me to leave before they begin their discussion. For a moment I have the urge to stay – I'm absolutely allowed to – just to spite them.

But Mathilde will argue better without worrying about my feelings, and the Elders might even listen if they aren't forced to be reminded of what a disappointment I am. It's only when the sounds of their voices become murmurs behind me that I remember the warning: YOUR CITIES DO NOT LEARN FROM THEIR CHOSEN ONES AS THEY SHOULD. THEY HAVE FLOUTED WISDOM AND TRUSTED POWER. YOU MUST DO YOUR BEST TO CHANGE THIS.

But the thought isn't enough to make me turn around. Change them *how*?

I decide to take a long way back to my hut, stopping off to look at the vine garden – where all the paths in Metis begin. On my way back across towards High Tree, I hear someone just out of sight behind me, but when I turn, the sound stops, and there is a creak like a giggle.

When I walk on, the footsteps behind me begin again.

I sigh and swing round. **Taurus?** I call. But there's nothing. No one.

I squint suspiciously into the vines covering this side of the trunk, but I can't see anyone. Never mind. I head for a bridge that leads to an observation platform where I'll be able to see the outer reaches of Athenas beyond the cliff above.

There is a noise like running.

I turn too slowly.

Someone lets out a laugh as they barrel into me, and I tip backwards and fall from the bridge.

The first instinct is to summon the vines to catch me. Power flares in my fingertips.

No.

I just miss the edge of the next bridge down, then I hit a lower observation platform hard. Tears burst into my eyes, more out of shock than real pain. I lie there, blinking and trying to restore the air to my lungs.

The world spins around me. When it stops, I move slowly. I'll have broken something, surely. But when I ease myself into a sitting position, run my hands tentatively over my body, nothing seems badly hurt. *How?*

I look around and here's my answer: the vines beneath me are only loosely woven. They must have bowed a little under my weight and absorbed some of the shock.

'Did she fly?' someone calls from above.

I peer up and see a girl frowning down at me. A boy appears beside her and shakes his head. They're no more than seven or eight. The humiliation of that makes my lower lip tremble.

'You idiot, Lana!' says the boy. 'You could have killed her.'

'Could not! She's *Chosen*. She's got powers, hasn't she?' the girl says, but she looks guilty. 'Sorry, Chosen One.'

'You all right?' the boy calls down.

I nod. *They didn't know what they were doing.*

'Sorry!' the girl says again, and they run back up the path giggling. I'm already forgotten.

I take in several shaky breaths. Try to get up and find I'm trembling too much to achieve it. Then Ade's voice rings out behind me.

'Oh, girl,' she says. 'My girl. My girl.' She approaches me from a right-hand bridge, clucking.

I'm trying my hardest not to cry, which is probably why, when I try to say, *not now, Ade*, I end up saying, **They hate me. They all hate me.**

Ade shakes her head. 'They want a Chosen One,' she says. 'They just don't know what that looks like yet.'

And what does it look like? I whimper, getting to my feet.

She looks at me as though *I'm* the one that's mad. 'Reckon that's a question for you,' she mutters.

87 Days

Aula

It's been six months of studying and training and studying and training and studying. Six months of forcing a smile on my face and pretending I know more about what will happen in Ariadnis than the day before. Six months since Ashir fell ill. I go to Ashir's ward every week and help the healer move her arms and legs to stop them from atrophying. Etain will come and watch, biting her lip, not saying anything.

Six months.

But I'm barely allowed to think about what that means. As if scarcely a day has passed, I am in the courtyard again, and Nadrik is making me work until my lungs are heaving and my skin is blistered with the heat. The only difference is that I used to get away with throwing him once or twice, but with less than three months to my eighteenth birthday to go now, I en't allowed to rest until I've taken his feet seven or eight times.

After we've washed we go to the city library and hole up in a study room. Before he makes me stare into books about wisdom until my eyes melt, Nadrik says, 'There are eighty-seven days until the Wise One's task. We know next to nothing about what obstacles you will find there. I think we should revisit the traits described to Kreywar by the Wise One; the skills that retrieving the book will require. It's all I can think of. It *must* be important.'

'*Again?*' I ask, but he just ignores me.

Joomia

'Joomia! Is you done communing?' Mathilde barks, somehow managing to make the sound teasing rather than aggressive.

Yes.

'Remember our lesson, kid.'

I didn't forget.

I'm safe in the Grove, trying to stretch my senses along the vines of Metis. I asked Taurus to come, and he hasn't. He was the first person I looked for today, and once again it seems he's gone to the top of High Tree. I've decided it means he's meeting someone, but I can't think who. I also haven't asked him about it. Everyone is allowed secrets. I can't share mine, so why should I ask him to do that for me? But these have been long months; I've felt each one crawl over me like a snail, while I do the same as I always have. It makes me feel cold and passive and means the pressure of my long-held secrets are starting to chafe at me. I should say something. I shouldn't.

'Joomia?'

I shrug the thought away and follow Mathilde's lead, sitting down and crossing my legs, then closing my eyes.

84

'Wisdom is gone from the world,' she intones. 'Wise One, help us return it.' This is her usual preface before any lesson, but today she adds, 'You enter Ariadnis in just less than three months, Joomia. There en't time for hesitation. No time for fear. You could be in there for weeks or ten minutes or a blink. It could be a battle, or a weighing. We don't know. We must be prepared for anything.'

Aula

'The values that the Wise One said would be needed to complete His task—' Nadrik waves a hand for me to begin.

I tip my chair back and squint in the direction of the window: 'Um. Love, Truth, er . . . Chaos?'

He looks like he's about to bite his own tongue off. 'Discipline!' he snaps. 'Willpower, Survival, Adaptation, Unity, Pleasure, Knowledge! And which values do you think you're *missing*, Aula?' he hisses, hooking the forelegs of my chair back to the floor with his foot.

I scowl.

'What *obstacles*, logically, would those values then produce?'

Joomia

Grief, Lies, Chaos, Shame, Fear, Stagnation, Singularity, Guilt and Ignorance, I say.

Mathilde nods. 'Good. And I reckon the obstacles you

face are gonna be along those lines.'

We exchange a thoroughly unenthusiastic look.

Mathilde smiles. 'Course, it en't gonna be easy,' she says, 'but at least we have a place to start.'

Aula

'Yeah, but *have we* ever started?' I ask. 'You've asked that question like sixty times and we're never any closer to figuring it out than we were last month, or the month before that, or the month—'

'*Aula.*'

'I'm serious,' I say. 'How the hell am I s'posed to prove that I'm worthy to be wise, huh?'

'By getting to the book first,' Nadrik says.

I slump back in my chair. 'Yeah,' I say. 'I gotta get the book to prove my worth; only to prove my worth I gotta get the book.'

He sighs, like I'm too dumb to get it.

'Well, I dunno why we're bothering,' I carry on. 'What's super-strength and super-speed got to do with wisdom anyway?'

Nadrik kisses his teeth. 'Aula, *you know this*. It is in every text that describes the Wise One's prophecy: Ariadnis is a test of *both* your physical and mental abilities. Wisdom is not simply the study of knowledge, but the practical application of it in *everything* that you do. You must live wisdom in the very fibre of yourself. That is why your powers have manifested in you physically, rather than

86

simply in your mind. He is asking that you reach for mental wisdom on your own.'

'So, in other words, me being strong is just the Wise One's idea of some great big symbol?'

Nadrik rolls his eyes.

'Come *on*. Why's it so important that I win against Metis?'

His skin goes waxy. He doesn't like it when I talk like this. 'You are being childish.'

'Telling me I'm being childish en't an answer.'

'That is because you are asking the wrong questions.'

Suddenly I've had enough. I'm on my feet and throwing the table at the wall before Nadrik can blink. 'Why can't you just *answer* me?!' I roar as we're both showered in splinters.

'Because I want you to think for yourself!' Nadrik snaps. 'What happens if Metis wins? I have taught you their values, their culture. What happens if they win? Tell me.'

Joomia

Mathilde says, 'Long ways back – long before even the Wave, the world was vast and untouched and unknown.' She takes a long breath. 'And then *we* came. And we dug it a deep grave. With our ignorance, our selfishness, our superiority. We built wars with information, we tore down forests with greed, we ended lives with impatience. But, kid, there *was* a time when we knew there en't none better than the world we live in. We cared about it. We lived alongside it. I'd give it all to get us back to that point. Start again. And the book can do that, Joomia. The Wise One's book can do that.'

Aula

I clench my hands in frustration, but there en't anything left to throw. 'They wanna start over,' I say. 'So what? It's the same as what we want. *Athenas* wants to start over.'

'But not like them,' Nadrik hisses. 'What do they embrace of human knowledge? Tree houses? Pretending the future doesn't exist? Sleeping with anything that moves?' He spits forcefully to the side. For a reason I en't sure of, it makes me wanna back away from him. 'We used to be *gods*,' he says. 'We used to have knowledge in buttons and screens, at the slightest touch of a finger!'

I know. I've read about it. Computers. A sprawling knowledge system known as the internet. Having access to that kind of knowledge . . . it en't imaginable.

'Would you have us return to bark and dirt as they have?' he asks fiercely. 'Would you have us scratch out wisdom from the wood?'

'No,' I say.

'*No*,' he agrees. '*That* is why you will win the book from them, Aula.'

'But—' I start, but he turns to fix me in place with a long, cold stare.

I open my mouth. I close it again.

He nods. His forehead and eyebrows full of *that's what*

I thought. 'We will need a new table,' he says pointedly.

I glare at him, but he just glares right back. I snarl, scuffing my heels and go to fetch us one.

Joomia

Mathilde quizzes me on the study of knowledge for another hour and then we have to go. She raises her hand to take down the shield that seals us into the Grove, but I stop her.

I just want to say, um . . . goodbye. To the trees.

'Well, kid, why don't you do it without the shield this time? You know you're gonna have to soon enough.'

I bite my lip.

'Look, I en't saying it's not to our advantage that everyone *thinks* you're powerless but it's like we been saying. You en't got long before your eighteenth birthday. It's time to start getting used to—'

Mathilde, I can't, I told you.

She puts her hands on her hips. 'Then what about the task? What you gonna do then?'

I . . . I don't know.

For a while, we stare at each other, her begging me to find my courage, me pleading, *not yet. Not yet. I'm not ready yet*.

She throws up her hands. 'Fine. Do your communing,' she says. 'But this conversation en't over.'

I give her what I hope is an appeasing smile, but she just grunts.

89

Then I stretch out my arms and wait for the vines to come to me.

This. If I could choose, I would just be this. It's not even about reaching or seeing. It's about *being*. Your roots in the earth, your branches stretching high into the blue, the air rich and close. Other magi might be able to manipulate them, but no one else has this: seeing what they see, listening as they listen.

My mind wanders to Taurus . . . I can't help it . . . *who* is he meeting?

But there is no one there now.

Stop it, Joomia, I tell myself.

I take a deep breath, and prepare to let go.

And that's when I sense it. It's like the smell of something rancid and sour – but out of sight, hidden.

'Kid, let's go,' Mathilde says.

Mathilde . . .

'Yeah?'

I look at her, and her expression changes. 'What? What's wrong?'

I sift through the tendrils of sensation in the bark of the trees, searching. Where is it – that sense of decay – coming from?

For a moment I think I've found the source, but the moment I reach for it my certainty disappears. The trees are as healthy and strong as ever.

'What is it, kid?'

Sorry, it's . . . it's nothing. I'm coming now.

Aula

Nadrik folds the book he's looking at and says, 'The Wise One celebrations.'

'Huh?' I say, and his mouth goes thin.

'The Day of the Wise One will be upon us in just under two months' time.'

'What about it?'

'I think, given the scenes you have been making, that I should remind you of your protocol during the lead-up to the day. A week leading up to the celebrations, you will need to be visible each day for your public. There will be time to train every day, but in the evenings you will present yourself to your people. You will be dressed accordingly, you will speak eloquently. There will be no appearance of *this*,' he snaps, flicking the point between my eyebrows which has furrowed itself into two deep crevices.

I glare at the cover of my book and twist my nail into the embossed title. En't I attended every opening of some stupid building or other that he told me to? Paraded through the streets with him so everyone can look at me while we pretend to 'have a look around the city'? En't I read every speech he's written from me – all without once saying 'en't'?

I can feel the acid of useless tears seethe under my eyelids. My fingers fumble with the corner of the book. I try to open it, but Nadrik yanks it out of my hands.

'There will be a demonstration tomorrow. You will remind this city that the powers the Wise One has given you are not just for destroying public property and private housing.'

'That was *months* ago,' I splutter.

He slams the book down on the table. 'You will go now and will come back here tomorrow in a better attitude.'

I don't wait for him to finish the sentence.

86 Days

Aula

They call for blood.

Well, here I am.

Nadrik and me wait at the open door, just out of sight. The crowd – wearing red and sporting headdresses fletched with owl feathers – roars like a tethered animal. The arena has been decorated, presumably for the pissing Wise One celebrations in two months' time. There are flags printed with owls and claws, banners with cogs and chimneys to symbolise the steam.

A magi is standing in the centre, one of Nadrik's, handpicked, ready to fight.

I've fought in demonstrations like this before. Nadrik likes to show off what he's taught me and Athenasians like to watch the blood of their Chosen One thudding in her veins; they like to be satisfied that though she en't perfect, she'll win them the Wise One's gift.

But this time is different. I en't sure I wanna go out there and hear my name shouted over and over. Etain would usually be here but she's helping the Cassandrae piece together some kind of prophecy – they've been working

93

overtime since Ashir got ill and they need looking after. I chew my lip as I scan the stands. Half the city's out there, by the looks of things. Don't they have anything better to do?

I glance at Nadrik. I want so badly for him to just look at me, but his eyes are on the magi he's selected to fight, not me.

'Are you ready?' he says at last.

'Yeah,' I say, tugging on the end of the plait I've wrestled my hair into, then I add, 'Nadrik . . . I'm sorry. I'm gonna try, really I will.'

'Good,' he says. 'Then go.'

I sigh, then jog into the ring.

The cry that goes up when they see me is like a tear in the sky.

The magi turns to watch me approach. She's just as tall as me, grinning with the same violent snarl as I am.

'FIRST BLOOD!' Nadrik bellows, and then a gong goes.

The magi cocks her head like *come on* and her silhouette blurs the same way Nadrik's does when he summons his shields. I crack my knuckles.

She digs her foot in, then suddenly outta the side of my vision I'm aware of five other magi running at me from open doors around the arena.

The gong rings again. One of the magi – armed with a bow and a quiver – fires in my direction. He misses by miles, but by then the first of them is on me. This one aims a punch at my head, but I've already knocked their fist aside and sent them toppling into the next magi running at us.

Just as I think *strike two*, a third magi manages to trip me with – of all things – a whip. He's so quick I don't even notice the tail of it snarling around my ankles and then *wham*, I'm down. I pretend to struggle on the ground, and wait for him to attack. When he does, I catch the foot that he aims at my face and put all my weight into rolling him over me. His shield stops me from twisting the foot right off – but only just. In any case, he's not getting up any time soon.

'Teach you to kick people when they're down,' I mutter.

Then three of them are on me at once: one knocking me down, the other clamping my feet, the third preparing a dust blast that'll tear skin. I know I need to get her quickly, but she's standing too close. Her shields are too solid.

Freeing my legs is pretty easy. I just kick upwards, knocking my opponent's head backwards. The magi who knocked me down gets treated to my best javelin throw – with him as the javelin. I launch him at another magi for good measure. *Five.*

I turn just in time. The magi preparing the spell is ready. Energy is throbbing through the air around her fingers. One flick will send it straight for me. She smiles like she's got me. So I run at her before she has a chance to move. I skid through her outstretched legs, snake up her back and pitch us both forward, slamming her hard into the ground. *Six.*

I try to let the roar from the crowd fill me up.

Nadrik is watching me from the side. He doesn't run out of the stands to lift me up with the crowd. He doesn't move.

And as I look at his I finally understand.

95

All this stuff – the training, these fights—
They don't mean anything.

He doesn't have any more of a clue of what's in Ariadnis than I do. He's just training me in what he knows, and what he hopes will work, and in the meantime he's raising citizen morale by getting them to watch me doing what I do best. In a controlled way, where no one can get seriously hurt and he can keep his people on side.

The gong goes again.

I win.

85 Days

Joomia

I rub sleep out of my eyes, and it's like I've been unravelled. The emptiness I've felt in me before is everywhere, stinging like an open wound. A dream lingers stickily in the air like some foul breath. But it's only the *feeling* of the dream. Even as I snatch for the details, they snuff out like candle flames.

I begin the process of folding and stacking my blankets in a corner, as much to restore order to the hut as to my head. In the end, it isn't that which distracts me. The floor of my hut is different. Usually it's unyielding, strong as rock, but when I run my feet over it this morning, it gives. I scrape aside the compacted leaves and dirt, and see the vines, which should be healthy, have an edge of rot. Just like the passage to Lore's study. Just like the hole in Mathilde's hut, all those months ago.

It is possible something's been nibbling at the fibres that make up my hut further down the tree, hurting their growth. Only . . . that feeling I had in the Grove a few days ago . . .

NOTHING LEFT FOR YOU TO SAVE . . .

When I leave my sleeping hut, I find Lear waiting for me on the branch below.

'I've been sent to keep you updated,' he says as I approach. 'The Elders went into another Meet last night. They've nearly reached an agreement about what to do with Ade's vision.'

I try not to roll my eyes, because Ade's vision was so long ago now that the initial panic of it has long gone from the city, whose real fear is based on the *idea* of *any* prophecy anyway.

Mathilde's been trying to bring it back to the Elders' attention every few months – especially whenever she spots another appearance of weakness in any structure. She says the first sign of weaknesses coincided with the vision. But, if I'm honest, even I have trouble toting that logic.

I nod to Lear though, to show I understand.

'Joomia,' he says tentatively. 'Did you really see that stuff Ade was moaning about? About bad things happening . . . about there being no one left?'

The rot, the Meet all those months ago, those kids pushing me. They've all hardened like scabs that pull on you when you try to move. I nod to Lear but when I turn to go, he catches my hand.

'What did she see?' he asks. 'What did *you* see in her vision?'

I sigh. I'm not in the mood to mime it to him, but his expression is earnest and Wise One knows I always need more allies. I go back to my hut to find some parchment and charcoal.

I write: *There were people. They were blank. It didn't seem like much then, but—* I pause in writing and feel like I might be remembering part of my dream. *I think I dreamed about it last night.* He pales at this, so I write out: *What is it?*

He hesitates, looking at me as if considering whether I'm trustworthy. 'I dreamed last night that my family couldn't remember my name. I dreamed that *I* couldn't remember my name. Is that what you mean by *blank*?'

I write: *I don't know . . . they didn't seem like people any more. I've heard that strong visions leave shock waves in people's subconscious sometimes. Maybe this is something like that?*

His mouth quirks, one hand moving anxiously to his hair. 'Yeah, maybe,' he says, without conviction. Unexpectedly, he takes my hand again. 'You don't think we should worry?' he asks.

I just shake my head, doing my best to smile easily as I get to my feet, but he doesn't let go.

'You haven't um . . . seen Taurus, have you? We were together last night for a bit, but . . .' He trails off. I think he's trying to sound nonchalant, but his voice is catching in all the wrong places. 'I can't find him.'

I think of what the vines have shown me. The top of High Tree where Taurus goes to . . . *what?*

Lear looks at me, a little desperately. 'Joomia, please. You're his best friend.'

I keep my face as apologetic as possible and shake my head again. He slumps.

Sorry, I say, but of course, he can't hear me. I turn from him and slip away along the pathways.

I need to clear my head, so it's only after half an hour or so of walking the paths that, by chance, I find Taurus in the garden of High Tree.

The garden is a large platform of branches woven in on each other, filled with earth and sown with grass seed. Most of the bridges in Metis start here. In some seasons, when you look at it from above and the earth is bright with yellow flowers, it looks like a picture of a sun, the bridges taking the shapes of rays as they lead away in meandering spokes.

Taurus is sitting alone, looking up at the statue that is the centrepiece of the High Tree garden. 'I never understood why you don't like my old friend Ramon,' he says, nodding at the statue when he sees me approaching.

I look at the wooden man with his laughing eyes, reaching out as if he'd seen a friend. Ramon was a mad old prophet much like Ade, whose last act before moving to Athenas was apparently to leave this effigy of himself behind.

That's what everyone thinks, because that is what Mathilde told them.

But if I close my eyes, I can hear Ramon's voice in my head.

Joomia, they're singing.

I shrug at Taurus, as if it's not important that we get off the topic. **Can I sit here?**

'Sounds cosy.'

Shut up.

He grins, hooks my legs out from under me and drops me next to him. I do my best to look at least a little bit dignified about it.

Lear was looking for you, I say.

He leans back against the tree and bites his lip.

I raise my eyebrow.

'I just need some breathing room. A couple of hours –

don't look at me like that. How're the lessons going?'

I make a face, and he ruffles my hair. He looks a little distracted, and I think again of asking him what he was doing at the top of High Tree, but I decide not to push it. We both have our secrets.

Will you please just talk to him if you're going to let him down?

'Who says I'm going to let him down?'

I'd **rather you didn't. I told you, I like him. He's definitely a lot easier than Nagesa. And a lot less shrill than Phaedra.**

We both shudder.

'I'll talk to him,' he says.

You *could* **just see how it goes from here, you know. See what it's like to be with someone for more than a few weeks.**

He wrinkles his nose. 'It's *been* more than a few weeks for quite a while. Anyway . . . Lear's nice but he's not . . . I don't know . . . he doesn't feel quite right.'

Mmm, I say. **Well, you'll let me know when someone does, won't you?**

He shrugs helplessly, still smiling as he takes my hand and kisses it, as if to say, not yet.

Something makes a sharp movement behind the rockery several feet away. My heart sinks.

Oh no. He followed me.

Of course he did. I see a smudge of black hair through the leaves.

Taurus starts. 'Lear?'

Lear emerges, his pale brown skin flushed, an angry but defiant expression flicking along his eyebrows.

Taurus glances from me to him, then takes a breath.

101

'Sorry I left so early. I like to come up here in the mornings.'

Lear says nothing.

'Joomia just came to tell me she saw you.'

'So, I'm nice, but I don't *feel* quite right?' he says to Taurus, his expression angry as a bruise. He turns to me. 'Didn't know where he was, huh?'

I blush. Taurus shakes his head. 'She found me here, that's all.'

'Finds you a lot, doesn't she?' Lear says. 'Pretty rare sight, to see you without her.'

I wince, because I know what's coming.

And sure enough: 'I reckon you saw enough of me last night without her. Don't you?' Taurus laughs.

I usually hate it when Taurus does this – turns on the charm for one of his flings – but today I'm distracted. Some other sense – innate, like the senses I use to summon the vines – prickles as if a phantom hand had brushed it.

Lear's mouth thins, and he turns to me. 'Mathilde and the Elders finished their Meet,' he says. 'Thought you ought to know.'

He begins to walk away, but he's only gone two steps forward when the pathway of vines under his feet . . . it ripples.

I stand up, feeling my senses twinge and spasm in warning. I see now that the pathway is reddish brown, the roots look gelatinous and wrong.

Stop! I shout, forgetting he won't hear me. **Taurus! Stop him!**

'Why?'

And before I have time to reply, he gets his answer.

102

Lear wobbles, turns back to us, eyes wide.

'Keep still,' Taurus whispers.

Lear tries to do as he says, but something snaps underneath him. His arms windmill.

When I was nine, and Taurus was twelve, we were climbing in the highest parts of High Tree when a branch snapped under me and I fell. I should have broken something; the distance to the nearest platform was ten yards at least. But I didn't.

At the last second, right before I hit the platform, I stopped. Inches from where I'd have snapped my neck. Vines had gathered around my body – my wrists and ankles and waist. They'd caught me. I didn't tell anyone about it, but there's no keeping secrets from Mathilde. She took me aside later and looked me over for signs of injury. Then I told her what happened and she'd smiled and said, 'Bless me, Miss Joomia. You is coming into your powers, sure enough.'

And I wonder sometimes what would have happened if what happened shortly after that hadn't happened; maybe I *would* have come into my powers and no one would think I was useless after all. I would have been ready, and able to do this. Able to stop someone mid-fall. But I never imagined that I'd *have* to. Never until this moment.

The path gives way under Lear's feet, and I raise my hands as if I can stop him from falling.

But it *did* happen.

So Lear falls.

And I let him.

Aula

Etain's forge is empty, but I go and wait in it anyway. It's been ages since we were in here together. Ages since we spent any time together, in fact. I'd caught her in the courtyard this morning on her way to Nadrik, and she'd promised we'd do some kiln work or blow some bulbs, or something else that will keep us busy tonight.

I go to her work bench, which, unsurprisingly for the daughter of a prophet, has been left in a mess. I sort a few of the odd nails into piles and then have a look around for where she might put them. There's a set of dusty drawers in the back of the workshop, and I spend a little while just going back and forth, putting things away. Her hammers all have leather-wrapped handles with loops sewn on to the ends to make them easy to hang up, so I find the right hooks for each one in the beams overhead. I stoke the fires and sweep the floor and sharpen all her blades on the whetstone.

An hour or so passes.

Maybe she's with Nadrik. I know he's been keeping her busy recently. And that could be something he's demanding of her, but some other, paranoid part of me doesn't think so.

I keep the fires going another hour, and the forge gets so hot I have to duck out. I watch the sun set on Athenas. There's the smell of thyme from the Earth plateau in the air and the sound of owls hooting softly to each other to wake up.

I nod off, and when I wake the moon is full in the sky.

I go to look for Etain again, and eventually I find her still in the prophet house, poring wearily over a book, quill in hand, straining her eyes by her lantern. I think about saying something, but she looks so tired, so I watch her for a few moments longer, and then leave.

Joomia

'Rot,' pronounces Head Magi Merryn of Wise Tree, her fingers tracing the crumbled mess of root fibres where Lear fell. 'We've been lucky. It doesn't stretch to the rest of the plant. Could be it was some kind of parasite and Lear was just unlucky about where he put his feet. Someone should have noticed.'

I noticed. My hut this morning. The strange feeling in the vines yesterday. And Mathilde . . . her hut . . .

No one has found a body but, given that the particular spot where Lear fell has no pathways underneath, it seems unlikely that anyone will. Thinking about that takes me back to dreams where the rules change halfway through – the stairs are a slide, your friend's hand is a monster's, the water you're drinking is blood.

I look at the hole, at Mathilde. 'It en't a parasite,' she says. 'It's more than that. Something en't right here.'

NOTHING LEFT FOR YOU TO SAVE . . .

My lungs feel small and frail, too weak to take a proper breath.

Deputy Magi Einar looks at Mathilde. 'Something else, Elder Mathilde?' he asks sceptically.

Mathilde looks at me, and Einar follows her eyes. 'But of course,' he mutters. 'Our saviour, who has even less power than most commoners, is convinced she knows more than us.'

Head Magi Merryn says, '*Einar.*'

Einar bows his head, but I'm not sure if it's to apologise or just to mock Merryn.

'She's right to be cautious,' Mathilde says. 'If it's rot – or a parasite or something else – we'd all be wise to check the vines carefully. As you well know, I've found other weakened structures before. Might be some explainable cause. Or . . . it might be something else. Now, if you'll excuse me, Magi Einar, Magi.' She bows slightly to the other magi gathered around the hole. 'Gotta fill the Chosen One in on the decisions we made in the Meet.'

'Of course, Elder,' Einar says, but his eyes are on me, like he's trying to scrape through my head to my thoughts.

Mathilde motions for me, and I grab Taurus's hand. It's cold. He's gone still.

Taurus, I say.

He turns to me, and for the first time in a long time, I can't read his expression.

They don't believe me, I say, once the three of us get back to Mathilde's hut.

Mathilde sighs. 'They don't believe you,' she agrees.

But *you* believe me, I say.

'There en't anything I can do, just yet,' she says, after a silence.

'You're the Head Elder,' Taurus says sharply.

'And the Head Elder doesn't impose her opinion on the other eight Elders in her city!' Mathilde snaps.

'Then what is the point of a Head Elder?' he says.

'To keep everyone together, kid. But I en't no one's leader.'

He turns to look at her. And then, slowly, he looks at me. 'Maybe someone should be,' he says. 'Maybe it's time.'

He walks me back to my hut.

Are you all right? I ask him.

'I'm fine,' he says.

But when we are nearly at the branch, he says, 'I was too slow.'

You can't think it was *your* fault he fell?

'No, I know it wasn't *my* fault,' he says. 'But I still feel responsible. Do you?'

Yes, I say.

'*Good*,' he says. 'I was wondering.'

I close my eyes. There is nothing to say. No way to defend myself. He walks past me without another word.

32 Days

Joomia

Tomorrow is the Day of the Wise One.

The last two months have passed so slowly. The Elders continue to do nothing, though the rot's getting worse. I'm called to every place it's found because it's still my function as Chosen One, but all I can do is look worried. The magi try to reverse it. Sometimes they can, but more and more often the fibres are too far gone to rescue. Some areas of Metis have had to be cordoned off. They called off the search for Lear's body after it was declared that every corner of Metis had been turned over.

It's almost over, I tell myself. In just over a month it will be over either way. If I can just get through the next four weeks without keeling over in panic.

The preparations for tomorrow have been especially elaborate this year because of the task. The celebrations don't start until the evening, and I'm trying to put my mind to other things because I can't breathe. *I can't breathe*. Unfortunately one of those things I have to think about is my least favourite part of my Chosen One duty: Audience.

I've had to attend Audience every few weeks since I was

nine, but it feels worse now – now that I'm older, now that they expect things from me. What happens in Audience is this: I sit in the courtyard of whichever tree I am supposed to be attending this time, and listen as the citizens come to me with their debates, arguments, their sufferings and woes. Then it is my job to advise them. It is not as bad as it sounds. Often, I know what their problems are already, because the vines tell me things about the troubles of the city.

But the last two months have been different. There have been many small problems, but the worst of it is Taurus. He usually translates for me, but he's let me down so often recently, and I've had to make do with Mathilde – or, worse, Ade. When he *is* here, he's distracted and moody and he only acknowledges me with nods and one-word answers, and I don't push him in case I make it worse.

He's here today, though. We are in Low Tree, and he stands next to my seat, sheltering from the rain under a canopy of waxed fabric and poles. I'm not sure if I'm relieved or anxious. He acknowledges me with a nod, but just barely. There are looping thorns in my stomach. **Thank the Wise One there's rain at last,** I say to him hopefully. He doesn't reply. For a moment we just hover in silence while people line up to talk to me.

They don't look happy, I murmur. Taurus raises an eyebrow slightly, but doesn't say anything. Something like fear ices the pit of my abdomen. Two months, and he still won't talk to me.

The first people to come up, as usual, are people with

112

petty problems: babies with colic, people with headaches that won't go away. I may not be able to demonstrate any power but I *do* know the herbal combinations for things like that. I recite them and Taurus relates for me.

'Thank you, Chosen One,' says one mother, Alma, patting her red-faced baby on the back. 'I swear I forgot my own name yesterday, I was that desperate!'

I am swamped momentarily by Lear's voice, *I dreamed that I couldn't remember my name.* But I tell myself not to be paranoid. This is nothing like that. This is a mother whose squalling child is keeping her awake.

The next group of people come to me with disputes to settle. This, I have less of a natural talent for. There's a man who was promised something at the market and never got it. A couple whose relationship has become tangled in lies. A mother whose son won't speak to her. They talk too fast and begin to shout over each other, and twice Taurus has to step in to settle them. I try to offer practical solutions where I can, sympathy if nothing can be done. For the most part it works.

But the man after these comes alone, with a smile.

'Chosen One,' he begins, 'the vines that make up my house have turned to rot. What shall I do?' He says the last part like a challenge, and I get the idea that he's asking not so much because he thinks I'll have a solution, but because I *won't*.

Tell him Elder Mathilde and the rest of the magi are looking into it, I say, and Taurus says this out loud.

But the man's eyes never leave my face, and his smile looks fixed in place as if someone has sewn it there. 'Oh, *looking into it*, are they? But surely that is *your* quarter – to be looking into it? Unless, that is, we are all mistaken, and you aren't the Chosen One after all?'

'She's the Chosen One, Ursus,' Taurus says stiffly. 'What she isn't is a magi.'

I stare at Taurus, more surprised at the fact that he knows the man's name than anything. *I* should know things like that.

'Not a magi.' Ursus repeats the words like he's chewing them. 'Not a climber or a weaver or a merchant. I could call her an advisor, but she doesn't even have a *voice*.'

'That's enough, Ursus,' Eros, Elder of Low Tree says. 'You've been given your answer; now move along.'

But Ursus just stands there, legs splayed, arms folded, and then a girl's voice shouts, 'Well, he's *right*, isn't he?'

I look up to see Oriha next in line. I rub my sticky palms on my skirt.

'Things are going wrong all over the place. My mother doesn't remember who I am,' Oriha says. 'And she's just sitting there!'

I stare at her, for a moment completely baffled. Lear's voice comes to me again: *I dreamed last night that my family couldn't remember my name. I dreamed that I couldn't remember my name.*

'What has happened with your mother, Oriha?' Taurus asks.

Oriha snarls, 'Aren't you sick of speaking for her, Taurus?'

My face brightens with blood. Taurus frowns. But I think I can tell what the answer to her question is. The

114

moment is like a bowl full of liquid – it's so close to spilling from me.

Eventually Oriha says, 'It happened yesterday.' She seems surprised by the words, and her voice sounds weaker than the last thing she said.

'Why didn't you tell anyone?' Taurus asks.

'Why would I?' she snaps. 'Did anyone give a damn when Lear fell? Did anyone *do* anything?'

Taurus bristles. I try to sink further into my chair. But the crowd have heard Oriha. There are murmurs.

'Why are you really here, Oriha?' Taurus asks.

'For *answers*,' she says. '*She's* the Chosen One, isn't she? Isn't she supposed to help us? Protect us? What is she going to do to help my mother? What did she do to help Lear?'

There are shouts of assent and rumblings of anger. I look, terrified, to Taurus.

The expression on his face as he looks back is hollow. 'What *did* you do to help him?' he whispers, not meeting my eyes.

'That's enough!' Eros shouts over the crowd. 'I will have order here!'

I couldn't *do* anything, I say. The words echo inside my skull. Liar.

'No?' Taurus says. 'Then what about when we were younger and you fell? What about how you used to make flowers grow out of their seed cases?'

'Step back!' Eros calls to the crowd.

That's different.

Now Taurus turns to me, his voice still barely more than

115

a whisper. 'How is it different? Are you even sad that he's gone?'

Of course I am! That's a horrible thing to s—

'Are you? Cause you're not *acting* like it!'

What do you mean? I ask.

But he doesn't seem to hear me. 'You know,' he says, 'I think they're right. You *are* the Chosen One. It's your *job*. It's what Mathilde's been *training* you for all your life. To protect us.'

Taurus . . .

He stands up. 'I don't know what you think's gonna happen, Joomia, but you're not gonna just *wake up* one day and find you aren't the Chosen One any more. If you don't do something to stop bad things happening, who will?'

A shudder goes through me. I'm not aware of getting out of my seat, or of obeying the impulse to run, until I'm halfway up the pathway that leads out of the courtyard.

31 Days

The Day of the Wise One

Aula

My throat is dry from reading the endless speech Nadrik wrote for me. My back is sweaty from the layered Ionic chiton I've been made to wear. As usual, the Day of the Wise One seems to have inspired people to have a crack at any style of Old World cultural dress they can mimic.

'Chosen One, wonderful speech,' says the Captain of the Guard, Linas. He's wearing what's clearly supposed to be a chief's war bonnet on his head, with a girl who I think is called Eilee on his arm. I recognise her from the palace guard too. They're both swaying out of time to the music, which is whining from somewhere near the centre of the palace gardens.

'Um. Thanks,' I say, and he beams like I just said something proper charming.

'Chosen One, I've got to ask you where you got your gown,' Eilee says. She clutches the folds of the chiton like she's never seen anything so nice. I gotta get something to drink. They've all been slamming back glasses since noon while I've been tearing my hair out trying to stop my accent sneaking out on me. I thought I'd be able to handle coming down here for a bit, but when you en't pissed yourself you forget how not funny it is when everyone else is.

Eilee still hasn't let go of the chiton, so I say, 'Um. I dunno his name. Some bloke on the Industry plateau.'

She adjusts her sari. 'It's just *beautiful*,' she says, grabbing my arm for emphasis. I bite down on telling her not to touch me.

'Everyone looks beautiful!' Linas says, gesturing around. Kimonos, al-Amira hijabs, sherwanis and lederhosen, tea dresses and turbans. I try and smile – I usually *like* this part of the Wise One's day. But this year, nothing feels right.

Maybe it's cos last year Sander and me danced until we were both red in the face and then went back to my rooms (and, you know).

Maybe it's cos Etain en't here. I've barely seen her over the last couple of months, and even when I have it's been weird between us, like something's in the way and she knows exactly what it is even though I don't.

Maybe it's cos Ashir's still unconscious. Comatosed. Whatever they are calling it. I've been sitting at her bedside for an hour every day and begging the Wise One to wake her up, but He hasn't.

Or maybe it's just cos I en't drunk yet.

I say something about the toilet to Linas and Eilee who en't listening anyway. I'm heading to the nearest drinks table when, *Wham*.

'Shit!' I blink as wine runs down the front of the chiton in dark red blotches. The boy who knocked into me is already getting to his feet, swearing. He's wearing healer's robes, with a cigarillo in one hand and a now-empty glass in the other. 'Watch where you're going!' I snap.

'Oh, Wise One,' he says, biting his lip as the wine stain bleeds. 'I'm so sorry. I was dancing and I ... er ... got carried away.' He looks like he's trying not to laugh. When his eyes finally catch up to my face and not the stain he does a familiar double take, which is what happens when people recognise me. 'You must be Aula,' he says. He doesn't say *Chosen One*, which is a plus, but what I like best is that he doesn't seem any more concerned that he spilled his wine on *me* than he would if it were anyone else.

'Yeah,' I say.

'Having a good time?' he asks. His accent sounds kind of Metisian, with a lazy, easier rhythm that feels friendly just now. I didn't know there were any ex-Metisians working in the healing quarters. The boy kind of looks familiar, but I can't place where from.

'I will be,' I say, as we make our way back towards a table where drinks are laid out. I help myself to a mug of ale. I down it in one and pour another.

He laughs. 'I'm guessing you didn't write that speech yourself?'

I let out a tiny snarl and finish my second mug. He turns the tap on the barrel so I can get a third. I look him up and down. 'You en't got a costume.'

He says, 'How dare you. I had to wait for *hours* to get a chance to steal this.'

119

'You're not a healer?'

He smiles. 'Do I look like a healer?'

'You look like an idiot,' I say. 'If someone here sees you en't got a costume they'll think you're skiving.'

He gives me a sideways look. 'I don't think there are too many people left here sober enough to think anything of the sort. Unless you're gonna chuck me out yourself.'

I realise then that I've been looking at him too long. It en't that he's the most beautiful boy on Erthe or anything. It's just that my eyes keep wanting to look. I cast around for something to say. 'Are *you* having a good time?' I ask, and I *almost* manage not to make it sound challenging.

'Not really,' he says. 'I'm not very fond of parties where people bastardise the clothes of our ancestors for their own amusement, without any respect for the cultures the clothes came from.'

'All our ancestors are dead,' I point out. 'There en't anyone left to offend.'

He smiles again, but a bit sadly. 'I thought Athenas was better than that. I thought they valued wisdom over ignorance.'

'We do!' I snap.

'If you say so.'

I stare at him. 'You're still Metisian, aren't you?' I ask. 'You en't moved here at all. You're . . . you're *visiting*.'

He shrugs, like I en't got him rumbled, but his shoulders tense up a bit and I know that I do.

I look around. 'Have you got a death wish or something?' I hiss. 'Do you know what they'll do to you if they find out you're here without the Anax's permission?'

'Who says I don't have the Anax's permission?' he counters.

'Cos if a Metisian were supposed to be coming he would have told me.'

He holds up his hands, like he's surrendering. 'Then take me to him, O Chosen One. My fate is in your hands.'

I suddenly realise he's *joking*, and with that realisation comes the even bigger one that I want to jump his bones. *Wise One*.

'Why are you here?' I ask him. I look at the healer's robes again. But deep down I know why he might be wearing them, and so before I have a chance to think I have him by the collar. 'Why were you in the healers' quarters at all?'

He looks alarmed, but not scared. 'Aula . . .' he says.

'Tell me!'

Someone nearby sees us and laughs. 'Don't get her too riled up, son!'

'Medicine,' he says unblinkingly. 'A rare medicine that we can't make in Metis.'

I hesitate. Then I let him go.

'*Wise One*,' he says, opening the top button of the robes where my hand's made a tear. I catch a glimpse of his collarbones pressing out against his earthy skin and my heart starts dancing outta rhythm. He looks back at me, a smile curling into one side of his face.

'You *are* strong,' he says.

A man's gotta feel like a man, I think hopelessly.

Only then he says, 'Would you like to dance?'

I make sure he can see me considering, then I say, 'I'd rather find a dark place to tumble if that's all right with you.'

Instead of being put off, he smiles, like he's surprised. 'I don't know if that's a good idea,' he says, but he's smiling like he thinks it's a very good idea.

I know this game. 'Fine, if you don't want to.' I turn to move away. This is the bit where they catch your arm.

He catches my arm. 'You want to,' he says. 'But why?'

God, of all the weird things to ask. 'Cos you're the most honest thing I've seen in months,' I say. He stares at me, but I do the brave thing and let the silence hang there. I mean it, I mean it. Then I add, 'And cos I don't want to be here. And . . . well, never mind the rest.'

He reaches for my hand.

My pulse.

'No dark places,' he says.

I take him to my room.

For a while we just sit and don't say anything. It's weird – it en't awkward. It's just sort of nice. He doesn't move to me, he just looks around. Between the soft pounding of the drums from the party and the far-off engines, I watch him close his eyes and it seems to bring him closer to me. My heartbeat has selected the rhythm known as HEY, THERE'S A BOY IN YOUR ROOM, which basically means that it's going so fast I dunno if I'm gonna be able to breathe soon. And I look at him, now I'm free to, and I stare. His shoulder relaxes slightly, and I think: a) how the hell is he so calm; and b) I don't want to be alone.

So I lean in and kiss him.

I expect his body to come alive all at once, like Sander's used to, but he is slower than that. He kisses me back, and then he takes my chin in one hand and kisses the underside of my jaw, and his fingers trace the shape of my ear. I close my eyes. He en't even opened his yet.

Before long neither of us has clothes on and I'm shaking a bit and staring dizzily at his body and shivering in mine. He en't particularly muscly or anything, but his body is interesting – like the rest of him. Like how his waist tapers, like how his arms are all ropy and the hair on his stomach grows up like a vine. He's like some sorta tree spirit. I suddenly notice how naked I am and how not like a tree spirit and I wanna cover myself up.

But his eyes are steadying and weirdly curious, like I'm someone he thinks he ought to know but can't quite place.

'Hang on,' I say, stopping him from coming in for another kiss, 'I should tell you, um . . . I'm pretty strong.'

He laughs. 'I think I can handle it.'

I laugh back, all sarcastic. 'No, you don't. I mean, I could snap you in two without much effort. So, um . . . you gotta be careful. Well, no, I mean *I* gotta be careful, but—'

I wanna curse myself, cos God how do I even get by with words like that coming outta my trap. But he doesn't look even slightly put off. He's stopped laughing though. He's taking me seriously. God, when was the last time that happened?

'I'll tap you if you're hurting me,' he says.

And then we move quite a bit quicker.

Compared to the kissing, it en't all that great so I cut out the niceties and give him a bit of direction, and then whadduya know he gives me some as well and after that our breath comes in snatches.

I clap a hand over my lamp and we do the rest of our

negotiating in the dark. There are a couple of times he has to tap my arm to let me know I'm hanging on too tight, but once we've settled into a rhythm, I get exactly what I was hoping for: total oblivion.

30 Days

Joomia

It's late enough to be early, and the Wise One celebrations from last night are finally winding down. High Tree is alight with small green illuminations – cast into the air and encouraged to hang behind the leaves like secrets. In the central courtyard people are dancing, weaving in and out of each other to the wail of stringed instruments and the trickling rhythm of rain sticks.

I sit out of sight on one of the higher paths. A little way below, I can hear the chanted prayers of the magi, calling to the Wise One in various languages of the Old World, asking Her to bless us on this day.

There's nothing for it now but to go to bed, so I stand and massage out the stiffness in my spine with my knuckles. The nearest path takes me away to where the lights are more sparing, the music ebbs and laughter floats through the trees to me like a kiss I can see but not taste. Loneliness always feels like old bruises being rolled over.

I'm almost relieved when Ade appears around the corner and takes my hand.

'Come, girl. Come, you must see,' she says, before leading

me off down a pathway to the right. Because the direction is *away* from the celebrations, I let her, though my relief curdles when she halts at the spot where Lear fell.

She crouches, muttering.

Are you investigating, Ade? I ask wearily, wondering whether I should have followed her after all.

'Death,' she murmurs, plucking at the rotten wood.

No one's been able to heal any of the spots like this, at least not permanently.

'Dead wood. Dying trees. Gone. All gone,' she huffs, and rocks back on her haunches. Her hair stands in fuzzy clouds and she smells sour. I don't think she's washed properly since her vision. She probably won't until Mathilde or I try and convince her to and, not for the first time, I can see what everyone else sees when they look at her – why they don't trust her words, or mine.

She blinks up at me. 'Is you crying, girl?'

No.

'They doesn't believe you. They doesn't believe me.' She shrugs and strokes the healthy wood around her.

You read my mind, I say, whisking my sleeve over my cheeks.

We both sigh.

Are the trees dying, Ade? I ask.

She wrinkles her nose. 'Maybe. Depends.'

On what?

She looks straight at me. 'You. You got powers all locked up,' she says. 'Help your trees. Help your people.'

I *can't*! I say. **You *know* what happened the last time I let my powers loose. You *know* what I can do.**

126

Ade just shrugs. 'Young girl, young heart, young power,' she says. 'Older now.'

She begins to sing softly under her breath, and I think about the rotten parts of the vines in my hut – of Ade's vision and what Lear said and what Taurus wants me to do.

STRONGER TOGETHER.

NOTHING LEFT FOR YOU TO SAVE.

I take a deep breath. **OK**, I say. **I'll try.** I look at Ade. **But if I tell you to run away, will you?**

Ade smiles. 'You not gonna hurt me.'

But I might. I only do this in the Grove. I don't know if I can control it.

'Time to try, girl.'

My whole body begins to shake, but slowly I reach for my power, the way a climber will inch themselves forward on an uncertain precipice. Just a little further . . . just a bit more . . . *there*.

The vines around me snap to attention, clamouring to tangle around my wrists and ankles, desperately trying to show me what they know. It's not like in the Grove, where the concentration of the magic is contained and safe. This magic depends entirely on my own power to control it.

I can't, I can't, I can't!

Frantically, I ask the trees, **The rot. Where is it coming from?**

As if in answer, the vines throw my senses along their length, and for a fraction of a second, I know they're going to show me. But something else catches my attention, and I swerve, my thoughts heading far down below us. A boy is

127

walking slowly, climbing up from where the first branches begin.

At the same time as my heart lurches, the power threatens to burst out of my skin, thudding against my inner barriers until, with a gasp, I sever my contact to the magic.

The vines around me slink to the ground.

Ade's head whips up, watching me as I steady myself against the trunk of Low Tree. Then she smiles.

'You saw something,' she says. 'Come now.'

What?

'Brave, girl. Be brave. Which way?'

I think for a second. 'That way,' I say, and then I'm running, and she's behind me. We take a sudden twist in the path and disappear downward.

It's a path I don't follow often. It corkscrews sharply, so that I'm running on the edge of my feet and each bend blurs into the next, my breath high and wild in the thick damp from the rain. The air smells sweet and wet and green.

Eventually I round a corner and stop. Ade nearly runs into me.

'Look,' she says, pointing. 'It's beginning.'

I follow her finger down. On the vast trunk of the next tree, a single figure walks up a pathway almost identical to this one. He is blurred by the rain but I know him.

A thrill whips through my stomach.

It's Lear.

Aula

I wake up with the biggest smile and stretch, and the imprints of lips and hands and sighs from last night stretch out with me. I open my eyes and turn my head. But he en't there. The boy en't there, and I never got his name. The brief lick of happiness withers and dies in my chest, and the ache comes storming in. I lie there, staring at the ceiling, and it builds and builds until I feel like I can't breathe and panic chases me outta my bed.

I pace around my room, trying to take big breaths. I knot my hair on top of my head and grab some leggings and a vest that's stuck under my bed.

Half an hour later I'm running alongside the aqueducts in the Water plateau, dodging between the arches and slipping between workers on a new construction site where they're updating some pipe system or other.

I gotta run this out.

Or do I mean *chase* this out? Chase out the feeling of that boy's hands turning me to water . . . And of course, thoughts like that make me think of Sander again. Sander. He never really knew me.

But that boy did. I wasn't *Chosen One*. He knew my name.

Who the hell *was* he?

I stop then, breathing hard. And I'm outside Sander's house. I don't remember deciding to come this way. I only remember concentrating on the rhythm of my legs and the thoughts I still can't drive out. I've stood here so many times before, under his window, waiting for him to go inside the house and open it for me. He'd say something to his pa, shout something at his sister, and then the glass would swing open and I'd haul myself up the drainpipe and into his bedroom.

I breathe. There en't any movement inside the house that I can see. I look around, but there's no one here, so I move closer. Peer in through a downstairs window.

Something smashes me so hard in the face that I actually stagger. Even Nadrik can't make me do that without his magic. I put a hand to my cheek, and it comes away wet. Blood dribbles down my face and on to the vest I'm wearing. I shake my head, trying to clear what's clouding there. There's pain, I guess, but it's abstract, unreal. And then I see Sander's pa coming at me again with an iron rod.

'What have you done to him?!' he says.

I could stop his next blow, but I don't. It hits me in the stomach. I'm ready for it, so it doesn't even hurt really. I sorta wish it did.

'WHAT HAVE YOU DONE?' He raises the rod again.

'What do you mean?' I say.

'Don't you lie to me!' he says. 'Don't you dare!'

'What's happened?'

He lets out a sound that I didn't reckon anyone could make and comes at me again, but I catch the rod and twist it out of his arms.

'What did you do to him? *What did you do?*'

'I dunno what you're talking about,' I say firmly. I feel a little shiver of fear though. What's happened to Sander to make his pa like this?

'You little bitch! Don't lie to me!' He thumps a fist into

130

my chest and yells. And then he begins to cry. He slumps against me and falls to the ground, sobbing. 'My boy,' he whispers. 'My boy.'

'Where is he?' I ask, but I don't wait for an answer. I'm in the door and up the stairs faster than he can gasp out the next sob.

Sander's in his room, looking out the window. His hair is shorter than I remember, and he looks thinner, but nothing awful. I take a step into the doorway, and it's like a minefield of memories the second I do.

He helped me draw a map on that desk for an art project at school.

I gave him that tunic hanging in his open wardrobe as a birthday present.

It smells of him in here – some sort of basil-scented perfume that would cling to my clothes after I'd left him.

That bed. He lost his virginity to me in it. I felt normal with him.

I have a revelation, there, on the threshold of his room. Nothing much, just how suffocating I must have been, because feeling normal and *wanted* were things I was so desperate for.

I say his name, but he doesn't look round. I go to sit on the bed next to him. He glances vaguely at me. It's just a glance, but my stomach plummets. Cos there's nothing in his eyes. There en't anyone there. Nothing.

'Sander?' I say.

He looks at me again.

'Couple of things at first,' Sander's pa says from the door. 'He couldn't remember the way home. Then, if I got him

131

back here, he didn't know his own room. It was his friends next. And then . . .'

'You,' I say.

He flinches. 'It en't just him,' he snarls. 'There are others, all over the city now. See you didn't know that,' he says. 'Charmed life you lead, huh? Bet you don't know about the buildings falling or the rot in the pillars or the damage to the mechanisms down in the great trunks. And now my son . . . he's . . . *this*,' he snarls. 'You. You're gonna pay for this.'

'This en't got anything to do with me.'

'You're the Chosen One. It's got *everything* to do with you. I shouldda known. The Wise One's Ninth Chosen One shouldda been a boy. It was in the stars. It's you that cursed us. It's *you* that hurt my city and my boy with your . . . unnaturalness.'

I stand up. I have to get out of here.

But Sander's pa puts his arm across the door. 'You stay here until he's fixed!' he says fiercely, squinting at me through tear-sore eyes.

'You're gonna move your arm,' I say. 'Or I'll break it.'

His mouth contorts. It's the first time in my life I've seen real hatred. But he lets his hand fall to his side.

'Don't you ever bring your taint into my house again,' he whispers to my retreating back.

Joomia

When I'm within ten feet of Lear I know something's wrong.

132

Ade wouldn't come across the bridge to the next tree with me, and immediately I'm wishing I'd brought her – if only so I could send her back to fetch Mathilde.

Lear's bowed over; his limbs and face are streaked with the green of bark mould and the brown of earth. He doesn't seem to have heard my feet on the path – and I'm making quite some noise. He doesn't respond to my continual waving, and when I finally reach him, he moves past as if he can't see me.

Lear?

I dart around him and stand in his path with both of my arms outstretched. He ploughs into me – not hard, but enough that we both stumble back. He tries to walk again. I put a hand in the middle of his chest and my bones melt in relief. His heartbeat thuds briskly to the right of my splayed fingers.

Still he continues to walk. I look into his eyes and recoil; they're blank and clouded. They're his eyes, but he's not there.

Lear.

There's no emotion in the way he walks past me – no anger or sadness . . . nothing.

I follow him, trying to think, trying not to look into the chasm of what could possibly be wrong with him, because I can't bear it. I can't.

I should get him to an Elder.

I catch up to him and he lets me take his hand and guide him to a vine bridge that is the fastest route to the courtyard of High Tree. We're twenty feet across the bridge before I think to look for faults in the vines under my feet and then

133

nausea tangs my mouth because Lear won't slow down for long enough for me to do more than glance at the places we're about to step. The thought of losing him again to rotten vines makes my breath come twice as fast.

Since slowing Lear down isn't an option, I take a firmer grip on his unresponsive hand and pull him faster. This, apparently, is something he will do, because his feet match my pace within seconds.

We make it across the bridge, but now we're running he doesn't seem to want to stop. I try dragging backwards on his hand, but my feet skid on the path and it's either trip and fall or try to keep pace with him.

I have to make split-second decisions at the cross paths that will take us to any of four other trees.

Mathilde? Taurus? Can you hear me?

It must be fifteen minutes before the courtyard of High Tree looms into view. I'm clutching at a stitch in my side, holding sweatily to Lear's strangely cool hand with my other arm, but he shows no sign of slowing.

The sun has fully risen now and the celebrations are finally dissolving, but there are still plenty of people dancing and eating the last scraps of the feast that was laid out. I have no way of attracting anyone's attention of course, but the fact that we're running does that for me and we're only a few steps into the courtyard when people begin to shout:

'Is that—'

'Lear?'

'Alive?'

'It is! Lear!'

134

'The Chosen One's found him!'

'He's alive!'

I fix my sights on Eros – the first Elder I spot, praying that he'll turn around and see me.

When he does, he calls, 'Stop!'

My legs can't find a way of digging in, hauling back. I could let go, but what would happen to Lear then? Would he hurtle off some other void?

I summon the loudest thought I can. **MATHILDE! I NEED YOU!**

Veins cord like tunnelling worms on Lear's temples.

My head throbs so heavily I am sure it will roll back off my neck.

And then Mathilde is there. She sees me first, then Lear, and her eyebrows settle into one firm line.

She moves her hand and I see magi in my peripheral vision, ready to stop us.

I try again to dig my heels in, to bring Lear to a stop, but if anything he tries to move faster and I have to let go. I dive to reach him again, but fall flat, smashing my nose into the floor.

'Lear!' Eros calls.

'Joomia!' Mathilde shouts.

I lie there, my sides heaving, blood thudding like a drumskin in my temples as the rain tickles gently against the back of my head and neck.

There's a hand on my shoulder, and a voice says, 'Chosen One, are you all right?'

You have to get up, I think.

I raise myself on to my forearms and peer out through

my hair. Something warm and slippery runs down my lip. I taste blood and mud.

Lear's still running. He's now just feet from the other side of the courtyard. How did he cover that distance in so little time? The magi, too slow to catch him, send vines to trip him, call on the bark underfoot to crumple into footholds, but although they're slowing him, he's still going.

'Someone stop him!' Eros is shouting, but unlike when I tried to stop Lear on the path, now he just dodges the people who hurry into his way. That is, until Taurus appears. He materialises into the right side of my vision, bolting forward, eyes set on his target.

He hits Lear hard in the chest, then takes out both his legs in one solid swoop of his own. Lear drops like a sack of stones.

Mathilde is the first to rally. She hurries over. Eros, wheezing as he jogs past me, reaches her a few seconds before the crowd. The others in the courtyard begin to really converge then, but Mathilde shouts, 'Get back!' and no one ignores Mathilde when her voice goes as brittle as that.

I try to stand up but my legs wilt under my weight.

You have to get up, I tell myself. *Get up*.

Somehow, I find the energy.

Between the shoulders and necks of the crowd, I see Lear, apparently unconscious, with Eros's fingers pressed to his neck.

'He's all right!' Eros shouts.

Everyone looks around at me as I limp forward. There isn't any cheering, but I can see they're all intensely curious.

Taurus? I say. But he's not looking at me. He's cradling

Lear's head in his arms. There's so much care in the way he does it, it makes something inside me ache. **Where did you come from?** I ask.

Taurus ignores me, instead saying, 'Quiet, everyone! He's waking!'

Lear's gaze, when he blinks his eyes open, goes directly to Taurus. I want to run forward, protect Taurus from what he'll see there – because I can tell from the way Taurus's shoulders stiffen that he already knows in that second that something is wrong.

'Lear?' he says uncertainly.

It takes the crowd a lot longer to understand. They press forward eagerly, shouting questions at Lear, trying to pull him to his feet. Mathilde has to snap at them several times before anyone takes any notice.

And then they realise: Lear doesn't recognise any of them.

Mathilde clicks her fingers in front of his face. But Lear looks past her, gazing peaceably at the middle distance, as if he were looking out on a wide, empty plain.

'What's wrong with him, Elder Mathilde?' someone asks.

'If you'd all give me a *minute*,' she snarls. Everyone lapses into silence. Her hands begin to glow as, gently, she reaches out to hold Lear's chin.

But he seems to hear something. Abruptly, he scrambles to his feet, head questing like a bird. This time there are several pairs of hands to hold him. Still he struggles.

'He's gone mad,' someone whispers. 'Mad, like Ade.'

'*Shut up!*' Mathilde roars.

But I think everyone can see that there's some truth in it. Because although Ade can respond to us, can interact and talk to us, her eyes have many times held that same empty look in them as Lear's do now.

The words of the previous Chosen Ones echo through the months to me:

NOTHING LEFT TO SAVE.

Aula

The street leading to the city temple is mostly empty, but even so I don't let myself cry until I'm in the entrance, and then I have to press my hands over my eyes and lean against some dark pillar and let the sobs shuffle out as quiet as I can make them. The ache seems to yawn wider inside me and, Wise One, I dunno how to shut it up.

What the hell is going on? What was wrong with Sander?

It was like he'd been leeched of everything that made him who he was. I think of that . . . that *nothing* in his eyes and my knees want to give way.

I stumble to the fountain next to the door, splash my face. The statue of the Wise One is waiting for me to look at it. A floor-to-ceiling carving of a man; his chiselled features are just about hidden by a mask shaped like the eyes of an owl. He has two owls perched on each of his massive blocky shoulders and another on his stone curls. Clutched to his chest is a book, which I guess is supposed to be his Book of Knowledge, and trailing from his dangling fist is a dead eel.

An otter stands by his thigh, sniffing the fish. When I was younger I used to think the otter was just to show that the Wise One liked animals, but now that I've read all Nadrik's obsessive notes on the subject I can officially tell anyone who wants to know that there was this ancient symbol in the Old World of an otter chasing an eel that was supposed to represent the quest for knowledge.

Buildings falling . . . rot in the pillars . . .

The Wise One's Ninth Chosen One shouldda been a boy.

Is it me? Did I do this?

I know it en't. But I can't help asking the question . . .

I get on my knees in front of the statue and I pray.

Um, I start.

I need a bit of help. Things en't going so well for me. I'm failing.

I swallow a few times to get myself under control.

I don't want much, but if you could just cut me some slack for the next month, I'd really appreciate it. And Joomia too, I guess. She can't be having it easy either. I heard a rumour she doesn't even have powers . . . Oh, Wise One, I wish I didn't.

I think of Etain and Ashir, who believe in me. And Nadrik, who wants to. I think.

OK, so there's a list of things I could use some help with. I'll just um . . . leave them with you. And you can do what you want with them.

I need Ashir to wake up.

I need Nadrik to be pleased with me.

I need Etain to understand me.

I need Sander to remember me.

I kind of want to ask about that boy from last night as well, but I reckon four things added to the first thing I asked is already a mite outrageous.

When I hear footsteps on the steps outside, I get to my feet, nod to the statue and move to the entrance.

I'm expecting to see priestesses, cos there's a distinct lack of them around given it's their job to mind the temple, but what I actually get is two prophets I recognise coming up the steps towards me: Igra and Yacin. Igra is the Deputy Head Prophet, under Ashir – and Acting Head while she's been unwell. She's old as hell and so wrinkled her skin looks like stewed prunes. Yacin is my height and has a very good profile, which makes me think of the old coins we have in the museum.

They're yapping at each other as they come towards me and I catch, 'Doesn't that seem off to you?'

'I've never seen them like that in my life.'

'Could it be something to do with the Wise One's task?'

'Or a change in the energies Ariadnis is putting out?'

Then Yacin spots me. 'Oh, the Chosen One!' She beams. I can't help smiling back cos she actually means it when she's happy to see me.

But Igra narrows her eyes and I know it's cos she's sensing my unhappiness somehow. 'Prayer for your thoughts?' she says. Her voice scratches like sackcloth.

'What seems off?' I ask, ignoring her question – like hell I'm telling her about Sander. 'Who haven't you seen like that in your life?'

Igra gestures upwards with her hands. 'The owls,' she murmurs. 'They en't happy.'

I raise an eyebrow, cos it's not like I noticed, or frankly, care.

'Um . . . not happy?' I ask.

'Not at all,' says Yacin. 'And other rumours have been circulating. People in the city have, apparently, been losing their memories.'

I take a sharp breath in.

'How are you, Aula? Keeping well?' Iqra asks, squinting at me. 'Is that – blood on your face?'

I shrug.

She grunts, loudly, and the scars around her eyes glimmer faintly. 'A man with a rod,' she says, looking strained.

'We're square,' I say. 'I broke his door. He got to hit me a few times.'

Iqra's eyes glaze. Yacin catches her shoulder as she sways. 'He did,' Iqra says, with some surprise. She blinks at me. 'Sure are lost, aren't you?'

This is so exactly what no one has wanted to say to me that something like a sob ricochets into the back of my throat and I put a hand to my mouth to stop it coming out like sick.

Yacin seems to sense it and tries to hug me, but I back up a couple of steps, saying, 'M'all right really. Just a . . . scare. And uh . . . worried about Ashir, you know . . .'

'Oh,' Yacin says, smiling now. 'No one's told you!'

What was left of the sob dissipates in a second. 'Told me what?'

'Ashir's awake!' she says brightly.

Joomia

Come on, have some food, I coax, holding a spoon of root mash up to Lear's mouth.

At last, he seems to understand what I'm offering and closes his lips around the mouthful, chewing like a baby.

When he swallows, some of the mash comes out of the corner of his lip. He doesn't lick it away so I wipe it off with a cloth already stained orange from earlier this morning, and feed him another mouthful.

Can you hear me? I ask, knowing it's hardly likely he'll hear me now if he never did before. **I'm so sorry I didn't catch you.**

Sure enough, his eyes pass over me as if I'm not there.

Mathilde stands nearby, massaging her temples. We're in a makeshift healing tent, near the Magi's Grove, where Lear had already been taken for investigative spells to see what's happened to him and if it can be reversed. They found nothing to explain it, and now he's here, with me.

Meanwhile, the rain of the last few days has given way to another blistering heatwave. Despite the gathering darkness, the sarong I'm wearing sticks uncomfortably around my middle and my armpits seem likely to become the source to a new river. To top it off, my period is coming like a punch in the gut.

Lear's father has visited every two hours to check on him, but each time I've had to send him away, disappointed, because there's no change.

There's nothing we can do, is there? I say.

Mathilde shrugs in answer to my question. 'I dunno,

142

kid,' she says. 'Tell us again how you found him.'

I didn't, I say, blushing. **Ade did. You shouldn't have told them it was me. It was almost like she knew I would find him.**

'Ade says it was you.'

But she's the one who made me use my power.

Mathilde lets out an aggrieved hissing noise. 'Miss Joomia, you've got to stop your downing on yourself. If your power alerted you to something then just *say it*. Lore knows this city needs to hear you felt *something* supernatural. I know you think you're powerless, but you en't. You're afraid. Only you can change that.'

I sigh. I know she's right. I *am* going to have to do something about it. I can feel something shifting in me, like an unconscious part of me is making a decision.

I try for one more spoonful of mash for Lear, but he ignores it.

'There's something else,' Mathilde says, watching me. 'What aren't you telling me?'

I put down the spoon and the bowl and press my hands over my eyes.

The morning it happened, I say. **The morning he fell, I mean. He told me about a dream he'd had. He said that he'd dreamed that his family couldn't remember his name. That *he* couldn't remember his name. And then . . . Oriha, the other day at Audience. She said her mother couldn't remember who she was.**

Mathilde's expression slackens. 'Einar forgot a spell today,' she says, 'and Renai in Wilde Tree said her soap-makers had forgotten how to boil the fat for soap properly.'

The heat presses into my pores. **Memory,** I whisper. **Something is affecting people's memories.**

143

A half-hearted wind flaps pathetically at the walls of the healing tent.

I hear distant shouts of laughter.

The trickle of water through the channels in the tree.

The creak of insects, the sway of branches.

This is my home and it is slipping from me bit by bit.

Wise One, what am I going to do?

'Nadrik,' Mathilde mutters, almost to herself. 'This has got something to do with Athenas. With *Nadrik*.'

I clench my hands round the fabric near my thighs to stop them shaking. It's time to do something. It's time.

'Where are you going?' Mathilde asks as I rise abruptly and lift the flap of canvas.

To find Taurus.

Aula

I en't allowed to see Ashir.

'She is fragile,' the healer at the door says. 'It was a very powerful vision. I think it may even have been a complete one. She still needs rest.'

I push her out of the way and go in anyway. The prophets have their own ward and I've gone in to visit before, so I know where I'm going. It's not uncommon for really strong visions to leave prophets on their backs afterwards, though usually only for a few days. Not for more than six *months*. Not that I had ever known before.

The healers don't take kindly to me barging in, and at one point I have three of them hanging on to the back of my tunic to hold me. When I reach the ward I kick the door in and stop dead.

Etain whirls around from where she stands by one of the cots and there – there is Ashir. She smiles when she sees me. 'Aula,' she says, her voice just a whisper.

'Ashir.'

I try and run to her, but now *five* healers are hanging on to me, and that at least makes it harder to walk forward, even if it en't enough to stop me.

'Chosen One, she is very weak!' one of them says. 'You *must* let her rest – even Miss Etain was just about to leave.'

'I was,' Etain says. 'Come on, Aula. You can see Ma tomorrow, I promise.'

I shake my head wildly, looking desperately at Ashir, who nods. Even that movement looks weird – strangely stiff. 'I am very tired, sweetheart. I *do* need to talk to you, but I'm – I'm just so . . .' Her eyelids flutter.

Etain reaches me, takes my hand. 'Come on,' she says.

'Ashir . . .' I say.

'*Tomorrow*,' Etain says, giving my arm a tug.

The healing staff tense, but their expressions soften when I don't fight back.

I let Etain lead me outside but no further. She sighs and puts her hands on her hips.

'I'll just wait here till they let me in,' I say.

'Then you'll be here until tomorrow,' Etain says.

'Fine.'

She stays there, staring at me. 'Aula. You're as good as my sister, you know that, right?'

'Yeah . . .' I say.

145

'Good. So as my sister, I gotta tell you if you pull something like that again, I'm gonna hit you with my anvil.'

'Yeah?' I snarl.

'Yeah,' she says, totally deadpan. 'You love Ma and she loves you and I know she's been your parent like she's been mine all your life and I wouldn't have it any other way. But she is *sick*, Aula, and that means her healing is more important than whatever mess you feel like you're in, OK?'

'You don't get to tell—' I begin, but she cuts straight across me.

'Aula, I'm being really, *really* diplomatic here so shut up and listen. You're acting like whatever's going on with you is more important than her healing, more important than how worried I am about her, more important than a team of trained healers' jobs.'

Her words hit home like an arrowhead. I open and shut my mouth like an idiot. I wanna try and justify myself, try and explain, but I can see in her face that actually, she knows *why* I charged in, but *why* I did it en't the point. I bite my lip and drop my head.

'I don't think I'm more important than you,' I say.

'I know you don't.'

'I'm sorry,' I say.

'Yeah,' she says. 'It's just that you're sorry a lot. Everyone's got their stuff, Aula. I know you don't really believe that, but try. I think you'd be surprised how often you en't the only one hurting.'

29 Days

Joomia

Taurus, I say.

He glances up from his book and gives me an expressionless stare. 'Yeah.'

I know you're still angry with me. I just need you to come with me, OK?

He nearly smiles, but doesn't quite. 'Why?'

I grit my teeth. **I think it's time I told you something,** I say. **About why I won't use my magic. About what happened with Lear before.**

He gives me this look like he doesn't know if I'm trying to trick him. Then he nods once, and I lead the way.

I take him to the High Tree garden, where Ramon's statue stands. I force myself to look at it before I turn to Taurus.

I purse my lips, blow out. Breathe in.

And I reach for my power.

It's not as bad as I thought it would be – even without Mathilde's precautions, I feel surprisingly grounded. Maybe the shield's been an illusion all this time. I wouldn't put it past her. The vines come to me quickly, looping

147

delicately over my hands and even weaving together at my command.

I can see along them too, I say, not wanting to read his expression. **And feel, and smell.** I take another long breath and let the vines go.

Taurus stares at me. Then he says, 'You could do that. All this time.' His voice is shaking, and I'm not sure if it's from anger or sadness.

No, I say. **It was only . . . only in the Grove. Mathilde said she put shields up but . . . but I'm wondering now if she really did.**

Briefly, he closes his eyes. 'You *could* have saved Lear. If you'd wanted. If you'd been training.'

No.

'Don't talk shit to me, Joomia! You could have been trying to get a grip on this all this time!'

I have been trying.

'Well, *clearly* you could have tried harder.'

I shake my head. **You don't understand.**

'What don't I understand?' He snarls.

I take a step back from him. Even knowing how angry he is, I didn't expect him to shout, and for a moment I lose my nerve. I can't tell him. Not like this. In a few words, a few minutes, I could kill what's left of our friendship, if I haven't already. I press a finger to my forehead.

'Why won't you answer me?'

Taurus, I'm *trying* to answer you, so can you *shut up* for *two* seconds?!

He blinks.

I take a deep breath and start to pace. **You remember**

Ramon? I ask, nodding to the statue.

He's thrown. 'Yeah,' he says. 'When we were kids he used to say he could hear the Wise One in the wind, and he left *that* here for us all to remember him by when he went off to Athenas.'

I nod. Another prophet like Ade who didn't catch his prophecy before he should've. But he didn't go to Athenas, like Mathilde said he did. Another deep breath. I killed him.

I say it to my bare feet, so I don't have to look at him. I find my breath and unclench my hands.

It was the same year I went to Ariadnis for the first time. He was in one of his frantic moods, and he saw me coming back from my lesson with Mathilde. He asked me to help him. He said that it was really important. He said he wanted me to help him make the trees sing. He reminded me of Ade, so I said I would.

Obviously, the trees didn't sing. He made me repeat a chant back to him which didn't sound like any language I knew and then we waved our hands about a bit. Then something changed. I think he actually recognised me for the first time.

He said something like, *Your powers can help. Have you unlocked them yet?*

I said I hadn't – not properly, but Mathilde was training me. He said it was simple – like finding a door in your mind and opening it. It didn't occur to me to ask how he would have known better than Mathilde. He made this weird humming noise in the back of his throat.

And the funny thing was – it was almost like he said it would be, only it was more like lifting dead leaves from a shoot so it has a chance to see the sun. My power had been there

149

all along and it was growling with energy.

And he said, *You extraordinary child*, and then he suggested I call the trees beyond our city and ask them to sing. And Taurus . . .

Taurus, I swear on the Wise One and on Lore and the Nine Trees that when I called them to sing – they *did*.

Taurus shifts then, and when I glance up, I can't see his expression.

'What did it sound like?' he asks.

I shake my head. I don't remember, I say. Because of what happened next.

'What?'

Ramon laughed, and he clapped and shouted a lot. And then he said, *Child, oh, let's go down to them – let's ride the wind and whistle through their branches.* And I grinned and laughed and . . . and I grabbed his hand. I close my eyes. I can see it so clearly. I felt the power running through me. And when I touched him it was – like what would happen if you tried to hold lightning. There was this shivering second, when he just looked at me. And then—

He looks at the statue that isn't a statue.

'You turned him—'

Wood. I turned him into wood.

The front of my tunic is knotted in my hands. I wait for Taurus to speak. The fibres of the Grove around us creak.

He says, 'It wasn't your fault, though.'

I wish I could tell him exactly how much I want to believe that. It could so easily happen again. Imagine what would happen if I . . . if I hurt someone else. If I hurt *you*.

Taurus exhales. Then he walks forward and pulls me

150

into a hug. It's what I want more than anything, to be held. I'm afraid to move. He kisses the top of my head and murmurs, 'You were only nine. You'd just awakened your magic. You can't think you'll hurt me now.'

There's a creaking noise in the background, but I'm not really paying attention, because Taurus is holding me and it's so long since anyone's done that.

I used magic yesterday. Just before Ade and me found Lear. I – *sensed* him, somehow. But Taurus, what if I lose control?

Another sound. I register vaguely that the High Tree garden doesn't usually creak.

'You won't,' he says fiercely, and he pulls away to look me in the eyes. 'Joomia—'

But he doesn't get to say anything else, because at that moment, the fibres of the High Tree garden fail.

In the second's grace I get to throw out a hand and grab hold, an entire side of the floor has collapsed – the fibres tearing like thin fabric where once they were so strong. The side we were standing on now yawns out on to a root bridge far below us, and below that – nothing. It's Lear, all over again.

I look at Taurus, clinging to what remains of the garden next to me. He is, *impossibly*, grinning.

Is there something I'm missing here?

'I was just thinking this is what you really need, isn't it? A bit of *motivation*.'

Shut up. Don't you *dare* let go.

He snorts, like he can't even believe I'd think that. My fingers are slippery. I take a breath.

'Do you think we can climb up?' he asks.

Are we children of Metis or aren't we? I say.

'Good point,' he says, and stretches out a hand.

There's a nervous jerk in my senses. **Taurus!**

I know the next place Taurus puts his hand will be rotten. I know it.

But he's just a moment too slow to react.

And I'm a moment too slow to grab him.

Our fingers brush, and he lets out a shocked, disbelieving breath.

And he falls.

He misses the bridge underneath us, and keeps falling.

NO!

I scream. I almost let go.

But it's there before I've reached for it. My power is there, like a flower in full bloom. I throw it out to Taurus and concentrate on the feeling of the vines under my hands – healthy and strong and *alive*.

Five feet away, vines go shooting down towards him.

Taurus's cry stops.

Taurus?

A sound echoes up to me but there's no reply. Oh, Wise One. Oh, Lore. I've killed him. The trees are singing and I've killed him. I crane my head.

TAURUS?

It's not trees singing. It's laughter.

I don't understand how I'm doing it, but I pull the vines in towards me.

Slowly, the laughter grows louder.

I'm giving myself neck ache straining to see – but there is Taurus, swinging where the vines caught him

152

by an ankle, laughing his head off.

   Taurus? I whisper, almost crying.

   'I was right!' he gasps. 'I WAS RIGHT!'

28 Days

Aula

Nadrik doesn't show up for my lesson.

I wait, thinking of what kind of explosion might happen if he turned up and I wasn't there, but fifteen minutes, twenty, thirty walk on by and I'm still there in the practice ring, standing there scratching my bum like an idiot. I know what I should do is go and sit in the library and study whatever sub-category of wisdom Nadrik's forked out for me. And I'm intending to walk over there – I am – but somehow I find myself loitering around the entrance of the healing house, looking in like a slum kid outside a kitchen.

Eventually, someone comes out. It's Head Healer Phythia, with her mouth puckered the way a lot of mouths pucker when they see me. She's very neat and very tall, her braids wound tight under her white headwrap.

'Morning,' I say.

She narrows her eyes at me and pulls an apple out of her pocket. 'Good day to you, Chosen One.'

'Nice day.'

She shields her eyes against the sun behind me and moves her head side to side. 'I heard there are owls about.'

'Yeah,' I say. There've been sightings all over the city this morning. Owls flying in strange formations. Owls out in broad daylight.

'And, if the gossip is to be believed, fifty or so people have fallen victim to a strange illness. Lost their memory. Just like that. Overnight.'

My body jerks, weirdly, like Sander is right there beside me. I see him staring blankly out the window with his pa behind him. 'Just like that,' I echo.

Phythia takes a bite out of her apple and eyes me like she's sizing me up. 'You can see her,' she says, after a while. 'If I have your word there will be no sound or untoward action from you in this house ever again.'

I bite my tongue, cos there's a nasty little comment just dying to wriggle off it. I do my best to look chastened. 'Yes, ma'am.'

She snorts and opens the door for me.

Ashir smiles when she sees me in the doorway and I let out a shaky laugh and run to her.

'You look tired,' she says.

'Not as tired as you,' I say. There are thin, dark scars tracing out from her eyes like cracks in dry ground. They weren't there before. They *shouldn't* be there now. Trained prophets en't supposed to have scars at all. Trained prophets have their visions under control . . . don't they?

'What's wrong, my darling?' Her voice is papery.

I tell her about what Phythia and me were just discussing.

'And?' she says, like she knew already. Maybe all of that was in the vision she had to recover from. But she's waiting to hear the last bit.

158

I tell her about Sander, and what happened when I went to see him. And then about his father and what he said to me yesterday. She doesn't say anything but her forehead wrinkles.

'What does it mean, Ashir?' I whisper. 'How can people just . . . just *lose* their memories? Is it my fault?'

'Your fault? Wise One, Aula – how on Erthe is this *your* fault?'

I shrug.

'Aula. Tell me what's wrong.'

'Just something that Sander's pa said.'

'What? What did he say?'

'That the Wise One's last Chosen One shouldda been a boy.'

'What do you mean?'

'You know. They say it's supposed to go girl-boy-girl-boy with every generation. But the last Chosen One was a girl so—'

Ashir thumps her fist down hard on the bed. It's such a powerful gesture even she looks a bit surprised, but she recovers before I do. 'Let me tell you this, Aula,' she says. 'There was a rebellion, not long after you were born. There were some who had . . . reverted back to the old ways, old traditions. There were some who thought that the Chosen One – the Ninth, that is – could never be a girl.' She sighs. 'People can bend truth in whatever manner they wish to, for whatever reason they think is the cause. They saw power in you – saw the birthmark on your neck – and they were afraid of it. There was nothing but the body you were born in that they could oath against.'

159

'What happened then?' I say.

'They wanted to select a Chosen One for themselves. They claimed there were prophets who had Seen an alternative. Someone "better suited" to the trials of Ariadnis.'

'*Better suited* meaning someone with a dick,' I say.

She smiles. 'I'm glad you can see how ridiculous it is.'

'*Had they* found someone better?'

'Of course not. Do you think *I* would have missed an alternative?'

'No,' I say, smiling.

'Anyway, Nadrik stopped them. He had them arrested and put on public trial, in front of all the city. He said that any person who dared to call themselves superior because of gender, love interest or ancestor, would face the same consequence.' She sighs again, seeing my look of shock at Nadrik defending me. 'Nadrik has done a many great things, but Aula, he has also done bad things. He has yet to do more of them.' The scars on her face glint even though there en't any light.

'What do you mean?' I say.

There's this long pause. And then: 'He is going to betray you,' she says. Quietly. Like it en't a thing she could say out loud and proper.

I make a noise like *tschhhhh*.

She says, 'You don't believe me.'

I say, 'Well, what am I supposed to believe, huh? One second you're telling me he'd stop a rebellion to protect me, the next you're saying he's gonna betray me. It's gotta be one or the other.'

'No, sweetheart,' she says. 'It's both. People aren't like elements.'

'Nadrik wouldn't—'

'Wouldn't he?' she asks. The room, with its small wooden bed, with its chipped basin and shuttered window, seems to shiver. Her scars shimmer along her cheekbones. My ears ring like something exploded.

I grip her hand, very softly. 'Stop!' It comes out as a whisper – the only sound I can make while I'm in the shadow of her eyes.

The room goes quiet. She falls back on her pillows. 'Water,' she mutters.

I hold the glass for her to sip. My hand en't steady. Some of it spills on her neck and on the thin shift she's wearing.

She pats herself down. 'I should have more control of myself.'

I find scabs to look at on my hands and wrists. Then Ashir's hand comes to rest over mine. There's not such a fierce contrast between our skin tones today: mine's still relentlessly yellow under the freckles; hers, usually so dark and weathered, is paler, washed-out.

'I understand why you don't want to believe me,' she says.

I raise my head slowly. Her eyes, pale green above the scars, are calling out, *trust me*.

I *do* trust her. But . . .

'Not all prophecies come true,' I say, trying to keep my voice steady.

'No,' she agrees. 'But this one will. It has already begun.'

'He wouldn't betray me!' I say, my voice rising. 'He lov—' But I stop.

Ashir's eyes are suddenly really bright. She winces like there's something that hurt her on the inside.

I poke my head around the door. Healer Phythia looks up. 'I'm coming in,' she says.

'Aula – listen!' Ashir whispers.

But Phythia's already here, carrying a silk blindfold and a sleep brew. The blindfold has marks stitched into it that will stop any more visions.

'You must listen!' Ashir says desperately.

Phythia reaches around me with the blindfold. 'Aula.'

'Yeah,' I say, helping Phythia lift Ashir's head and wrap the blindfold around securely. The second it's pinned properly the shaking in her body stops.

'Prophet Ashir, I will need you to drink this,' says Phythia in a very healer-ish voice, waving the sleep brew. It smells of earth.

'Could you just give us one more minute alone?' she asks.

Phythia looks at me. 'Can I trust you to help her drink it?'

'*Yeah,*' I say. It comes out harsher than I meant but I'm too worried to apologise.

She raises her eyebrow but doesn't say *I think you're too unhinged to help anyone drink a healing brew.* She just straightens up and says, 'She will fall asleep quickly once the brew is drunk. You can stay with her till then.'

'Uh-huh,' I say.

She nods and leaves.

Ashir looks like she's going to sleep already, but I help her sip the brew down.

'Listen,' she keeps saying.

And I say, 'I am,' thinking that she'll say something else but she doesn't. She drains the cup, leaving slimy dregs.

'You will need to be strong, Aula,' she whispers.

I try for a cocky smile. I know she can't see me but I'm hoping it'll nut and bolt some swagger on to my next words. 'I dunno if you noticed, but I'm pretty strong.'

'Strong here,' she agrees, touching my arm. 'But can you be strong here?' Her fingers move to my chest. 'And here?' She raises her thumb to my head and presses gently.

'I'm gonna try,' I say.

'Good.'

She lapses into silence then – for so long I think she's asleep, and I'm about to get up when her hand finds my sleeve.

'The books . . .' she mutters.

I lean closer. 'The book? The Wise One's book?'

'It's your last chance . . .'

'Last chance?'

She yawns. 'Yes. In a few weeks they'll be gone . . .'

I ask her what she means, but she's asleep and I en't gonna bring her out of it just to tell me what kind of brew makes you prattle about reading.

13 Days

Joomia

Barely two weeks have passed by, but I don't recognise Metis.

Hut doors stay shut during the day. Journeys back and forth around the city are conducted only in pairs. People are wary to touch each other, or even speak to each other. They are afraid the memory loss is catching.

Since Lear returned, nearly a hundred people have been taken. In *two* weeks.

Obviously, everyone blames me, but they're too afraid to be vocal about it. For once, I don't care what they think. I'm not silly enough to think that the memory loss is my fault, but I'm still frustrated at my inability to find out what's causing it.

As one of the only people convinced this thing isn't contagious – because if it was contagious, Taurus would *definitely* have caught it – I've been helping care for those who can barely feed themselves. Enough people gave up their homes in Black Tree for us to move all those affected to the same area, but convincing other people to help has been a task on its own.

And now, this:

Ade had snagged my arm on my way back from ferrying fruit to the memoryless. 'Library,' she'd said. 'Thought you should know.'

I stare now at the books in the library. They look the same, but they're not. I've yanked them down, one by one, and every page is wiped blank, as if nothing was ever printed on them. I try to release the scream that wants to tear from my lungs, but nothing comes out. I kick the shelves. I grab handfuls of pages and rip. My hands massacre spines, bindings, leather, paper.

'Makes sense that *this* is when you really start to crack,' Taurus mutters from behind me. 'When the *books* get it.'

I collapse where I stand and he comes to sit beside me. I leaf through the books on the floor miserably, tapping the spines gently against my hand as if words will spill into my lap.

'That really is it, then,' Taurus says. 'Should we pack up?'

What?

'Well, didn't the voices in Ariadnis say that you and Athenas's Chosen One have to unite, or it's all doom and gloom?'

How did you know about that? I say, turning to him.

'You told me, the night you came out of there.'

No, I didn't. I *know* I didn't. I haven't told anyone that. Already, his eyes have given him away. **Taurus, who were you meeting that day I wanted you to come to the Grove with me?**

His fingers find an empty page lying between us. I watch him pinch the corner into a tight fold. 'I'm thinking this is the doom and gloom part,' he says.

I press my hands over my face in an attempt to stymie some of my frustration. **Don't evade the question.**

'Don't ask me questions I can't answer, then.'

I frown at him and he gives me a big grin. He is so maddening.

'Is it time to go, Joomia?' he asks.

I stare at him. *Go where?* I want to ask. There's the most obvious answer: go and find Aula, unite with her, like the previous Chosen Ones advised. Or . . . or does he mean go away? Run from all of it. Find out if the rumours are true that we can't escape the cities, that we are trapped here.

He's leaning against a shelf now, waiting for my answer, and I know from the look on his face that he's already decided he'll stay with me, whatever my choice is.

Which is why this is my answer: **I don't know. I need more time.**

'More time for what? To keep stalling? Wait for *more* people to lose their memory? Wait for everyone to go all zombified like Lear? Wait till you have to risk it all? And for what? Some mythical book that might come too late anyway.'

Taurus, stop! I don't know, all right. I don't know what I have to do! It's not like I got a list of instructions when I was born.

But I *have* had one little piece of advice: unite with Aula. So why haven't I? *Why haven't I?*

How's Lear? I say suddenly.

That look he's been giving me falters. 'Look who's changing the subject.'

I can't *think* about it right now, I say. **How is Lear?**

166

'Don't try and change the subje—'

How is he? I say more forcefully. **I've been meaning to visit this past week, but I've just been . . .**

Taurus sighs, shaking his head. 'Distracted? Yeah. Well, he's fine.'

Working out your feelings for him? I prod. I know it's probably cruel, but it nettles me how easily he can touch my weakest points. I feel like I have to remind him that I can get at his as well.

He rolls his eyes. 'No, I know how I feel about him.'

I wasn't expecting that. **Was it . . . the fall that made you realise?**

'Realise what?' Taurus says.

How you feel.

He laughs. 'Joomia, I'm not callous enough to think I'm in love with someone just because I thought they might be dead.'

I didn't say you were. It's just . . . you were so *angry* with me. You really thought I didn't care if he was gone or not.

'No,' he says, 'I didn't.' He puts his tongue between his teeth, I think so he can taste his next words. 'Joomia, you're not *great* at showing your emotions. I've always known that, and I'm sorry, it wasn't kind of me to accuse you of not caring. I was just . . . angry.'

At me?

'At everything. And you—'

I what?

'You were the nearest person to lash out at.'

You mean, I'm an easy target.

'I was a prick.'

So you think I won't face up to the life laid out for me, and worse, you don't think I have the emotional tools to communicate how I feel about it.

He begins to shake his head, but then he stops. He sighs. He won't lie to me.

'I think you can't expect people to help you if they don't know how you feel,' he says. 'I think you scared yourself with your power, and you've been running from it ever since.'

I used it two weeks ago. I saved you.

'Then why do I feel like you're still running?'

12 Days

Aula

It just all happened so quickly. First Sander, and then one or two others, and the next thing you know, Nadrik's ordered a city-wide curfew. People are so twitchy they jump and clutch their skulls if you so much as *say* the word 'memory'. All the healing houses are full, and not one prophet is free when I stop by the kitchens any more. I go in and try to feed them when I can, but I en't exactly Miss Free Time any more – when I'm not doing all the studying Nadrik's got me on, I'm having to literally *hold* houses together while someone does another quick mortar job cos so many of them are suddenly on the point of collapse. And if it en't that then I've taken to filling all Etain's orders for parts needed to fix the city engines cos they're malfunctioning at a rate I can only describe as ridiculous.

But none of that, *none of that* is as bad as this:

'Aula.'

I'm on the floor of my room, surrounded by all the maps and books I pulled towards me. They're all blank. Even the ones I drew myself. *Despair* doesn't cover it. Joke's on me that I didn't really listen to that thing Ashir said about the books. I was just knackered and glad she was awake, but now . . .

'Aula.'

Someone's hand, picking the tome out of my lap. It was called *The World as We Know It* and had all these amazing diagrams of the world from outer space which were so amazing I'd always drag it towards me whenever I felt like the most important screw in a big machine, which everyone's relying on turning smoothly. Cos looking at the world when it was green and beautiful reminded me I am so, so small that I don't really matter. I en't gonna be able to do that again. The picture en't there any more.

I look up and jump outta my skin.

'What the hell are you doing here?' I say.

The boy I slept with at the Wise One celebrations grins. 'Happy to see me, huh?'

My insides do something complicated, and my right hand considers knocking that stupid grin right off his face. It's not like I *expected* him to stay that night but, the thing is, I'm usually the one who sneaks out in the morning and it en't so good for my pride to have the sandal on the other foot.

He seems to guess what I'm thinking cos he says, 'Sorry I didn't say goodbye.'

I en't gonna dignify that with a response. 'Why are you here?' I say, all haughty.

'I had to check something. I'd tell you about it but it's kind of—' He shakes his head. 'Never mind. I *can't* tell you about it.'

'Uh-huh,' I say, cos if he thinks I'm gonna bite on a titbit as lame as that he's got another think coming. I start to close the books and shuffle the papers, mostly so I don't have to look at him and his stupid parted lips and that stupid stubble on his jaw and especially not his stupid beautiful collarbones making clean, hard lines above the open collar of his tunic.

'Also,' he says, more quietly.

I look up, and he's really really close.

I feel dizzy which is ridiculous cos I'm already sitting down. I try to clear my throat. 'Also?'

He raises one eyebrow, very slowly.

Oh, just do it. You're only human.

I want to. Tear off each other's clothes and forget. But I got a feeling the heaviness in my stomach en't gonna move just for a bit of a tumble. I scrub my face with my hands. 'You want an escape from something too, huh? What's your thing? Bet it's not as bad as being a Chosen One.'

He looks surprised, but then his face settles. 'Nah, probably not.' He sighs. 'Sorry.'

'What for?'

'I just . . . I don't want you to think I was trying to use you or anything.'

I shrug. 'I'd be a hypocrite if I got offended. I get it. Sex is good for forgetting. But it just . . . doesn't last.'

He sits down beside me. 'Tell me about it.'

For a minute or two, we just sit there. It's weirdly comfortable, an understanding sort of silence.

Then he says, 'Two weeks to go.'

I grimace. 'I bet your Chosen One's got it all sorted.'

He laughs. 'You don't?'

171

I raise an eyebrow at him. 'Nice try. Like anything I tell you en't gonna get straight back to Mathilde or—' I sit up, thinking I should have listened to my instinct that night after all. 'Is that why you're here? Is *that* what you were doing when we—'

He rolls his eyes. 'I don't know if you've ever tried to get information out of someone while you're having sex with them, but I'm guessing I could think of better ways. Besides . . .' He runs a hand through his hair and yawns. 'I'm not sure I really buy any of this Ariadnis stuff. A book that makes the reader omniscient?' He wrinkles his nose and gives me a look that says, *am I right?*

I press my lips together. It's the edge of a conversation I don't even want to get into. Not that I haven't thought about it.

'You think it's real?' he says, somehow reading my silence.

'I dunno if it matters if it's real,' I say. 'It's like a fairy tale – the point en't the dragon or the witch or the poisoned rose, the point is what you get out of it after it's been told.'

He grins at me. 'I like that,' he says. 'A fairy tale. So the story of Ariadnis and how it's made – that's all a metaphor?'

I raise my eyebrows. 'Pretty bloody literal, for a metaphor.'

'You think there's some sort of magical task in there for you and the Chosen One of Metis to race to complete?' he asks.

'You *don't*?'

'Where's the proof?'

I pull my hair over my shoulder so he can see the mark on my neck, but I can tell from the look on his face that he doesn't reckon that's proof enough.

'I guess you don't believe in the Wise One either,' I say.

'Ten points,' he says.

I sigh and hang my head. 'Well, that's easy for you.'

'Yeah?'

'Yeah. There en't any consequences for you if He—'

'Or She,' he puts in. I frown at him, but his eyes glitter. I nod reluctantly. 'Or She exists. But there are for me. If the Wise One en't real, if there en't anything in Ariadnis. If the book en't there to be won, then what the hell is the point of any of this?'

'Power,' he says instantly. 'Who gets to do what.'

'I don't want that.'

'No,' he says. 'Neither do I. And I bet my spleen that the Chosen One of Metis doesn't want that either.'

I look at him, startled.

He shrugs. 'What? Who's it gonna harm, you knowing that? It doesn't matter either that you don't want it – that's what it is.'

I bite my lip, strain against the knot in my throat. My eyes feel hot. I turn away and stare at the blank pages. I can't look at him. I can't look at how sure he is about something I've never felt sure about in my life.

I feel his hand, warm on my shoulder. 'Or maybe,' he says softly, 'maybe you're right. It's a fairy tale. And the point of it – all of it – real or not, is to help you be wise. I think I like that better.'

'Don't try and placate me,' I mutter.

'I'm not. I think it's a good point. A lot wiser than anything anyone down in Metis is saying anyway.' His

173

turn to rub his face. I see that he looks tired. Really tired. Just like Etain.

'Are you going back to Metis soon?' I ask.

'Yeah,' he says.

It's like that thing where you can see a glass about to topple from a table. Your instinct is to catch it – you don't even think. Something like that makes me put my hand over his.

But I can't blame impulse for making me say, 'Stay.' He looks surprised, and I'm cursing myself cos this is exactly what gets you into trouble of the slushy, emotional kind. 'Just for a bit,' I say hurriedly. 'I mean, if you want.'

Ugh.

But he turns his hand over, so our palms are facing, and slides his fingers between mine.

I wake in my bed, hours later, and when I turn over, he's still there.

It's the first time in my life that I've fallen asleep with a boy fully clothed. Where I've fallen asleep holding someone's hand, *wanting* to kiss them, but not doing it cos I know where it leads. It's the first time that *not kissing*, not even talking, just feels like enough.

I've been lying a bit awkwardly, and I'm just shifting myself into a more comfortable position when he opens his eyes. He looks at me and smiles.

That is a bit too much. I lean in. He raises his head, but pauses.

We hear a door opening and closing and then – *footsteps*. Coming up my stairwell.

We jump up at the same time.

174

'You need to go,' I say.

'You don't say,' he says.

I hold up a hand and listen. 'They're coming up the back staircase. Quick, go left out my door, along that corridor and then straight down when you come to the steps.'

He stops at the door. 'My name's Taurus, by the way.'

I dunno what to do with that. What comes out is, 'Hurry up.'

He grins. 'I hope I see you again,' he says. Then he disappears.

I make a business of trying to pick up clothes, but I've only managed to throw three things on to my bed when the door opens.

I spin around. Etain walks in and my stomach drops at her expression.

'What? What is it?'

'It's Ma,' she says. 'She's been fine all day but I think she had another vision or . . .'

I can't bring myself to speak.

'She's asking for us.'

'Why?'

Etain's shaking. 'I think she's gonna die.'

In the last few weeks Ashir has been weak, mostly sleeping, but smiling and talking a bit and asking how I am, how's the training going, don't let Nadrik get you down. Not now.

She is barely moving. The scars are glowing lava lines on her face. Her eyes are wild and blazing. Her skin has cracks and crumbles in it like weathered paint.

The blindfold, when they try to put it on, goes thin and

translucent, like netting rather than silk. Nothing can stop the visions now.

When she grips my hand, her fingers slide with sweat.

Her voice is more like an echo than a real sound. 'Aula. Etain. I need . . . a potion.'

'Potion?'

'A mixture that will kill my vision. You will need to go to . . . Metis . . . to retrieve it.'

The healer on hand looks at her like she's gone totally mad. God, Nadrik's sure got this lot whipped, hasn't he? I know that unless you're a messenger, going to Metis without permission is technically illegal and all that, but there's no need to look like we just killed her dog.

'Metis?'

'They do not like prophecy in Metis. They know how to draw it out.'

I glance at Etain, sure we're about to exchange an incredulous look, but she's staring straight into Ashir's eyes. I get the sense they're communicating something but a second later Ashir winces as she coughs.

'I'll get Nadrik,' I say. 'He'll know what to do.'

'*No!*' Ashir shrieks. 'Not him! Not him!'

We both step back at her outburst. She looks so contorted – so *not* Ashir – I think for a second her mind must've broke.

'There is . . . no . . . time . . .' she chokes. '*Don't let me die. I don't want to die.*'

This is it: the scariest moment of my life. Salt in my nose. My throat closes.

'You en't gonna die,' I say, with as much strength as

I can. 'Come on, Etain. Let's go and get that potion.'

'I love you, Ma,' Etain says.

Don't say that, I want to say. *Don't say goodbye.*

Etain finds my hand through her tears and together, we walk out of the ward.

Of course we're going. En't any choice.

Etain detours to the prophet house to get some things but she's back in my room within fifteen minutes. 'I'm ready,' she says.

'Yeah,' I say, thinking of the entrance to Ariadnis. Knowing there is a route down to them just like there's a route up to us.

She says, 'I should leave in about an hour. After it gets dark.'

'Yeah, yeah, I know. I'm coming too,' I say, looking for some kind of cloak that will blend in with the darkness under all the crap on my floor.

'No, you en't.'

I stop packing and stare at her. She's wearing an expression I en't seen before. She doesn't look patient or calm. She looks hard and unyielding. 'Did I hear that right?' I say. And I *do* manage to say that, rather than snarl it.

'Yeah,' she says. 'You did.'

'I'm gonna pretend I didn't,' I say, and start rummaging again.

'Aula, I'm going by myself.'

'No, you *en't*.'

'Yes, I am!' she shouts.

Etain *never* shouts. I stand up. 'They'll never let you,' I say.

'*You* en't gonna tell anyone,' she says.

'Oh yeah? How'd you figure that?'

'Aula, for fuck's sake!'

I swallow. Etain *never* swears. 'What?' I say.

'Why do you have to make this difficult? Why has it always got to be about you?'

Ouch.

'I *en't*—'

'You *are*. Come on, *think*. You have to be here. It's breaking the treaty for either of us to go. I'll just get a smacked wrist and maybe some extra time working on the mechanisms in the trunks for not having the Elders' permission, but the *Chosen One*? You'd start a war faster than a Metisian could cross one of their root bridges. Anyway, you have responsibilities. You have your lessons with Nadrik. You have to *prepare*. You have hundreds of people to send hope to – especially now, when people are losing their memories, when all the books are wiped blank. You have to stop following every single instinct your gut sends you. She's *my* mother. She's *my* responsibility. So I'm going.'

'But . . . but . . . you don't even know the way.'

There's this flash of something on her face – an expression I can't understand cos she smothers it too quick.

'Wait – do you?' I ask. '*Do* you know the way?'

She shakes herself. 'No, I . . . hadn't thought of that. You'll have to show me.'

'What if I won't?' I say.

She just looks at me.

Something gives. I say, 'She's my mother too.'

178

Etain blinks a lot and bites her lip as if she's getting it under control. 'I know,' she says, in a slight voice. 'But you still have to stay here. You know that, don't you?'

I don't say anything.

'You don't always get to be the hero, you know,' she says. 'Every now and then, it's my turn too.'

I shiver, though it en't cold.

There's a long, long silence, as I look at my now-blank map parchments, my empty books.

Better to be anywhere but here.

I say, 'Fine. I'll show you.'

Like she'd said, we wait for night.

Someone comes to tell me that my lessons are cancelled, cos Nadrik heard about the books and had to go and pacify the uproar that came about as a result. I don't bother to tell them that my lessons would've been up hours ago anyway.

The palace courtyards are empty.

We sneak out and begin to run. The owlery is silent, which is what makes the guard that greets us so pissing scary. Not guard as in human, guard as in *owls*. As in maybe all the owls in the city, perched on the roof, on the little wall that runs along the outside, clustered together with their wings all hunched up like they're expecting a high wind. I slow up pretty quick as soon as I see them.

'Uhhh,' I say, but Etain just marches past them, not sparing a glance.

'Aula,' she says impatiently.

I'm still in a don't-blink competition with the owl closest to me, and then I have to give in cos my eyes are watering.

179

It occurs to me that it's a bit weird she en't saying *why the hell are we at the owlery* but then we've both got other things to think about so I step over the threshold (holding my nose), find the trapdoor and pull it up.

In the dull echo of the lights outside you can only see the top of the ladder. The rest of the climb down is just inky darkness, and I realise with a groan that I didn't think to bring a light for her. But then Etain takes something out of her pocket. It's a kind of night light that people usually use for their kids' bedrooms or for lighting badly lit hallways – a rock with a glyph for light spelled into it by some magi or other. It en't bright exactly, but it shows us a good two yards down as Etain casts its beam before her. I wouldn't have thought of that.

I tell her the directions best I can. I remind her that she'll have to guess where to go once she reaches the entrance of Ariadnis but I'm pretty sure that the way to Metis goes straight down. Then I realise I'm babbling so I stumble to a halt. She's been peering down into the trapdoor the whole time I been talking, but now she raises her head to look at me.

'OK, I'm going,' she says.

My throat is suddenly aching without warning. Her chin shivers. We step into each other's arms and she's holding me tight and I'm holding her tighter until she says, 'Ribs! Ribs!' And I let go and we laugh even though we're both crying. And then she says, 'Take care of her.'

'Well, *yeah*,' I say.

She steps on to the first rung of the ladder and I shut the door after her before I have to watch her light disappear.

Joomia

It's been a long day, and I need to clear my head, so I decide to wash in one of the openings in the tree veins. We have to make the openings ourselves. Over time, when old veins of the vishaal trees no longer channel sap and start channelling water from somewhere in the cliff, we send the most skilled magi to harvest the hardened sap and hollow out the vein, to better allow water to pass through. It's a painstaking process, but it means we get to wash in running water. The bathing openings are quite high up in the city, almost up to the rock ceiling that towers over Metis; a few branches away from the entrance to the pathways up to Ariadnis.

I used to think it was risky, having the baths so close to the pathway to Ariadnis, but you wouldn't be able to tell the entrance was there unless you knew it was. It's covered almost completely by brambles and ivy. Only a few people in Metis know the exact location, and when messengers come we guide them out blindfolded so they won't be able to find their way back without one of these people escorting them – though that hasn't happened for many years now.

The water is cold enough to make my teeth shrink, never mind the warmth of the evening sun. I am up to my waist and making hissing noises as I brace myself against the cold when I see the splinters of wood in the water, which would usually be bright and clear. The shards are black and gritty and the water smells different. Like the forest floor, not the air above. It still looks clear enough to clean myself in, but suddenly I don't want to.

I breathe deeply, to stop the tightening panic in my chest.

Because I'm in now, I give myself a cursory splash and climb out as quickly as I can, combing my fingers through my hair. Then I look up and there's Oriha, watching. I fumble for my clothes and manage at least to get my sarong wrapped around me.

'Do you remember?' she asks me.

I use my eyes and my shoulders to ask: *Remember what?*

'Us?'

I knot the sarong over my chest. *Do I* remember us?

Only last year I was never more at peace than when she looked at me. I try not to think much about it any more, because there's so much ugliness and resentment between us, but sometimes I remember the way her lips made me solid, and how safe it felt to move in her arms. What happened after – it still hurts, but in a distant way. I just wish the sight of her wouldn't make me feel like I'm about to lose an argument I haven't even started.

I nod my head once. I crook my finger and signal upwards. *Why?*

'My mother. She's gone like Lear.'

Oh, Wise One. Why is she telling me? Why isn't she telling someone who can help?

Because there's no one to help. It's supposed to be your *job.*

She looks blankly at the water vein behind me. Then she asks, 'Why didn't we work?'

I stare at her. I'm not sure, even if there were any paper to hand, that I'd be able to answer that. We were sixteen and it was doomed from the beginning. She wanted to help me. I think perhaps she even thought that she'd be able to help me with my powers, with my voice. When it didn't happen, she was so disappointed. I wrote her so many silly notes to make up for it that my hands ached constantly.

I tried.

When she got jealous of Taurus, of our ease together, I explained that I've never had a choice about who hears me. Taurus, Mathilde, Ade. That's all it's ever been. She didn't believe me.

But maybe that's not why *we* didn't work. Maybe it's just this:

I don't work, I mime. *I am broken.*

She shakes her head.

'You are . . .' She sways, catches herself on her right foot. She looks at me. Her eyes are hazy and unfocused, but she brings me back into her sight. 'You're not broken,' she says, but she sways again. Then she staggers.

I run forward and catch her arm.

'Joomia,' she says, her fingers brushing my shoulder. Then she sags in my arms.

Oriha. I shake her. ***Oriha.***

When her eyes open, they're blank.

Blank as Lear's.

Blank as every book in Metis.

I stare at her helplessly.

Oriha?

And then, suddenly, she's out of my arms and out of my reach in ten seconds.

Running headlong, right towards the entrance to the tunnel as if she knows it's there.

Oriha! Come back! I shout, but I think of Lear and how unstoppable he was (was this where he was heading?). I take

183

off after her, springing across the paths where they run parallel to each other. I've never seen Oriha run so fast. She's disappeared through a gap in the ivy already. She's in the tunnel, she has to be.

Oh, Wise One.

I run as fast as I can, but stop at the entrance, gasping for breath.

ORIHA! I bellow.

How is she supposed to hear you? Go after her, idiot!

I stumble upwards, running blindly into the dark, wincing as my bare feet catch on the shale and grit and pebbles of the tunnel floor. I run, hands groping in front of me in case she's stopped and I can guide her back.

I don't know what trips me, but I skin my wrists against the rock, smacking my chin against a bulbous lump in the floor. My head snaps back and my consciousness is swallowed like a pebble in a well.

It can't be more than a few seconds before I'm blinking my eyes open again, but it's dark of course, so I can't tell for sure. I can't believe how stupid I've been. I'm alone, in the dark, without a light, having lost another friend to whatever's causing this memory loss, wearing a sarong and no shoes. I don't even have the energy to get up and inspect my wounds. I just lie there.

If I had the gall to use my power at least, I think, *maybe I could have stopped her. But I didn't even do that.*

I didn't think. I didn't—

I am a failure. What am I going to tell them? That she lost her mind and then I lost her?

And then a heavier voice sounds. It's my voice, but from

184

the very bottom of whatever makes me up. It's dripping with disgust. It's *glad* I'm on the ground, with grit on my face. I deserve it.

It's not just the darkness of the tunnel, or the loss of a friend, or the disintegration of my home. It's the fact that I'm supposed to be Metis's best hope for the future. It's that Mathilde and Taurus have such painful, unrewarded *faith* in me, and here I am, lying on the cold stones of the inside of the cliff, wondering if it wouldn't be better for everyone if I were dead. I curl into a ball and put my hands over my head.

The hand on my face is warm.

I don't want to open my eyes and find it isn't real, so I keep them closed.

When I do blink, there *is* a hand on my cheek, a light beside me. I give a start.

Oriha, I say.

'Easy,' says a voice. 'You sure messed yourself up here.'

Is that . . . is that an Athenasian voice? I try to sit up.

The girl in front of me is illuminated by a small glowing stone. She's about my age and wearing distinctly Athenasian clothes – tunic and chlamys all belted and clipped with buckles. Nothing like the thin, brightly patterned cloth we weave to clothe ourselves in Metis.

I look around. **My friend . . . did you see her? She ran up this way and . . . and now . . .** I peer up the tunnel, away from the light. **I can't see her,** I whisper.

'I en't seen anything,' says the girl (yes, she's definitely Athenasian). 'But . . . maybe . . .'

185

Maybe what?

'I felt something pass me just now.'

That must have been her, I say, trying to get to my feet.

'No,' she says. 'Not on foot. Something . . . over my head. I thought it was a bat. Or a bird.'

A bird?

'Yeah.'

But it can't be . . . I—

A thought hits me then. Hard. Adrenaline has my heart in a tight wind and my veins throbbing in a millisecond. I can only think that my fall must have rattled my head more than I thought.

You can hear me, I say.

'I wasn't gonna comment,' she says. 'But yeah. You don't seem to be using your mouth.'

How . . . how did you know it was me who was talking?

She looks around, and for a second something like a smile, or at least the ghost of one, appears on her face. 'I reckon we're the only two people around. Who else would it have been?'

She says it so *reasonably*.

I want to say, *There are only three people in all the world who can hear me. How can you be the fourth?*

What happened to you?' she asks.

I lost something, I mumble.

I can tell that she knows I'm lying, but she doesn't press me.

'Do you live here? In Metis?'

I nod. Is this real? What is she *doing* here?

'My name's Etain,' she says. 'I need to speak to Taurus.'

186

My skin jangles as though I've been licked with flames. *Taurus?* What does she want with him?

'I can't explain right now,' she says, as if reading my thoughts. 'But it's urgent.'

I stare at her.

'We're friends,' she says. 'Please, will you take me to him?'

I say, **He's never told me about you.**

'No,' she says. 'He won't have.'

I hesitate. But what else am I going to do? Sit here and cry? I use the walls to stand. I look around. I have no idea which way is which.

'Is your head all right?' Etain asks.

It's been better, I say.

'Well, I came from that way,' she says, pointing. I nod, brushing grit from my face and arms, and lead the way, limping on my cut feet.

When we emerge, she gasps, and despite the heaviness I feel, I don't blame her. This high up, Metis is quite a sight after dark: the roots of Athenas tangle in the branches of our vishaal trees; the colours of the vishaal leaves turn the moonlight pastel green; the breeze carries the smell of the ocean, far off.

'It's beautiful,' she says. And then she turns to look at me, and her smile falters.

'You're Joomia,' she says, 'I mean . . . sorry, you're the Chosen One. Metis's Chosen One. You have to be.'

Of course. She's recognising Aula, not me. I nod uncomfortably.

For some reason I don't want to have to explain to her about fetching my clothes but once we get to the tree vein she sees the pile of discarded garments and turns away so I can dress properly.

We make our way towards the herb garden in High Tree, which is usually pretty empty. It's not a particularly tricky way down but I can tell she isn't used to the lumpy, uneven platforms, the weave of the root bridges and the occasional vine-net ladder. Just to be sure, I spread my awareness out in every direction to make absolutely sure we don't accidentally stumble into rot. I have to steady her several times – once on a ladder and twice on a branch – until eventually I have to take her hand and place it on my shoulder in case she moves too quickly and falls.

'Thank you,' she says, and her voice, for that moment, sounds very old and sad.

I nod, and then I call Taurus. **Wake up. Wake up. There's someone here. From Athenas. If you can hear me, will you come to the upper pathway near the herb garden? Will you meet us there? I think it's urgent.**

When we get there, Taurus is waiting for us, his fingers apparently unable to keep from knotting together. When he turns, I'm proud of how much he exemplifies Metis at its best: hands brown and calloused from climbing, hair snarled with twigs, back straight and tall.

I'm about to say something, but then Etain makes a mournful sound. She stumbles into Taurus's arms, and he holds her tight, whispering something into her hair.

'Is it . . . ?' he asks, but she doesn't answer him, and he doesn't seem to need her to.

My brain can't get any further than: *They are almost the exact same height.* I stare between them with my mouth open, unable to process what I'm seeing.

'She needs the potion *now*, Taurus,' Etain is saying. 'She's – she's going—' But she can't go on. She breaks down, and it's like she's wilting.

'We'll fix it,' Taurus says hoarsely. 'We'll find a way.'

'But it might be too late.'

'Shh.'

They stay there, clutched against each other like survivors for what seems like hours. I can't move. My head spins.

And then, finally, Taurus looks at me. His eyes are red. 'Joomia,' he says. 'Mathilde can't know. She can't know Etain's here. It's against the laws of the treaty for someone from Athenas to come here without the Elders' consent.'

I glare at him. What is he talking about? Why would he think my first reaction would be to run off and tell Mathilde about it? But all I say is, **Messengers from Athenas are always welcomed**, thinking belatedly of how I didn't blindfold her when I brought her down.

'She's not a messenger, Joomia.'

No?

'No. She's my sister.'

Aula

When Ashir wakes, she screams.

When Ashir sleeps, she screams.

I sit by her bedside anyway.

I hold her hand when there are lulls.

I layer blindfolds over each other. But it's useless.

189

There en't anything I can do.

Except sit here as the room fills with her rasping breath and the silence whines around us.

I can never stand it very long.

So I go to the forge, pound out my frustration with a hammer.

I go to my room and retrace the lines of my maps as if something hasn't erased every sign of them.

Then I go back to the healing house, where Healer Phythia en't ever far away from Ashir.

Sometime during the night, she wakes me. I've been drooling on to my arm as I sleep by Ashir's bed in a chair with too many corners, so I have to wipe my cheek and pretend to look awake. Phythia's braids have found every available escape route from her headwrap and her face looks like sleep's been trying to drag it down for ages.

'No one can find Etain,' she says.

'She's down in the trunks with the engineers,' I say like I've rehearsed – though no one's really asked. Everyone in the prophet house and at the forge just assumes she's with Ashir. 'Meathead engine builders can't get her screws to fit even though she's told them a hundred times.'

'You will need,' Phythia says gently, 'to fetch her back.'

For a second I don't understand but then I hear Ashir's breathing – and it's different. Slower now. Harsher. Her skin looks oily and wasted.

The words come, but only just barely. 'How long?'

'I don't know. I'm sorry, Lady Aula. You should prepare yourself.'

'But how long?' I ask.

'Hours at most,' she says, her mouth tight. 'I'm sorry.' She gives me a tired nod.

The door closes behind her. A scream surges out of my chest and into my mouth. I squeeze it through my fists and let the panic and grief pour out of my eyes.

She has to be wrong. She has to be wrong.

But Ashir is barely moving on the bed.

'I'll get Nadrik,' I remember saying. *'He'll know what to do.'*

'NO!' was what Ashir shrieked. *'Not him! Not him!'*

I won't have time to get Etain, I know it. I won't have *time*. The ache yawns open. I'm gonna fall into it. If Ashir goes, I'll drown.

'Wise One,' I say. 'Help me. *Help me.*'

Don't let me die. I don't want to die. That was what Ashir said.

I gotta stop panicking cos my breathing sounds more like a gurgle. I'm still rigid, frozen on the seat, but I know a minute more and I won't ever get up.

So I get up. I take Ashir's hand. I say, 'If you die before she comes back, I'll kill you.'

Then I kiss her cheek and go to the window . . . just to check. The courtyard is empty, and the palace is dark. Except for one room, right at the top of the western tower.

Nadrik's study.

He's still awake.

What else can I do . . . ?

When he doesn't answer my knock I kick the door open and get splinters in my leg for my trouble.

'Perfect,' I mutter, and snatch the ones I can see out

191

before they get worked in too deep. I look around. He wasn't ignoring me. He really en't here. I try and breathe deep. He probably went for a piss or something.

I hesitate where I'm standing, cos even though the study's empty, it feels like if I go in any further I'm violating something between me and him. Not that it matters. It doesn't matter. I don't care.

I go to the desk. It's a big wooden thing – more like a kitchen block than anything else. There are books open on every inch of it, and every one of them – like all the books now – is blank.

Except, wait . . . there is writing in one. It's his writing, I know, cos it's all tidy and neat. It's filling every inch of this spread with annotations and little diagrams I don't get. I glance back at the door. I look down, pull off a tobacco pouch that's covering a bit of the page.

Circles, it says. *Memory works in circles.*

And other stuff. I squint and look closer. *Memories need an anchor—*

There's a sketch of his circlet, the jewel on it—

Panic lubricates sanity.

Begin again.

I stare at the words. I don't even wanna think about what they mean, so I move on. I open a drawer. More blank pages. Then something else. I pull out a piece of paper. It's a sketch of a woman. She kind of looks like me but not. Or, at least, the artist has captured someone whose face sort of looks like it's laughing, and there's something about the eyes or the chin or the way the hair falls that reminds me of me . . .

'Can I help you with something?'

I skitter round so fast some of the books get knocked off the desk.

Nadrik.

My thoughts are everywhere. I can't find the one I need. And then—

'Nadrik. You gotta help. It's Ashir. Healer Phythia says she's gonna – she's only got—'

I want to finish, but at that second, everything spins out of focus. It's like every part of me wants out of my body – wants to spill out into the air and go spiralling into any direction that en't here, in a place where I en't dealing with this on top of the usual stuff.

He just stares at me, expressionless. 'If you finish your sentence, Aula, I might be able to help you.'

I pull myself together enough to gasp it out. 'Healer . . . Phythia . . . she says Ashir's gonna die. Soon.'

'How long does she have?' he asks.

'I . . . I dunno. Healer Phythia said only hours.'

He presses his lips together. 'Is it that time already?' he murmurs, and he's gotta be talking to himself cos he en't looking at me.

'What do you mean?' I whisper.

He looks at me as if he only just noticed I was there. 'So? What do you want me to do about it, Aula?'

I stare at him. 'I want you to save her.'

'Why?'

'What do you mean *why*?' I say. 'How can you ask that? She's the only person who ever treated me like anything other than the Chosen One. She's been a mother to me all

193

my life! You save her! *You fucking save her!*' I scrub my eyes with the back of my hand.

Finally he takes a breath, as if he had been waiting for me to exhaust myself. 'The visions are killing her,' he says calmly. 'There is an old concoction they used to use to take away a prophet's vision. We use spells more often these days to ease visions, of course – but since removing a prophet's vision is just as dangerous as letting her keep it, the potion hasn't been used for years. Still, it exists.'

'Do you know how to make it?'

'I don't need to, I have some.'

'Why?'

He lets out a tiny laugh. 'Do you want it, Aula, or don't you?'

'Are you gonna give it to me or not?'

He gets to his feet and goes to his desk. He opens a drawer, below the one I was looking in. The drawer rattles. He takes out a phial and gives it to me.

I stare at it. At him. 'Just like that?'

I recognise his expression. It's the one where he's trying not to roll his eyes at me. 'My city isn't run by my foresight, Aula. If I didn't treat the prophets well, how would I rule at all?'

'Why don't the healers have this then?'

'As I have explained, the removal of a prophet's vision is considered too dangerous – not to mention *sacrilegious* to our way of life.'

I hesitate.

'How long did you say she had, Aula?' he asks mildly.

I jump and run out the door.

Joomia

'You've got to let me explain,' Taurus says.

I take a deep breath, to steady myself. I say: **I'm listening**.

But he can't seem to say the words out loud. His voice catches in his throat. His eyes go very bright.

I'm listening, I say again, softer this time.

Taurus bows his head. Etain runs her hand through his hair. 'Our mother is sick,' she says. For some reason, I don't want to look at her. 'She's a prophet, and her vision is taking her from us.'

Don't you have spells for that? *We* do.

'Would I be here if we did?'

There is a long, long silence. Then Taurus takes a loud breath. 'Ade? Do we have time to tell her?'

As if on cue, Ade steps out in the moonlight from a shrub a few yards away. Her hair is as wild as ever, but her posture is straight and she seems focused. Etain tenses, but Taurus's face is impassive.

I look between them, frowning. **What's going on?**

But Ade shakes her head. 'No time, Mathilde is coming. Listen, Joomia,' she says, and that's how I know she's having one of her lucid moments. There's still something slightly mad about the way she's looking at me, but it's like she's able to squint through something clouding her vision and just pay attention to what's in front of her. 'Time I told you something. Time for you to know. Taurus. Etain. They were there when you were born.'

She looks straight into my eyes as she says it. That blankness that usually haunts her face is gone.

She knows me. She knows me.

'Etain barely one. Taurus only two. They were there with their mother. While I was giving birth . . .' My hand snatches her sleeve as I understand her meaning, and her arm lowers me to the ground as my knees give in.

Ade says, 'You were dead when you came out of me. Ashir knew you were dead, but she was trying to get you to breathe. You wouldn't.'

I search her face. I can't see anything else.

'Then they came. Mathilde and the Athenasian Nadrik. Knew that the Ninth Chosen Ones would be born that night. Each of them wanted you for their city. Tried to draw you to them. It was Athenas magic against Metis. Same, but different.'

The full moon gleams brightly between the branches. I close my eyes, trying to imagine, but it turns out I don't have to imagine for long.

'Come see,' Ade says, and she pulls me towards her, so our foreheads meet.

I'm not on the branch any more. I'm watching Etain and Taurus, but they are children, crying because the light of the magic is too bright and they want their mother to hold them. Their mother Ashir, so like them, is nearby, looking between Nadrik and Mathilde, horrified.

It's one magic against another. You can't tell by sight whose is whose, but you can smell the difference: oil for Nadrik, sap for Mathilde, and a sickly burning smell as they meet. They strain, desperately trying to win the fight.

And then something happens. Something snaps like a

bone. Nadrik falls backwards; Mathilde falls the other way. Both of them are holding a baby. Both babies are screaming. So is Taurus. So is Etain.

As Nadrik turns to run, I catch a glimpse of that baby's tufted hair – it's red. And the baby with Mathilde . . .

In another world, apart from my body, I see Taurus, Etain and Ade staring at me. My *mother*, staring at me.

So we *are* sisters, Aula and I . . . twins. And you're our—

But Ade ignores me, and keeps talking. 'Chosen Ones told you. Told you what you have to do.'

If you do not unite before your eighteenth birthday . . . before the Wise One's task, I say numbly, **there will be . . .**

'Nothing to save,' she finishes. 'Two cities. Two Chosen Ones. Two. Always apart, always struggle. Not Wise God, not Wise Goddess. Wise *One*, Joomia. Wise *One*.'

I take this big, shuddering breath. I say, **Yes.**

'Ashir,' Ade says, suddenly turning to Taurus. She sounds like she's going to cry.

'I have the mixture,' he says, and the look he gives me is mortally apologetic. 'I *will* explain everything. But I think that's our time up.'

'There is a cave, boy. The Cave of the Ancestors,' Ade whispers to him urgently.

'I know of it, on the edge of the Cliff that Stands Between,' he says. 'Ma told us stories of it, but—'

'Remember it well,' Ade insists. 'You must meet there. Together, all of you . . .' She blinks, struggling to focus, to know if she is telling us of today, or yesterday, or tomorrow. 'But first . . . Ashir. Go, both of you. Go to Athenas . . .'

Etain jerks her head once, like a pupil receiving

instructions. She grabs my hand and my heart jerks unexpectedly.

Ade—

'Go now.'

And for better or worse, the insistence in her voice and Taurus's eyes and Etain's hand press in on me, and I find I'm running with them, trying to look back, but the path turns and that's it. My mother is gone.

Aula

Ashir opens her eyes almost as soon as I've coaxed the last of the potion into her mouth.

I sag in relief and press my face into her shoulder.

She moves slowly, gently running her hand over my head. And then she frowns, and blinks. Her hand moves to her head.

'What is it?' I ask.

'Oh, my darling,' she says. 'You went to Nadrik, didn't you?'

Like I'm still some lying little kid about to get caught, my instinct is to lie. I shake my head, but it's no good. She knows. Of course she does. 'I'm sorry,' I say. 'I didn't reckon there was any other choice. Etain's not back yet, and I—'

But Ashir's sat up in bed, breathing like she's gonna be sick. 'Oh Wise One,' she whispers. 'Oh, sweetheart. I told you. I told you not to trust him.'

'Why? You're all right n—'

But she leans over the side of the bed and heaves. It's not

198

vomit. It's blood. As dark and red as life. Shock presses out all my nerve endings.

Blood. Blood everywhere.

She doesn't stop heaving. She won't stop.

'HELP!' I scream. 'SOMEONE, HELP!'

But no one comes.

'Aula,' Ashir chokes. 'Aula, it's all right. I—' She heaves again.

I scream, clutching at her, sobbing. 'I'm sorry, I'm sorry, I'm sorry, I'm sorry . . .'

'It's all right,' she says, spitting.

The blood pools around my toes. My throat constricts. It's as warm as Ashir is suddenly cold.

'Is this it? Is this what happens when you lose your vision?'

Ashir shakes her head. 'Poison. To see my last vision. To—'

'But why? Why would he want your last vision?'

But she's vomiting again.

'SOMEONE FUCKING HELP!' I roar.

And the door opens. It's Nadrik.

'What did you do to her?' I scream. 'What did you do?'

He looks at Ashir. At the blood. He *smiles*.

I run at him. But he's prepared, and I'm knocked sideways into the wall.

This can't be happening. My mind won't believe it. I pick myself up. But he sends an orb of energy in my direction, like it's nothing. It hits me so hard I dunno who I am. He's done that before – flattened me out – but only in lessons. Only ever in lessons.

And all I'm thinking is *no, no, no, no*.

But I can't make sense of anything . . .

Ashir's still on the bed. Nadrik's squatting in front of her. The back of his heels are stained in her blood.

'Now,' he says. 'There's that one vision I need. You know that. They say the last vision completes the circle. The last is the same as the first, but with more clarity.'

'You won't be able to See it,' Ashir says. Her voice sounds as red and raw as the floor.

'I have done a great deal of learning from the prophets,' Nadrik replies. 'Come on now, I know you're holding it in there. Hurry up.'

'It will not end well for you, Nadrik Sawnem,' she whispers. And then she raises her head. It's like watching the oldest person in the world, she's that shaky. But she does it. And she looks at me. I wanna stand and run to her, but I can't. I can barely move my eyes. I'm paralysed. 'It's all right, Aula,' she says.

And then something begins to build in her. I can feel the energy of it. The scars around her eyes gleam. Nadrik raises his hands and I see he's holding a cloth with the same marks on it that would hold a vision back.

He's gonna catch it, I think. *Catch the vision*.

And that's almost exactly what happens.

Something silvery, pearly, leaks outta Ashir's eyes like tears. It en't a liquid though, not quite. It holds its shape as it comes out of her, then drops into the cloth with the softest sound.

And then she falls back. Just falls back on the bed. Gone. Nadrik stands and ties the cloth carefully. Then he looks at me. 'Don't think I don't regret it,' he says softly. 'But it was necessary.'

I scream. It's the only sound I can make. He raises his hand and the air is sucked outta my lungs. I cough, splutter, heave.

'Even after all these years, Aula. You never *think*.'

I can't even sob as my lungs painfully try to refill. Even if I could speak, I couldn't say anything. Cos he's right about me. He's right.

And Ashir was right about him.

Nadrik spins a circle with his finger, and the air is stained with traces of shimmering blue.

I try to struggle to my feet. But it en't any good, cos whatever spell he's weaving hits me hard and the world is only heat and noise and nothing.

VI

11 Days

Joomia

Long after we pass the entrance to Ariadnis, we are still climbing upwards in darkness, with Etain and her odd stone-light as our guide. It's airless and strangely cool considering there are engines in the column next to us. The metal stairs feel bizarre under my bare feet, and my legs – however used they are to climbing – take a while to get used to the evenly spaced steps. 'The night you were born, Ade and Ma Saw their first prophecy,' Taurus says.

He and Etain share a glance.

'They Saw that one day Mathilde and Nadrik would dishonour the treaty of the ancestors. They Saw them try to take power, as the ancestors knew was inevitable. But they also Saw you and Aula uniting the cities. And they Saw . . .' He sighs.

The pause is so dramatic that I find myself saying, **What? Saw *what*?**

'Etain. They saw her—'

'Ruling,' Etain says, as if the word is bitter.

'*Leading*,' Taurus says, giving his sister a look. 'So Ma left Metis, to bring Etain up in Athenas, where she could see what ruling looked like for herself.'

'Whether I agreed with how Nadrik does it or not,' Etain interjects.

Taurus nods, 'She could read everything she wanted, study everything she wanted. Oh, and it helps that she's basically Nadrik's personal assistant.'

I rub my forehead. **And you?** I say to Taurus.

'Ma left me in Metis to help you. And to watch Mathilde, learn how she works, learn what ruling's like from her perspective. Everything I learned from her, I taught to Etain.'

I meant, what about your destiny? Are you going to be a leader too?

Taurus smiles at me. It's only because I know him so well that I catch the bitterness there before he smothers it. 'No,' he says. 'I'm just the help.'

'You are *not*,' Etain says.

He shrugs. 'Not everyone can say their future is the same as their destiny. If they did, why would we need Chosen Ones and leaders and all of that?'

I rub my forehead again. Already the skin there feels chafed.

'Is this too much?' Etain says.

Yes, I say. **All of it is.**

They wait.

I say, **I don't suppose they Saw *how* we might be uniting the cities? I mean, are we supposed to make that happen in Ariadnis or . . . ?**

'The prophecy of the Chosen Ones and Ariadnis was made way before this one,' Taurus says. 'I don't know if it's real any more than you do, but—'

206

'But,' Etain interrupts, 'Ma and Ade's prophecy isn't contradicting that prophecy. It's just another possibility. But it's a better possibility than *this* city or *that* city ruling, holding the other one down, don't you think?'

So, *no*, they didn't say *how*, then, I mutter, and their silence does the answering for them. **So . . . when they Saw you . . . us . . . uniting the cities, it was good? I mean, there was peace?**

Taurus hesitates. 'There will be peace,' he says. 'It will be hard. But we can do it. Us four.'

I shake my head, trying to clear it, trying *not* to think about what he means by *it will be hard*.

What about Nadrik and Mathilde? I say. **How have they violated the truce?**

Taurus blinked. 'The memory loss. The rot. You didn't think that was normal?'

I'm suddenly furious. How on Erthe am I supposed to be a judge of normality by *anyone's* standards? But I remember Mathilde's fingers, and the magic winking along them, fixing a hole in her hut. But was that all she was doing? Fixing? And Nadrik? Is he capable of the kind of magic that will pull memories from people's minds? I think of his unfathomable stare. Yes?

But why? I say. **Why would Mathilde put rot in our trees?**

'Your trees are connected to Athenas's,' Etain says. 'What happens to you also happens to us.'

Oh, please. It's *Mathilde*. She lives for trees and green and—

But I stop. Because she also said she'd do anything to protect her city, didn't she?

I look at the walls of the trunk we're now climbing.

In the gloom, I can see tiny veins of phosphorescent light, pale green against the dark – which means that these trunks really are made out of the vishaal trees. Which means – somehow – it's possible that they're still alive, even though they're hollowed and filled with machinery and staircases. When I reach out to the walls in my mind there's a faint, faint recognition there. It's not quite like with the trees in Metis – where I am more or less a part of them. This is different – I am different. More separate, but no less connected – as if I were a relative of these trees, or a pet. And there's something else. A rancidity that's just beyond my reach. I recognise it this time, though. These trees are rotting just like the ones in Metis. Oh, Wise One . . . I try to eke out the places where the damage seems to be spreading, but just when I get a grasp on the connection, something will clank or grind or jerk in the machines working in the centre of these impossible structures and the connection gets lost and all I can see is a stuttering light. **She's killing our trees**, I say. **To kill these ones.**

'That's what I said,' Etain says wearily.

But ours will survive, I say. **Because they're still trees. They're alive, and they can regenerate. These . . . aren't any more. Not quite.** My chest is heavy. *Mathilde. How could you?*

There's a silence.

'You see why we have to hurry?' Taurus says.

Yes.

We speed up, even though the pace Etain has set is already pinching my thighs and the metal under my feet jars horribly.

'Etain and me have been relaying messages all our lives,'

208

Taurus tells me. 'We started four or five years after you were born, when I was seven and Etain was—'

'I was six,' Etain interjects ahead of us, looking back to roll her eyes at Taurus. She smiles at me.

'But it didn't become a regular thing until the first year you and Aula went to Ariadnis,' Taurus continues, rolling his eyes back at his sister.

Guilt stipples in my stomach. My past is suddenly full of sacrifices. Ade gave up her sanity for all of this? For me? And Ashir, their mother, gave up her son so he could relay messages between our cities illegally? I glance at Taurus, a few stairs ahead of me, and wonder how it's never occurred to me to ask him about his birth parents. I'm sure I must have. But his answers must have been predictably vague, or he sounded happy enough with not knowing so I just shrugged it off.

And your father? I ask. **Was he part of this?**

'No,' Etain says, but there's a question lurking in that one word too. 'Not that we know of,' she adds, catching my eye. 'Ma said he died not long after I was conceived and Taurus doesn't remember him.'

I look at Taurus for confirmation and he shrugs. 'I remember *someone*,' he says. 'But I don't think he meant much to Ma.'

My mind stumbles before I find my next question. I want to tell them to stop, that I can't hear any more of this. But I find that I have to know. I have to know all of it now, and think about it later.

And what about Aula? I ask.

'What do you mean?'

209

Does she know any of this?

Etain hesitates, then says, 'Nah, she doesn't. She's with Ma now. Probably threatening to kill anyone who touches her.'

I hear a lot of fondness in that description and find myself wondering if it's sisterly or another sort. Wise One, what is the matter with me?

Will she help us? I say. **Will she listen?**

Etain barks out a grim laugh. 'Help and listen en't words Aula really understands,' she says. 'Oh, don't worry, I'll help you convince her, Wise One knows I've had enough practice.'

Thank you, I say, and try telling myself that the heat in my face is something to do with the climb and not the look she just gave me.

It's a long time before we reach a dead end. Etain stops and shines her light-stone upwards, and instead of another stairwell I see a ladder that must be twenty feet high, leading to what looks like an old trapdoor in the cavernous ceiling.

I've barely enough energy to glance at it before I collapse on all fours. I try to heave air into my body as the limited light blurs around me and my head pounds. Taurus comes over and puts his hand on my shoulder.

He's breathing heavily, but no more than if he'd done a lap of the courtyard in High Tree. *How often has he made this journey?* I wonder. Etain looks like she's trying to clear the black spots from her vision as much as I am.

'I'm sorry,' he says. 'But we can't stop.'

I take a deep breath, shaking out the last of the cramps in my feet, and do the same.

Only, at the foot of the ladder, Etain pauses. 'There's something up there,' she says. 'What is it?'

Taurus squints so she raises her light. 'An owl,' he says disbelievingly. I look myself and see he's right. There's an owl flapping around the trapdoor, as if it's looking for a way out but can't see one.

'Hold on there, little bird,' Taurus calls. 'We're coming for—' But he doesn't finish. Instead, he raises an eyebrow and looks around. 'What's that sound?'

I listen, because almost every noise has been drowned out by the wheeze of my own breathing and the chorus of gears, pulleys and steam taps in the heart of the trunk. But he's right – there's something else.

A rumbling noise like—

'Footsteps,' Taurus whispers, frowning.

'It would have to be a lot of footsteps to make a noise like that,' Etain says. I put my hand on the railing and it's vibrating like it's about to break.

'Joomia . . .' Taurus says.

I look back the way we've come, but I can't see anything, even when Etain comes up on my right with her light-stone held high over both our heads. I'm distracted by her proximity, even as exhausted as I am. She exhales, and air hot from her mouth hits my cheek. In that second, I am more solidly there in my own body than I ever have been before, as if whatever makes me *me* is pressing against the ends of my fingers and driving itself into my toes.

The railing is shaking now, the metal under us creaks and groans.

Taurus takes Etain's light and runs back down the stairs to investigate. He's gone for barely thirty seconds, and then he's pounding his way back towards us.

'Up the ladder!' he shouts. 'Now! Now!'

Etain goes first, surprisingly quickly considering she's from Athenas. She's at the trapdoor in no time, setting her shoulder against it and heaving, but she's not strong enough to open it.

What is it? I ask as Taurus throws himself after Etain to help.

'You'll see!' he shouts. 'Climb!'

The sound is so loud now. I hop on to the ladder and fling myself up – jumping rungs rather than climbing them.

Etain lets out a snarl and pushes her whole body into the trapdoor. As Taurus reaches her, puts his body into the effort too, the cacophonous sound resolves itself below me. It's people. A dozen of them at first, but then more and more. I look back as I climb, and catch sight of their faces – their blank eyes.

They're Metisians. There are so many of them, it must be every Metisian who has lost their memory. They reach the ladder, and immediately try to climb after us. It's like watching frogs scramble for purchase on the same leaf. They are expressionless, and yet their fingers grab and pluck, their limbs scramble. The ladder screams a high metallic warning.

There's a yawning sound as Etain and Taurus finally manage to push the trapdoor open. The trapped owl zips out.

212

'Joomia!' Taurus calls.

But I can't move. I watch, transfixed, as a memoryless scrambles up the ladder towards me. It's Lear.

I call his name, knowing he won't hear. I cling to the ladder as he closes the distance between us. I keep calling him, even as his eyes look straight through me. And then he's climbing past. His foot finds my shoulder. It's like I'm not there . . .

'Joomia!' Taurus roars, though I don't know if it's because he's concerned about me or because he wants me to stop Lear.

Morning sunlight is streaming in through the trapdoor. Lear stretches out towards it.

Then something strange must happen to my eyes. The light bends the silhouette of Lear's hand. It makes it look longer: a slippery, fluid shape. And then something else altogether. Not fingers. Feathers.

Not an arm. A wing.

Taurus lets out a yell but I don't hear the words.

And in the next second, Lear is gone. In his place is an owl. An owl the same dark sheen of Lear's hair. It flies through the open trapdoor. I don't understand.

The sun finds the memoryless crowding up the ladder towards me.

'Joomia!' Etain shouts from above me. 'The ladder is going to collapse! Climb! Climb towards me!'

I see Taurus, gripped by whatever's going on below me in a kind of fascinated horror. Then his eyes find me, and it's like whatever had him spelled releases me too. I climb.

The ladder creaks.

There's a sickening lurch as it moves strangely beneath me.

There's a sudden clap like muffled thunder, and then the air is full of wings. They stream past me in clouds of white and grey and speckled brown. Their talons brush my hair. Their beaks hiss as they pull alongside me.

And then I reach for Etain. She hauls me up by the wrists and Taurus grabs a handful of my tunic and then I'm tumbling up through the trapdoor with them. The air throngs with the wings of all the owls now swirling out around us.

We huddle together, but the room around us clears surprisingly quickly.

'What. The hell. Was that?' Taurus says.

'Oh, of course, because Joomia and me have all the answers,' Etain snaps.

'Those were Metisians . . . and they just *changed into owls*,' Taurus says. 'I didn't even know that kind of magic was possible.'

'It's Nadrik,' Etain says, shaking her head. 'I don't know how or why but it's got something to do with him.'

For a moment, we stare after the birds. They have joined another flock already spiralling overhead.

'At least we know why all the owls here are acting so weirdly,' Etain says.

'Come on,' Taurus says as the last owl swoops out of the owlery. 'Etain, you should go ahead and get the medicine to Ma. We'll find somewhere to hide.'

'I know a good place to hide you,' Etain says. 'If we get split up on the way, go to Aula's rooms. They en't well-guarded.'

I don't suppose they would be from the stories I've heard about her formidable strength. **Where are they?** I ask.

Etain leads us out of the owlery door and points. 'See that tower there, with all the balconies? Her rooms are right at the top. Like I said, it en't well-guarded so you should be able to get in. And she won't be there – she'll still be with Ma.'

Without another word, Etain takes off at a jog and we follow.

Aula

There are specific funeral rites in Athenas.

You do it as early as you can, you carry the one who has passed on your shoulders to your plateau's viewpoint, where you can look from the edge of the city to the forest below, and the sea, if it's a clear day.

You wrap the body of your loved one in the colours of the sky.

There are magi on hand, of course. And priestesses.

You and your family are allowed to choose some hymn.

After you've sung it, the magi will blow on a whistle made of bird bones and carved in the shape of a feather. The owls will hear it and come.

The priestesses murmur the rites and utter the farewell oath. They bring out the funeral knife, and the blade sings its own hymn as it's pulled from the scabbard.

Your loved one is unwrapped, so the head is exposed.

And the priestess brings the knife down on their neck.

The owls will arrive then. In their hundreds. The great greys are usually the first.

It's your job to offer them your loved one's head.

You pick it up gingerly.

You hold it out.

The owls have been trained to take the head back to the owlery to devour it, but sometimes they don't.

As you cry your tears, or not, a priestess does a speech about the bullshit metaphor: 'May the wisdom of their life take its course through the Wise One's creatures, let the Wisdom flow from them to Him, from Him to Athenas and in turn, may the Wise One keep us Wise.'

Then the priestesses and the magi will wrap the body back in sky colours, and they'll attach small parachutes which float the body through the air, to the sea.

As your loved one glides gently from sight, most people sing the Athenasian Sky Song, which is depressing as hell and sounds like a cat being strangled.

So when I hear the notes of the song I know what it means.

I en't awake, but I en't asleep either.

I'm trapped somewhere in-between.

And they're giving her body to the sky and I en't there, I en't there, I en't there . . .

Joomia

We hear singing as we approach the palace and Etain stops short. 'No,' she whispers, then, abandoning caution, she runs forward, making a sharp left into what I assume is another courtyard like the ones we've passed through already.

Taurus is after her in a moment, and I follow them with some unnameable dread sticking to my throat.

When I catch up with them, I'm just in time to see Etain folding like a puppet whose strings have been cut. I see the palace's colossal open doors and through them, the procession, dressed in white.

At the front, is what I assume is a magi – the clean, plain robes look similar to the ones magi wear in Metis, though there are few other similarities here. Behind him are women, all holding huge swathes of fabric in light blue and cream. I know before I see the body carried behind them what it means.

Etain falls forward.

She screams.

She screams.

And above her, above us all, despite the light that clearly signals dawn, a cloud made of owls circles in strange formation.

We can see the courtyard through an arch in a wall. As the procession looks up, I grab Taurus and yank him back with me. He doesn't resist. I don't think it occurs to him he can. All I know is that we can't be seen. Etain's screams go on and on, and my heart is small and hard as a bitter fruit. Taurus crumples next to me. I step over him and peer around the arch.

I look for Aula, but I can't see her anywhere.

There are so many of them. Women and a few men, all dressed in white. I suppose these are all prophets. A few of them move towards Etain, but someone else is quicker. A tall figure – the only one in black – whose silvering hair is knotted at the back of his head.

Nadrik.

I stiffen, but he doesn't see me. He strides to Etain, but she carries on screaming. I don't think she even knows where she is. He stands there. Watching her.

'Get up, Etain,' he says.

Taurus seems to come to himself then. He hauls himself to his feet but I throw out a hand. I shake my head. He takes another step, till my hand is against his sternum. **No, Taurus**, I say. **If he sees us, who knows what he'll do?**

His head sags.

'Get up, Etain,' Nadrik says again. 'Your mother needs her daughter.'

Etain stops screaming. She lies there on the paving stones at his feet.

'Get up, Etain.'

She gets up. She wipes her face, takes Nadrik's hand. Walks towards the funeral procession.

I don't watch any more. I turn back to where Taurus has sunk against the wall again.

'You're crying,' he says. His voice is raw, as if it's been him who was screaming.

We stare at each other. And then he reaches for me and I put everything I have into holding him together until I can get both of us up again.

It hadn't occurred to me to worry about getting lost, but in the end it doesn't matter, because the second I step inside the cold dark stone of the palace I know where Aula's room is.

If I weren't so tired, I'd be tempted to be suspicious of this sudden sense of direction, but I *am* that tired. So I give in, and follow my instincts and we find our way to Aula's room.

Inside the door, Taurus collapses against me and we go staggering into a pile of books, knocking several on to the floor. I can hardly bear to look as each page shows me its blank face.

After shutting the door behind us, I look around. There's a strange wooden box in the corner that, judging by the knotted mass of clothes sprawled underneath, must be for storage. Next to it is a huge structure with curtains. I've heard of beds, but I've never seen one. This one looks like it was made for three people, its dark wood frame carved with endlessly spiralling curlicues. There is a stale smell that is part yellowing pages, part food spices, part engine oil and something else – a smell that lingers on my own clothing when I haven't washed them in a while. I help Taurus over to the bed, and he falls back, asleep, before his hands leave my neck.

I watch him for a moment, trace the salt staining his cheeks with my eyes.

Oh, Wise One. I think: *this could have been my room.* If Nadrik had taken me and not Aula. And Etain would have been my best friend, and it would have been me at that funeral . . .

I try to lie down, next to Taurus – I don't remember the last time I slept, but I'm wide awake. I keep expecting Aula to come bursting in through that door, or at least for Etain not to be far behind us. I turn over, close my eyes, trying to imagine my way out of here.

Etain's face is the first one I see in my head. And we're in a world, in a place that isn't this one with all its complications. We're lying on a branch, somewhere in Metis, and my head is in her lap, and she is stroking my hair, and she leans down to kiss me.

I blink, shake myself. *Of all the times to get a crush on someone. Stop it.* The fantasy fades away, but my mind won't give up this one thought: her hand on my shoulder and my back as she pulled me through the trapdoor.

Hours seem to pass.

But Etain doesn't come. And Etain still doesn't come.

As my head droops, the emptiness rises. It's gentler than usual, less frightening. I sink into it.

Deep.

Deep.

Something prickles. Something reeling in pain and anger and sorrow. The emptiness throbs inside me.

There's something distinct about it this time as if it is pointing somewhere . . .

Aula?

* * *

I open my eyes. It's hot now. Late afternoon light is blaring through the window. It's brighter here in Aula's room than it ever is in Metis. The light is more naked and raw somehow, and the air is thinner.

I look around, but nothing's changed. No Aula and no Etain. I look at the bed, and Taurus's curled back rises softly. I want to reach out and touch his shoulder, but at the last second I hesitate because I hear a sound on the other side of the door. It's the sound someone makes when they've walked a long way and are finally allowed to sit down.

Cautiously I stand. I walk over and press my ear to the door.

Etain?

There's no answer. I peer round the door.

She's sitting on the topmost step of the stairs to Aula's room, her head bowed, her shoulders stiff.

Etain?

She flinches as I touch her shoulder. I take my hand back.

I'm so sorry.

She wipes her eyes with the heel of her hand. I don't know what to say now. I wish I knew her better, so I could offer her real comfort, but I don't know if that desire is for her sake or mine.

I sit down beside her. We're still for a few minutes. And then, slowly, she sinks against me. She doesn't make a sound, but my shoulder grows wet, and every now and then a tremor goes through her like she's sick.

'She's dead,' she whispers. 'She's dead. She's dead.'

It's such a horrible, stark truth.

I hate myself for saying it, but I have to. **I need to find Aula. We've got to do what we were told to do by the Guardians of Ariadnis – the Chosen Ones who came before us. And Ade.**

Etain laughs, but it's not a nice sound. 'Aula?' she says darkly. 'Aula only does things on her own. She doesn't take help, or give it. She just *does*.'

Etain . . .

'Ma didn't just *die*, Joomia. I've just seen the Head Healer. She saw what happened. Aula went running to Nadrik about how sick Ma was and he took Ma's last vision. Do you know what that means?'

I do. The last vision a prophet has is the same as their first. A closing of a circle. I shiver.

'Do you know what happens when you induce the last vision, before it's ready to come?'

I don't say anything. I can tell by her face it isn't good.

Etain swallows. 'He poisoned her. After everything she did. After everything she sacrificed for him.'

What do you mean, he poisoned—

'Ma *told* her not to go to him. Ma *told* her. And what did she do?'

I blink. **Etain, I don't understand.**

'Aula!' she bellows. 'She got asked one thing. *One!* And the first thing she does the moment Ma's fragile enough is to run screaming in his direction! Now he has exactly what he wanted! The prophecy about you, the prophecies about me and Taurus . . .'

Etain—

I don't get to finish because at that exact moment, the

emptiness yawns and reverberates inside me so powerfully I have to clutch my head. And through that infinite space, through some unseeable door, I hear Aula's voice.

Aula? I ask. But as quickly as it struck, it's gone.

'What's going on?' says Taurus. I turn around to see him at the door, glancing between us. His eyes are swollen but he looks alert.

When Etain doesn't answer, I say, **I think your ma warned Aula not to trust Nadrik when she was getting sicker but . . . Aula asked Nadrik to help anyway. He . . . didn't help her.**

He presses his lips together tightly before expelling a breath. 'Well. It's done.'

Etain stands up. 'So am I.'

He frowns at her. 'What do you mean?'

'You heard me. I'm done, Taurus.'

'Etain,' he says gently, walking towards us. 'You need to sleep.'

'No, I am *finished*. I don't care about the prophecy. I don't care what was laid out for us nine generations ago, because I am *never*, *ever* allying myself to that girl who betrayed our mother and who wants to be the lapdog of the man who killed Ma *ever* again.'

She tries to walk back down the staircase, but he catches her arm. She swings on him then, pushing him back with all her strength. He staggers against me. Etain turns away again, but doesn't move this time.

'Etain,' he says softly. 'Please.'

She is breathing hard, everything bristling. I can see the grief in every rigid line of her body. I move away from them, but don't go back into Aula's room. This isn't my fight, but

223

I feel like it's my burden to hear.

'We can't give up now,' Taurus says. 'Ma sacrificed everything for this. She wouldn't have wanted us to—'

'*Don't*, Taurus,' Etain snarls. 'What the hell would you know about what Ma wanted?'

He hisses in a breath through his teeth. 'Fine. You're right. I *don't* know what she would have wanted because when I was two years old, the Chosen Ones were born, and Ma had her first prophecy, and she sent me to live in *Metis*, without her, without you, without anyone.'

She turns then, her face hard and bitter and disgusted. 'Oh, like you didn't love it. I know what Metisian life is like. Drinking and songs around your torch flames and *tree whispering* and sleeping with anything that moves. Meanwhile I had to *sit here* pretending to be the good little servant, listening and spying and waiting and keeping his Chosen One happy while Ma got sicker and sicker, but told me how *we* were the ones in control, *we* were the ones with the right hand, and if we kept our heads down and played the game everything would be all right. But our heads were down and we played the game and everything's *ruined*, Taurus. It's *ruined*. So don't you talk to me about what Ma would have wanted, because I know everything her and Ade had planned out for us and they were wrong and I am *not* gonna just play along any more.' She chokes back a sob.

The silence that follows is like the curl of smoke from a snuffed-out flame. If any of us move, the smoke will be gone, and the door will shut between these two, and it will be the end of something. I hold my breath and wish, because I can't bear it for either of them if that happens.

224

Then Taurus takes a long, ragged breath and I watch two tears that have gathered in each eye spill, like dropping flowers on to a grave.

And I think Etain must see them too, because she lets out a mourning sound so soft it's barely audible. She lets her head fall against his sternum, and he holds the back of her neck and presses his lips against her hair. He sings softly under his breath, just a few notes, and to my surprise she sings them back. The fine hairs on the back of my neck lift. I feel like I'm listening to something ancient.

They stay like that for a minute, and then Etain lifts her head and looks at me like she's forgotten I was there, which is equally a relief because I was trying not to be, and a jab in the ego because, despite everything, I want her to be looking for me.

'I need to go and see Ma's rooms,' she says to Taurus. 'There's some things I want to get.'

'I'll come with you,' he says, before looking at me. 'Wait here?' he asks.

I can't, I say. **I have to find Aula.**

He shakes his head. 'You can't go by yourself.'

We've got twelve days until the Wise One's task. And I can find her better than anyone else. I want to tell them that they need to come with me, that this is the most important thing. But what kind of person would I be if I did? Their *mother* just died. **Let's meet back here . . . OK?**

He squints at me. 'You know where Aula is?'

Something in me does.

He gives me a ghost of a smile.

'You're being cryptic.'

225

I raise my eyebrows, and he holds up his hands in mock surrender.

'Good luck,' Etain says, and I think she might even mean it. She turns and walks ahead down the staircase.

Taurus, I say as he passes me.

'Yeah?'

I just . . . I love you, OK? Whatever happens. And I'm here, even if your ma isn't.

He comes back up the stairs and wraps me in a hug that nearly cracks my spine. 'Love you too,' he breathes into my shoulder. 'Be careful.' He lets go.

I stand there for a second, fighting the fear that wants to follow him and not have to make any decisions on my own. When I've pushed it all down, I go and stand by Aula's bed, and for the first time in my life, I open my mind to emptiness.

The first thing that happens is that all the physical things seem to stop meaning anything. Sound, sight, smell; they all get swallowed up in the emptiness. But I do not feel swallowed. I am not afraid of it, because I'm not separate from it. I am part of it.

Then I'm vaguely aware that I'm moving. My feet are taking me down this corridor and then the next, climbing this staircase, slipping past these people as they talk in panicked whispers. No one tries to stop me. Maybe it's because all they see is the Chosen One. Athenas. Metis. Is there really a difference?

I'm outside. It begins to rain. My knees are still aching from the climb to Athenas, but they draw me on – and every pulse of my heart is like another hook that's caught on me, leading me down the ladders in the dark. Like a hurricane wind that pushes you forward. Like being swept up in a current. I can no more resist than walk backwards through time. The rain gets harder.

I smell wet stone. I smell engines. I hear them, feel them throbbing under me. That's when I realise my power – my magic – is unravelling as well. Moving out from me like liquid, finding every living thing around me. I'm surprised to find that even though the connections that make up Metis aren't here, there are still connections, synapses between things. It reassures me.

My feet tumble me forward. My hands move to push an enormous door open.

I smell the books first. They're towering above me from every direction. A library. The sky lets out a roar behind me. Thunder. And then lightning splatters illumination on the polished floorboards. I can see the bookshelves now – looming impossibly high like dark sentinels.

I'm slowing now. There's a shelf right at the back of the room. I pull a book down, seemingly at random, but not truly. There are marks on the wood. I trace them.

The shelf opens. There's light, just beyond it. I step through.

Here, the ceiling is lower, and to my right are yet more bookshelves. Tables are filed against the wall to my left, and all but one are staggered with papers, scrolls, spilled ink wells and several stacks of dusty glass phials. The last table is a desk of sorts, cleared to make space for writing. Elsewhere, books are piled up to my waist at random intervals. There are small white lights, which I know must

227

be conjured, hovering neatly over each stack, strewn around the room like stars in a tiny solar system.

It is so familiar and so alien that I pause. But the emptiness beckons me on. I want to stop and look closer. My fingers itch with it.

But then I see a different kind of light – larger and brighter – hovering just behind one of the bookshelves. I hesitate, and then, moving slowly, I weave my way through the strange chaos of the room towards it. As I get closer, I see it's not a singular orb as the other lights are, but a gathering of many smaller ribbons that move silently over each other like a shoal of sleepy fish. I frown, fascinated. The ribbons – they seem to hold some kind of meaning, almost a language – but I can't make it out. I am only steps from it now, and I see that all the ribbons seem to be drawn to what is beneath them – a round band of silver with a colourless jewel set into it which I assume you'd wear on your head. The jewel is emitting a light – very pale but just about visible, and every ribbon seems to want to stay within sight of that light. I can feel a kind of polarising desire gather inside of me – to stretch out my hand to touch the jewel myself and at the same time, to turn and run in the other direction. I stand, shivering at the point of doing one or the other, each desire fighting for dominance.

In the end, it is not me who decides.

It is the voice from just behind me, saying, 'You found us. I was wondering if you would.'

I know it's Nadrik's voice, but I see Aula first.

She's lying on a long cushioned seat, just beyond the orb. Her eyes are closed and Nadrik is crouched in front of her.

There's a towel in his hand, and a bowl next to him, as if he's been dabbing her forehead.

She's not moving, I think. *She's dead.*

The relief is cruel. I won't have to beat her in Ariadnis. Metis has won and that's the end of all of it. Except . . . no . . . that's not why I'm here. I'm here because we have to do something other than beat each other. I'm here because we have to unite . . .

I take a deep breath, and with it, see that Aula is breathing as well. I feel a different kind of relief – this one I'm not so sure of.

Nadrik is looking at me. He has lizard eyes that keep flickering and appraising. I wonder if he always looks as unimpressed as he does now. I wonder what it's like to have a mentor like that.

What is that?

I don't look at the glowing ball again, but I trust he knows what I mean.

'You have an interesting voice, Joomia,' he says.

For a moment, I'm back on the upper pathways, watching the scene of my birth as Ade presses her fingers to my forehead. And I realise, everyone who has been able to hear me all my life was there when Aula and I were born, as if we're connected by that moment somehow. Was it always going to be like that, or is it a side effect of the magic that Mathilde and Nadrik were using to fight over us?

There's no time to dwell. Nadrik is looking at me, and he's smiling.

'To answer your question, it is *memories*,' he says.

Whose memories? I ask.

229

'Quite a few people's by now, I should think.'

So it *was* you taking them.

'Yes,' he says.

And the owls? Is that part of the spell?

'It is a . . . safety precaution. And a convenience. And a symbol.'

Is that why Aula's like that? Are her memories next?

I try to hold his eyes, but they carry on flicking. Upwards. Down. My face. My hands. He sighs.

'No. I haven't and I wouldn't touch her mind, although it would make my life a lot easier if I could. I admit, I am not entirely in control of whose memories I take. I can touch no one's mind who carries prophet blood in their veins. Did you wonder why Mathilde and your friend Taurus remained fully functional?'

I hadn't. I suppose I assumed that Mathilde was invulnerable. I assumed that Taurus would keep his memories because Lear's were already gone. Never mind my own. I feel very, very afraid of those assumptions, because here is a man who assumes nothing, which means I can't afford to either and – oh, Wise One, how does he know Taurus's name?

What's wrong with her then? I ask, trying to buy myself some time to think.

He sighs again. 'I am afraid she is very sick. You won't know, of course, but my Head Prophet died yesterday. A terrible loss. She was like a mother to Aula and I think the strain of her death has taken its toll.'

It would be very easy to believe him. But I don't, and he knows it. Is that why he's smiling?

Why . . . why are you doing this?

230

He holds up his hands, like he's relenting. 'A few reasons. Because I am in deep admiration of the ancestor we both share, Kreywar Brenwar, and the aims he had for rebuilding humanity. Because I am unfortunate enough to have watched two generations of Chosen Ones make the wrong choices. Because I do not want to live in a world choked by ignorance any more. Because your mother made a promise to me and broke it. Because you are my daughters and I would like to show you what I have spent all your lives building. An . . . alternative prophecy.'

I hear the words, but they don't sink in. *You are my daughters*. A wave of white noise hisses around the words like a storm of flies, drowning them out. Maybe it's because his face is completely impassive as he speaks, but I get the sick feeling that regardless of whether what he said is true or not, this is a trap; there was nothing I ever could have done *not* to step into it.

It would be easier to kill me.

He laughs, but it doesn't sound like a laugh. What do you call that sound? His eyes are flicking again, taking me in and then Aula.

'Almost no difference, physically,' he says. 'Well, I suppose, given your unusual beginnings . . . I wonder sometimes if I'd taken you instead, would it have been *you* who developed remarkable strength and an inability to think further than your nose? Would Aula have grown up in Metis, like you, without a voice, communing with trees? It is a lovely coincidence though, isn't it? That Aula's powers reflect her city's values – the impossible speed and strength of industry, the reckless, ruthless spirit of human command.

Whereas you – you reflect that slow growth of nature, naturality. Quiet, but dangerous to underestimate. Well, I can't deny that humanity needs nature. Your city is just as much a parasite to it as mine is. The difference between them is that mine has dominated it. Mine does not shame the legacy of human knowledge our ancestors in the Old World worked so hard and long for.'

I can't breathe. Because that's it, isn't it? He wants Aula and me. To control us both. Manipulate us. Make us retrieve the book for him. He's not even trying to hide it. He's testing me. Seeing if I'll guess. Is it a game to him? Does he want a chase before he tries to capture me?

His eyes flicker. He raises his fist and the air around it blurs. I duck just as something shoots over my shoulder. I turn back and see air moving so fiercely it's formed a shape: a ball that ripples the space around it like heat hazing a horizon. It comes for me again, faster than I can dodge. It hits me in the shoulder. My right hand and most of my forearm go numb.

I stumble on my feet, trying to sense the air around me, trying to find where the blow will come to next. The answer is my legs. It takes them out as it flies into them, and I smash my head into the nearest bookcase as I fall.

The next thing I see is his blurry outline standing over me, laughing his not-laugh. The word for it comes to me as I lie there. *Mirthless.*

'That was worse than Aula. Are you telling me that nearly eighteen years haven't prepared you for a fight?'

Fight? He wants me to fight him? Is that how it ends? With me cowering and him eliminating me from the competition? My heart, flopping like a beetle on its back, tells me it's true.

The wood of the shelf behind me. I can feel it under my left hand and sense something. It is dead. Dead wood. A long time before Ramon, when I was a child, I remember a moment when I was experimenting with the vines of my hut: something went wrong and instead of flourishing, they wilted and died. I could feel their deaths, but I could also feel how the vines – even when they were dead – still felt like vines. I remember how, in that small childish moment, I accepted that death was just a little way over from life: not that far, not even that hard to cross. And as soon as I knew that, I knew how I could bring them back. In the next moment, the wilted vines grew again—

Nadrik gazes down at me.

I take a long breath.

I'd forgotten what it was like, when Ramon turned to wood in front of me.

But I remember now. Dizzying, with your blood hot in your hands and pulsing like it's ready to throw out a current. It thunders through me – through my hand – and into the wood of the shelf.

And a second later Nadrik is flung backwards.

I blink, my vision clearing, and look up.

There's a branch over my head. It's growing from the bookshelf behind me. I shuffle into a sitting position and stare. I reach out a hand to touch it. There's no varnish now. It's wood. *Living* wood. I did this.

I hear Nadrik's gasping and turn. The branch struck him hard in the sternum and he looks winded, but his gasping isn't in pain. He looks . . . *elated*.

'Well. Now,' he says. 'That was something.' And he raises his fist again.

This time I'm faster. I duck his next attack, roll forward and slap my hands on the wooden floor. I hear his yell of surprise mixed with satisfaction and look up to see vines curling from the boards up his legs with unbelievable speed. He kicks at them, and they splinter and break before they can finish their transformation from dead thing to live wood.

I'm already stumbling up though, heading for Aula, my heart like a bludgeon in my chest.

Another of his shots misses me by a hair, but the second hits my leg. I collapse and my nose breaks as I hit the floor. The pain explodes into scattershot pieces through my skull and the room is spun into spray and fog. I can't move. I can't.

My head lolls to the side, pounding in agony, but I open my eyes. I see Aula, muddy and distorted through my splintered vision, exactly where Nadrik left her, just inches away.

'Interesting,' says Nadrik, from behind me. 'That was very interesting.'

I reach out, my hand brushing Aula's.

It's the smallest touch, barely even that. But Aula's eyes fly open, and everything changes . . .

Aula and Joomia

. . . and I'm Aula, I'm Joomia.

For a second, **that's who I am.**

234

I'm lying on the floor with my nose broken.

I'm the person who betrayed Ashir and Etain. The girl who can put her hands through a brick wall like it's nothing.

I'm the person who can call the vines, see along their reaches, feel out their weak spots. The person who can make branches grow live from dead wood.

WHO

I

AM.

Aula

It was sort of like watching two shapes blurring into one, or the opposite of that. For a second, I didn't know who I was. Or I did, I knew exactly – but it was like I was looking at it from *her* eyes. Now I'm me again, and I'm more awake than I've ever been in my life.

I sit up, and my heart goes *bud-de-bud-de-bud-de*.

Joomia's lying beside me, her eyes just visible through her hair, blood pouring outta her nose. For some reason, I wanna cry. 'You came,' I whisper. And I *remember* it. I know how she got here. I know everything she knows.

Nadrik is right behind her. Oh, Wise One. Nadrik, what have you done?

'You're awake,' he says, and he's surprised. No one and nothing surprises Nadrik. But Joomia has.

I sit up slowly, raise a hand to my head *slowly*.

I catch Joomia's eye. I raise my eyebrow, just a bit, but she gets it. She lets out a whimper.

Nadrik. I can just see his hands, clenching and unclenching, like he doesn't know what to do next. What's that Old World saying? The one about a dog chasing a car? I read about that somewhere.

'Aula . . .' Nadrik says. 'Are you all right?'

I know he wants me to look at him, but I keep rubbing my head. His hands are glowing now. It's slight, but I know what he wants to do. Send me back there, to that prison, until he figures out a way he can control me. Control *us*.

I make my voice fuggy and thick. 'Where am I? What happened?'

'You've been sleeping,' he says softly. 'I've been keeping you safe. And then . . . *she* got in. Aula, she was going to kill you.'

I nod, like I can't quite hear him. 'I've been dreaming. A really weird dream. I dunno where I was . . .' I make my voice crack.

'It's all right,' he says. 'I'm here.'

I don't pretend about the tears. They come all on their own, cos I remember this: I remember his voice like this. When I was a kid, and I was scared and he said *I'm here*. And he was.

He comes slowly, picking his way over Joomia, to rest a hand on my shoulder. 'I have been hard on you. I hope that you can understand why. I needed you to be strong. The world they want to build,' he says, sneering at Joomia's collapsed form, '*debases* us.'

My breath hitches. 'I dunno,' I say, getting to my feet, letting him steady me. 'I reckon you've been doing some pretty decent debasing all on your own.'

I hit him before he can move – right on the temple. He collapses – and at exactly the same moment, the orb, the light he told Joomia was made of memories, disappears. I whip round looking for it, but I can't see it anywhere.

For a moment everything is still. Joomia just lies there. Then, all tentative, she pulls herself up, cupping her bloody nose. **Aula—**

I flinch, cos her voice appears in my head instead of coming outta her mouth. I'd heard she was dumb. She says my name again, and this time I hear the tone of it.

'*Don't*,' I say. 'Don't be nice to me.'

She bites her lip, and looks back at the shelf with a branch sticking out of it. It's weird – I remember that happening. I remember . . . I shake myself, but it's too late.

'You got a plan?' I say. 'Now you . . . rescued me?'

Before I can stop her, she grabs my hand. And I feel it again. Strange, shifting shapes. Clarity.

Sort of. There's lots to tell you, she says. **But there are things even I don't understand yet. We need to find Taurus and Etain first.**

'Taurus?'

A friend. He's – he's Etain's brother. And my friend.

Taurus . . . *Taurus* . . .

'I remember . . .' I whisper. 'But I wasn't . . . but you weren't . . .'

Cos the memories I have of Taurus are suddenly not just mine – they're *hers*. *Her memories*. They're still hers, but it's like they've been in my head the whole time.

I can't concentrate, cos my world's getting thrown open by things I suddenly know. That Taurus and Etain are

237

siblings. That Mathilde is destroying the trees of her city to destroy ours. That what's happening to people – the *memories, the owls* – it was *Nadrik and he's our . . . he's my . . .*

We stumble back from each other and turn away like we're both naked and ashamed, and I guess we are.

There's this long silence, and I'm reeling from it which means she must be too.

What is this? she whispers. **What *are* we? How are we sharing . . . ?**

'I dunno,' I say. 'I dunno.'

We sit there, I think both just trying to rally ourselves. I find, after a few minutes, that if I focus, I can separate my past from hers. I can still hang on to myself. I open my eyes and see she's already figured this out, cos her shoulders have relaxed and she looks calmer. She meets my eyes.

Another memory rises to the surface. Joomia's memory. It's her and Etain and Taurus, and a woman – Ade, I guess, very obviously an untrained prophet cos of the markings under her eyes. Ade is telling Joomia about when she was born – and what happened—

I stop.

Joomia looks at me. **What?**

'Is it true?' I ask.

What?

'We're sisters?'

She gives me a look that's grim and sad.

'I guess it's obvious,' I say. '*Look* at us.'

It's such a completely stupid time to have this conversation, and if I were her that's what I'd be saying. But she doesn't, and I can hear the relief in her voice that she can share it with me.

She says, **I guessed, but I didn't know for sure.**

'I guess I thought so too,' I say. 'But it never seemed to matter. Either way it was always gonna be you against me.'

That is, until the other Chosen Ones got involved, she says. **I suppose the prophecy needed two halves. We each have something the other needs. Do you think that's why the emptiness is less when we're together?**

The emptiness. The ache.

I grunt, because she's right. 'I hadn't even noticed until you said it.'

She smiles, but suddenly the whole plateau lurches.

Something's really wrong.

Come on, she says. **Before he wakes up.**

I look at Nadrik, sprawled on the floor.

You are my daughters, I hear him say to Joomia again. *He is our father*, a part of my mind mocks me. It dares me to look at him and apply that name. Instead I say, 'He trapped me. Inside my own head. How could he do that?'

I don't know, Aula.

So why do I want to stay here with him? I grit my teeth and tear my eyes away. She leads the way to the door. I'm about to ask where we're going, but then, of course, her memory comes to me again. I'm so confused. It *feels* like mine, but it en't. Ade. *Our mother. The Cave of Ancestors? Is that where we're going?*

Joomia raises her sleeve to her nose to blot the blood and stares at me over her hand, like she knows what I'm thinking.

'Are you reading my mind?' I ask, trying not to sound like I'm scared.

239

I don't think so. We're remembering each other's past, but I don't know what you *thought* about any of it. I know what you *did*, but not *why*.

I shake my head, and I'm crying again. I'm crying and I don't even know why. 'This is too much,' I say. 'Everything is . . . too much.'

Joomia blinks a lot. I know, she says. There's so much heaviness in her voice. It's like everything that's in my heart, put into those two words. She bites the inside of her cheek and raises her head. Then she offers me her hand.

I look back at Nadrik. At the branch coming out of the bookcase and the flowering vines in the floorboards.

I take it.

That's when the ground under us starts shaking.

Outside, in the pissing rain, everything is thundering. There are clanks and rattles and screeches from below us and it en't anything like the noises I'm used to. Everything is wrong.

'Is this Mathilde's spell?' I ask as we run through the bookshelves.

I think so, says Joomia bleakly. She's panting from having to keep up with me so I slow down to let her. But Aula, I don't understand. Where is everyone?

I feel guilty, cos I hadn't even noticed. I mean, yeah OK, we're in the middle of a thunderstorm, but the plateau feels like it's coming down and no one's around to yell at me to do something or shriek about the end of the world.

'I dunno. I dunno anything.'

I start running again but I en't up to my usual pace anyway. I feel wobbly and, I dunno, not like myself. In fact,

I find I have to stop a second time, catch my breath. It sets off little alarm bells in my head. I must be more spun out than I thought. I curse; force myself to get moving.

And that's when the owls come.

They come outta every house, rippling down the street. More owls than Athenas ever had. The shaking under my feet stops. The only sound is the rain and their wings.

'Where are they all coming from?' I yell, but don't expect an answer. As the owls tear in, the rumbling starts again. We gotta go, yet we stay put.

'Wise One. We're gonna die, en't we?' I say, taking off again.

Taurus and Etain are in your room, she says.

The plateau beneath us is shaking like the end of a snake. I can hear bricks groaning, metal shrieking, wood splintering, and thunder from the sky above and the ground below. My home is falling apart. Everything is falling apart.

I turn to Joomia and she looks really bad. I'm sure I en't exactly the pinnacle of human beauty right now, but at least my face en't caked with my own blood. It's more than that, though. However horrible being trapped in your own head is, at least I've been unconscious. She doesn't look like she's slept in a week. It makes her face look hollow and fragile, like a doll's. A really scary one with blood running down its chin.

We've got to get to your rooms, she says. **I said we'd meet them—**

She's cut off by a particularly oh-god-we're-gonna-die sounding vibration beneath us, and she trips.

241

'Oh, for the love of—' I reach down and lift her up on to my back.

What are you doing?

'What do you think I'm doing?' I snap. 'Outta the two of us, who's got super-strength? Plus I don't think you can afford to fall down again. No offence but your nose already looks like a tomato. I en't sure you can risk smashing it again unless you wanna end up with half a face.' I don't think she hears me over the din of all of it. 'Keep your head into my shoulder,' I bellow. 'Else you'll get whiplash.'

I wait for her to do it. Then I dig my feet in and run.

I can see my window when I finally stumble.

The ground I'm running on just en't there. I go bum over tit and lose my grip on Joomia. She's sent flying. Everything's quaking and rippling and my teeth clatter like coins in my mouth.

I crane my head – chin skinned on the cobbles. The air en't in my lungs.

Coming down on us is a rain of water and plaster and fragments of crumbling grey stone as the buildings I've lived in all my life wobble and crack.

Aula! We're almost there! Joomia's already on her feet – barely keeping her balance – but offering me her hand anyway. I take it.

'You gotta get on my back again!' I yell.

She doesn't protest. She jumps up and holds on tight – it's awkward cos we're the same height, but her grip is strong. I pelt with everything I am towards the door to my part of the palace. An archway falls with a bone-juddering crash that nearly steals my feet again, but I manage to get away with a stumble and then I'm up again and sprinting.

There's the door.

And just under it—

'ETAIN!' I roar.

She hears me. Taurus turns too and my heart leaps just the tiniest bit. I'm ten feet from them. Five.

Joomia gets off my back. But the ground's sloping. The slabs under our feet are moving.

HOLD ON TO ME! Joomia yells, and I try to gather us all together.

Then we fall.

10 Days

Aula

After a lesson or a long morning shut in the forge, I often go out and lie under the trees in the palace gardens, and enjoy the flashes of sun between the leaves overhead. Sometimes Etain comes with me and reads one of her old engineering manuals. Sometimes I bring my maps or whatever but mostly I just lie there and listen – to Ashir on her breaks from prophet duty, knees in the soil, raking back crumbs of earth for seed beds; to the sound of Etain's finger turning the page.

I spent ages thinking about stuff under these trees last summer – duties and Sander and what happens after I turn eighteen, whichever way the task goes? It's so nice to be back, even if I don't remember how I got here. It's funny . . . the leaves under these trees don't look anything like how I remember them.

I blink. It hurts to blink.

I lift my hand. It's mottled grey and black and white.

Huh. That's weird.

I try sitting up.

Oh.

Bad idea. Very bad idea. My stomach muscles give me

one last shredding burst of pain just to make sure I got the idea. Still is best.

What the hell happened? It's all blurred, but eventually, some of it starts to make sense in strange, daubed images.

Wings.

Stone.

Hands.

Joomia.

Etain.

Ashir.

Nadrik.

I sit up.

I choke.

Nadrik. *Nadrik.*

Joomia asking, *Why are you doing this?*

You are my daughters.

I clap my hands over my ears as if that'll block out the memory. Can't think. Can't think.

Look, then.

I'm in a forest. Surrounded by tree trunks. The floor is a red-brown mass of twigs, leaves and mud. There are strange sounds coming from every direction; flurries like wing beats, snapping twigs like footsteps, chattering and calls like I've never heard in my life. I'm not in Athenas any more. I'm under it. In the forest on top of the cliff that, along with the rest of the island, we en't been allowed to touch since the truce all them hundreds of years ago.

Where are the others?

'Aula?' someone says.

I make a yelping noise like I just stubbed my toe

248

and jump up so fast my body shrieks in outrage. When I see Taurus I snap out a few curses and kick the nearest thing to me – a log. It smashes into a tree and showers us both with splinters. He puts his head back with a wince and closes his eyes.

'Are you OK?' he says.

I remember: falling, trying to hold on to them all, the wind pushing us apart, losing hold of Joomia as we crashed through the canopy. I managed to keep hold of Taurus, manoeuvred us so that I'd hit the ground first, but—

'What happened to Joomia and Etain?!'

He grins. 'My Chosen One did her own trick.'

I don't remember seeing Joomia doing anything. Would she been able to – I dunno – summon the vines to catch them or make some tree branches cushion their fall? I decide to trust that Taurus saw something like that happen or else he wouldn't look so relaxed.

'Did you see where they fell?' I ask.

He gives me an incredulous look. 'Yeah, I managed to pinpoint their exact location while we were falling through the air at terminal velocity from a city in the sky.'

I mutter something about how helpful scarcasm is, then I look up for the silhouette of Athenas's pillars and plateaus between the trees. They're there, so much smaller from this distance, but the tallest pillar – the one *I live on* – en't any more. A kind of buzzing starts in the back of my head.

We must have been thrown a lot further than I thought? It's still there. If I climb that tree over there I'll see it.

I climb. Taurus yells something after me, but I don't

249

hear him. I climb up through the branches, craning my neck. A bit higher, and I'll see it. A bit higher, and I'll see my home. It can't be – it won't be gone.

But it is.

I'm almost as high as I can go, and in the grey morning light, I can see far, far out. Across an ocean of trees. Eight pillars looming over us, taller from here than I ever imagined. But the tallest one is gone. Smoke is rising from a dark area where trees have been flattened.

I risk another branch. Just a bit higher—

The branch snaps and I'm falling again.

I don't put out a hand to stop it. I let the twigs snag at me. I smack my head on something. Then my shoulder.

'AULA!'

The ground meets me.

'Aula? Aula. You're OK. Breathe.'

But I'm not OK. I want to scream, or cry – *something* that would get all this pain out, but I can't do it. I can't. All I've got is my lungs struggling to work and my mouth struggling to speak.

'Gone. Gone.'

I feel hands on my face and know that Taurus is leaning over me.

'Gone,' I choke out. 'She's gone. Ashir's gone. It's all my fault.'

He gives me a look. His eyes are kind. His hands stay there on my face, like he's grounding me. Like he's guiding me back. I remember how his dreadlocks felt, surprisingly soft under my hands, how those arms – brown as bark and knotty with climbing muscles – felt as they

250

followed the line of my shoulder blades.

Bit by bit, the ache settles back over my heart and hangs like phlegm in my chest. It's so much heavier now. It's so much.

'Sorry,' I say. 'I'm sorry.'

He says, 'I don't think she would've made it anyway, Aula. Not if Nadrik was planning on getting that vision. He knew Ma was never really with him. Don't you think he would have known that Etain was meeting me in the owlery all these years? Don't you think he knew where she'd gone this time?'

'But *I* went to him. I . . . poisoned her.'

He shakes his head. 'I don't know him, but I have a feeling he's been spinning webs for years. Ma thought she was ahead of him but she wasn't, and now we've seen how deep the trap was.'

It's such a generous thing to say. I can't believe a word of it.

There's a long, awkward silence. All I can think is how tired I am and how close he is and how much I want to kiss him again. Apparently, watching the woman you call *Mother* die, being betrayed by your mentor who is actually your father who is stealing everyone's memories, and finding out you're actually a twin, still doesn't stop you from being suddenly, stupidly horny at the most idiotic moments. How about practicals, Aula? Like food, water and where the hell are Joomia and Etain?

'Aula, what's that?' Taurus asks.

I don't have to ask what, cos movement catches my eye. There's a shadow creeping towards us through the trees.

It dapples the ground as it glides forward, like a cloud. It's ten feet away – it's five—

A smatter of screeching I know very well—

I know their feathers are designed to give them perfect predatory silence and all that, but it's still something when you see this many of them and you can't hear a single flap. The shadow reaches us.

There's a second's delay, and then they're overhead, blocking out the sky. Not hundreds. *Thousands* of them. More owls than I've ever seen in my life.

'Where are they going?' Taurus whispers. He stands up, craning his neck.

'Towards the city,' I say. 'They're heading to Athenas.'

'But what for?' Taurus murmurs.

'Not what. *Who*.' I don't say his name. I can't say his name. But somehow I know. 'We gotta find Joomia and Etain,' I say instead.

'Judging by the fact that you don't see a thousand owls all together every day I'm guessing they'll be heading that way too.' He pauses. 'Unless . . .'

'Nothing's happened to them,' I snap. 'They're fine. They have to be.'

He nods, but he doesn't stop worrying his lower lip with his teeth. He glances at me. 'Are you all right? You look pale.'

'I'm always pale,' I say, hauling myself up. 'Don't rub it in.' But I find once I'm on my feet again that I'm dizzy. I stagger against him.

'Careful,' he says, pushing me back upright. I close my eyes and plant my heels. I take a long breath in. 'It's OK,

I got it now,' I say. 'Get on my back.'

He laughs. 'Can't you carry me in your arms, like a prince in a fairy tale carrying a princess?'

I blink. 'All the boys I know would rather choke on their own vomit than be seen being carried.'

'I'm not all the boys you know,' he says. 'You're strong, I'm not. Pick me up.'

Joomia

When we see the owls, Etain is on her feet and running before I can blink.

I stumble to follow her, but she's fast and the ground is strange and springy. Another alien terrain to navigate. My nose is throbbing.

Where are they going?

She turns her head and roars, 'It's got to have something to do with Nadrik!'

I pick up my feet. Blood thuds dully in my ears.

Etain! You can't stop him!

She doesn't answer, and that's when I realise stopping him hasn't even occurred to her – her only thought is her mother. He killed her and she wants revenge.

Etain, wait! We've got to wait until Aula's here too. And Taurus! We've got to *think*.

I don't expect her to respond, and she doesn't. She's much faster than I am.

The trees to my right suddenly whip and shake – as if a great wind has lanced through them. For a fraction of a

253

second, I see two figures – one running, the other in their arms. **It's them! Aula and Taurus! They're here, Etain—**

But she's already slipping through the trunks ahead, almost out of sight. I sigh and follow her. We've barely gone a hundred yards when the trees stop abruptly. I haven't been able to stop looking at them, despite my uneven footing, because they're so small. I wonder how they manage to even sustain a single leaf. Their trunks are spindly – many of them barely even the width of a single branch in Metis. I can't quite believe that they're real.

Etain slows, and I sigh in relief – there are Aula and Taurus, standing where the trees end. The owls are circling high above, and before us lies what was once one of the pillars in Athenas. It's ruined – the metal casing has caved and split like impossibly vast fruit. Metal shards stick high out of the rubble – broken and skeletal and somehow fragile. A weird amalgamation of nature and industry; so different – and yet here, they don't look so far removed. The structure could almost be the bones of the tree that stood.

Beneath, the wood looks pitted and blackened. How has the rot spread so fast here? Perhaps the fault lies in removing everything that is essential to the living thing – the branches, the leaves. Everything but the root and the trunk itself.

When we are next to Aula, she gives us both a shrewd look, as if she's making sure we're all right, and then she shudders and her knees collapse.

Mathilde, I whisper. **Why? Why would she do this?**

Taurus opens his mouth, as if to reply. But Ade gets there first. She steps softly out from around the nearest tree.

254

'*Ones who survive will know whose city is strongest,*' she mumbles, eyes looking past them. 'Meet at the *cave*, boy!' she snaps, flicking Taurus's ear. 'No one listens to Ade!'

Aula

How did you find us? Joomia asks.

'Prophet,' the woman – Ade – mutters, slapping her chest violently, as if this explains how she knew we'd be here, not even mentioning how she made the journey from Metis to here.

Joomia glances at me and Ade follows suit. She makes this weird, involuntary movement like she wants to come over, but en't sure if her feet will hold her. I want to look at her too, but I'm tired and there's only so much I can fit in my head. This is the woman calling herself our mother. Really looking at her feels like it will cost me too much.

Ade appears to brace herself. 'Potion for Ashir?' she asks. No one answers. She looks steadily from Taurus to Etain and back. Then she looks at me again. I realise I'm crying.

Ade's posture sags. 'Gone, then.'

'Didn't you *See* that?' Etain sneers. 'Didn't you know that with your *collection* of futures?'

'Saw this one. Saw another.'

'Yeah? So what happened in the other one?' Etain says, dangerously softly.

'Etain,' Taurus warns.

255

Etain doesn't look at him. 'What happens in that other future?'

Ade rubs her fingers wearily across her mouth. 'No, no, it doesn't matter. Gone, now.'

'Of course it matters! Tell me!' Etain starts towards her, but Ade holds up a hand and Etain stops as if she's been slapped.

Ade takes several long breaths. 'My burden to know. Not yours, girl.'

Etain splutters. 'She was my mother!'

'And I loved her,' Ade says, her eyes clear for a moment, her voice hoarse and strained. 'I loved her.'

There is a silence in which, distantly, I think about how that makes a lot of sense about Ashir, but not Nadrik. I have no idea where he fits into all this. How, if it was Ade and Ashir, could it ever have been Ade and him? Finally, Etain lets out a shout of frustration. It stirs some instinctual part of me that makes me try to take her hand.

'*No!*' Etain shrieks and I stumble back, feeling like I've been slapped. In a kind of panicked whisper, Etain hisses, '*Don't touch me.*' Then she walks away into the woods and I crumble to my knees.

Out of the corner of my eye, Taurus moves like he's gonna go after her, but Ade stops him.

'Been brave, boy,' she murmurs. But I don't hear his reply – sound blurs. When it comes back, Ade is sitting in front of me. 'Girl,' she whispers.

My eyes feel so heavy as I raise them to her. But when I do, it's the weirdest thing – I recognise her. Not from Joomia's memory, but from mine. 'There's a sketch of you in Nadrik's desk,' I say. 'I never asked him about it. I was gonna, but Ashir, she was dying . . . and I asked him for help. I shouldn't have. She told me not to.' I swallow, and try to take a breath, but it feels like there en't enough air. 'It's all my fault. I shouldn't have done it. I was so scared she was gonna die and then I sealed the deal by telling him about it.'

'No, no, no,' Ade says, and I guess she wants to make it sound caring or something, but I know what happens to prophets who en't been trained, and even their best efforts can't make emotion like that happen in their voice.

Joomia moves towards me, I think to say some word of comfort in Ade's stead, but Taurus shouts across us before she can speak.

'Etain!' he yells.

And Etain can't have gone far, because she is there a second later, looking panicked. 'What is it?'

'Look!' he says.

We all crane our heads.

The owls are coming in to land.

They descend one by one, with a lot of ruffling feathers and pointed looks like, *this is my space so back off if you know what's good for you*. And then, I dunno how to describe it, their shapes seem to smear. I'm looking, but my eyes can't find a way to translate it to my head.

My hand reaches out without thinking and finds Ade's. *Wise One, Wise One, Wise One*. It's like the light shifts around the birds, in a way that it en't supposed to. And now there are people, standing, totally naked, in front of all this wreckage. They are silent. They don't show any shame.

They just stand, looking up at the ruins like . . . like they're waiting for something.

Or someone.

A huge metal sheet rises from the heap, almost silently. It rises – moves backwards, and falls with a sound like thunder. Ade's hand squashes mine. But I don't feel it.

Then Nadrik comes, gliding upwards like he's some sorta bird – or – what was it? An angel. Yeah. Like an angel. One of those terrifying statues with blank eyes and no expression. Like Sander. Like someone without a memory.

Only he's got memories all right. Between his hands – pulsating like a heart – a thousand thousand starlight strands of what made all these people *people*, stripped from them and balled up into something he can control. Anger scratches under my skin.

The memoryless begin to wail. It starts with a few of them, and then it spreads – voice rolling over voice until it fills the air with this keening that sounds horrible and longing, nothing human.

I whip round in time to see Joomia lose her struggle to hold Etain back. Taurus makes a dive for her, but Etain gets past him and runs for the space between me and Ade. I think for the tiniest moment that I'll let her past, cos she deserves her anger at me and at him, and I'm so tired. But then I'm tackling her, pinning her arms and forcing her back under the shade of the trees and holding my hand over her mouth as she tries to scream.

'I'm sorry,' I whisper. 'Etain, I'm sorry.'

The voices of the memoryless get louder and louder.

She's kicking me, punching me and Taurus tries to stop her and Ade is making soothing noises but I think, *No, let her*, not just cos I deserve it, but cos I can take it. I can take all of this and she can't.

Nadrik speaks to the throng. 'I have your memories.' His voice reverberates so powerfully I can feel it in my throat and chest. 'I will keep them safe.'

There's a fracture in the noise. He is – impossibly – completely unharmed, though his robes are ripped and pale with dust. He's still wearing his circlet, its colourless jewel flaring brightly, as if there's some sort of light caught inside it . . .

'Why is he talking to them?' Taurus asks. 'Can they even hear him?'

'They hear,' Ade says.

Etain is sobbing beneath me. I dunno what to do. I dunno how to help her. But Joomia puts her hand on my shoulder. I let go and Joomia draws Etain away, and in my head I hear her voice murmuring something to her and, who knows, maybe it will help.

I roll over. My arms and legs feel like water.

'We stand on the brink of the rightful path. The path that our ancestor, Kreywar Brenwar, planned so many years ago, defiant of Lore, his nemesis,' Nadrik intones to his army of the mindless. 'I have collected your thoughts and feelings so that you, like me, may find this path for yourselves. But that time is not yet. The Chosen Ones must still compete, the Book of Knowledge must still be claimed. The non-believers of Metis must be . . . pacified. I see you, my Wise Ones. I see Metisians and Athenasians alike. Let us

259

speak no more of truces. Let us become one, as we should have – long, long ago.'

One.

One. Like the ancestors planned before their interests separated.

Aula, Joomia says, **I think we need to go.**

'Yeah,' I say. I blink. Everything seems hazy. 'But en't that . . . en't that what we got to do, Joomia?' Her face swims in front of me. 'You know,' I say. 'Unite them. Make them one.'

'The Chosen Ones have fallen in among the trees,' Nadrik says. My heart slaps into my stomach like a mistimed jump. And I swing around to see him pointing his finger almost directly to where we're hiding in the treeline. The memoryless turn in slick unison. We are frozen – even Ade – like five stupid animals.

'They are accompanied by three very misguided accomplices. Spread out. Find them, and bring them here. Bring them to me.'

Joomia

They move smoothly, fluidly. Their bodies are wildly varied, but somehow their movements translate to something like symmetry.

It's not just their memories, I say to Aula. **If that were all—**

'He wouldn't be able to order them all like some kinda puppet master,' Aula mutters, nodding. 'They're mindless now.'

'Cave of the Ancestors!' Ade hisses. 'Follow!'

I see one of them cock his head in our direction.

We back up quickly, slipping as fast as we can back through the trees. There's a crack as someone steps on a branch. I look back. Four mindless still now in sight. They haven't seen us yet, but we break into a run. We only stop when we're sure we've lost them.

I turn to Ade, who seems to know where she's going but isn't exactly taking what seems to be a straight path, and for a while we hurry along after her, weaving left and right, until we find a stream. The island has lots of streams and rivers, some of which you can see from Metis, but I've never been this close to one. The running water cuts through the quiet, and I feel safer here, where at least something is moving. This forest is so *still*. I know the trees of Metis are old, but these are something else: old in the way that comes before memory, like elements: rain or clouds or earth. Their bark is thick and deeply grooved and moss grows dark green over the roots.

'You know where you're going, Ade?' Taurus says, jolting me out of my thoughts. 'You seem a little lost.'

Ade stops muttering to herself for a moment to frown at him. 'Not lost. Not been here for a long time.'

'But you can't have been here, Ade. No one's supposed to be able to leave the city at all.'

This is the first time that's occurred to me and I look at Ade sharply, cross with myself for not thinking about that first. Is it possible Ade *doesn't* know what she's doing? Is it possible this is all part of her madness and we were so desperate for something to happen that we just went

261

along with it?'

But she's already shaking her head. 'Did my service to Ariadnis. I'm free.'

'What about us?' Taurus wonders.

Ade shrugs. 'We'll see,' she says, and with that another thread inside me snaps. Reality and myth. Truth and lies. Was this all just another story to keep us in line?

Taurus blows out his cheeks. 'So which way next?'

Ade grumbles darkly under her breath.

Taurus makes an impatient noise. 'Well, I mean, *take all the time you need*, it's not like Nadrik is looking for us or anything.'

Taurus, I say. **Let her think.**

'We need to be moving!' he snaps.

But hurrying her isn't going to help.

'I'm not hurrying her. I just think we should be moving while she picks a direction.'

'Ade,' Etain says suddenly, her voice firm. It's like she's pulled a veil down over her face, masking the pain that was clearly visible before. Her face is serene; practically radiating calm, and we're all turning to her like weeds seeking light.

'This cave,' she says. 'It's important?'

Ade nods vaguely, and then her eyes light up. 'That way,' she says, pointing straight. 'That way, that way.'

'Is there food there, Ade?'

'Yes, girl. Yes. All prepared.'

'Aula,' Etain says, without looking at her. 'You have the strength. Take Ade ahead to find it and then come back for us.'

'That's a good idea,' Taurus says.

Aula's gaze is on Etain, but Etain looks purposefully in the opposite direction.

At last Aula nods. 'OK. I'll go now.' With apparent ease, she picks up Ade and practically tosses her on her back. In the next moment the trees have swallowed them.

We wait, a little on edge now that we've separated.

Taurus and Etain doze together on the forest floor. I stand wide awake and watch the trees. Finally I go back to the stream to clean my face, gingerly removing the blood that's dried there, then give in to my nagging bladder and find a shady spot to pee. The forest feels even quieter, even older now I'm alone, and my skin prickles despite the late morning heat. It feels hard to get air.

I'm just getting the horrible, crawling feeling of being watched when I hear a loud *snap* of a branch behind me. I stand up quickly, pulling my breechcloth tight. Even if Aula *is* a half of me, it doesn't mean we have to throw privacy to the wind.

I turn and nearly scream. Because it isn't Aula.

It's three mindless, staring right at me, their heads slightly slack, as if they can't keep upright, their arms loose, their eyes dead.

There's a horrible pause.

And then they're on me.

All of them reaching for my wrists and ankles.

Hands grabbing me roughly, tangling themselves in my hair and clothes, shoving me on to my knees. I don't have time to run and my voice won't work itself up to a scream. I am seized, they are dragging me. I'm struggling but it doesn't matter. They're taking me to *him*.

I let out a roar and yank one of my hands back. They almost drop me and my nose narrowly escapes hitting the ground again, but even so a searing pain lances down my face and neck and I'm howling as my freed hand finds the floor – wood chips and dead leaves and earth.

There's a sound like cracking wood. The same sound that I heard as the Grove collapsed around Taurus and me. And I find I'm free.

I get to my feet, breathing heavily. There are three people surrounding me, their hands still clenched as if trying to hold something, their limbs stiff, mouths set, eyes blank and unmoving. They're not breathing. Not breathing because they're not human any more.

Their skin is grooved with wood grain, bark crusting to the ridges of their shoulders and backs. Roots have grown up around their feet and slithered around their ankles, joining them to the earth. Small branches grow from their limbs, out of their heads, leaves shining wetly – as if morning dew is still clinging to them. Just like Ramon.

Another sound – this one I can't name – and I turn in a half circle, a scream crouched in my mouth.

But this time it is Aula. She's back already.

'What did you do?' she says. 'Joomia, what did you just *do*?'

Aula

I killed them, she says. **I can't be trusted. I can't do this.**

I've never seen anyone burst into tears but that's exactly

264

what she does. Like a little kid who got the stuffing knocked outta them.

I run my hands through my hair. 'They might not be dead,' I say finally, looking at what used to be people.

She stamps, and leaves go flying back from her. **Do they look alive to you?**

'They've got roots and branches and leaves. En't that alive in a tree's book?'

I can't do this. I can't *fucking* do this. Every time I try to be the Chosen One everything goes to— I've had enough!

She gets up, clutching her hair, and a seedcone by her feet explodes into life, curling dark wood that ripples upwards in weird spirals. She screams, a nearby log dissolves into the earth like the last bit of water in a pan evaporating. Weeds grow up fast underneath it. They grow up around my feet before I've moved an inch, tangling around my ankles, my legs.

Everyone I touch, I hurt!

The weeds thicken, turning to wood and bark. Another tree erupts skyward in front of her, but the growth is all wrong. It's weak and brittle and gnarled like something that grew in the dark.

The weeds tighten around my waist and slither over my chest. My throat. I don't do anything. I don't move. The weeds edge over my mouth to the corner of my nose. They'll grow up into my brain and out of my head.

'Me too,' I whisper. 'Sander. Ashir.'

Joomia swings around like someone sucker punched her and sees me. Everything that's growing and dying around us stops. She stares. Her whole body tightens like a

265

pulled thread, about to snap.

'Me too,' I whisper. My voice wants to tear around the edges.

For a long time, we just look at each other. Then I reach up and tear off the weeds. They come with a lot of snaps and cracks. I lift my feet, and the wood splinters open. It en't easy cos the wood's strong – stronger even than some metal I've worked with Etain before, but it bows to the force I'm putting into it.

Joomia's still looking at me, still heaving in breaths. Then she sags. The trees slide back into the earth. The weeds shrivel.

I walk over, but she holds her hand up, looking down.

Don't, she says. **Don't touch me.**

And, Wise One, I know how that feels. Being scared that people will get too close and you'll hurt them. But the flipside of it is worse: what if people don't want to get too close *ever*? So I go and stand in front of her, and I take her hands. I just hold them, cos I think that's what Ashir would've done, and even though her breath comes in small gasps, she doesn't try to take her hands back. We stand there in silence.

'I reckon we're the first people to stand in this forest for something like three hundred years,' I say. 'It's something I dreamed about when I was a kid, walking through these trees.'

She closes her eyes, and it spills the last of her tears down her cheeks. Something like confusion crosses her face for a moment, and then she puts her fingers gingerly to her nose, pressing it.

'Healed,' I murmur. 'That was quick. Kind of like how

trees regenerate, huh? Not all bad, being you.'

She bites her lip and turns away. And then she says, **We could go.** She doesn't know it, but she's saying the thing I've been thinking about in the back of my mind since I woke up on the forest floor, and I get this thrill right through my body just hearing it. **We could go and leave them to their war. Nadrik and Mathilde.**

I take a deep breath. 'Yeah,' I say. 'We could.'

She looks up at last, and there's a bit of surprise there, and a bit of hope. We stand there for a long time, letting ourselves feel that possibility. 'Only then . . .' I say, eventually, 'what's been the point? What's been the point of any of it?'

She says, **I don't care any more. Mathilde lied to me. She *lied*. None of it matters, nothing that she taught me. Did you really believe it, Aula?** she goes on. **Did you really believe my city debased yours?**

'I dunno. Yeah, I guess. But everything I knew came from Nadrik. I just . . . went along with whatever he said. I guess I thought I wasn't sharp enough to understand it.'

Me neither, she says. She looks at me then, like she's really seeing me.

It's funny, she says. **I always thought you'd have bought into it. The Chosen One thing. I thought you'd be so much better at it than I was. But you're not, are you?**

Last week, I might've said something defensive to that. But I don't have anything to say now.

Slowly she leans her head against my shoulder, and after I get over my discomfort, I put my arms around her.

Joomia

We return to Etain and Taurus, then Aula takes us to a cave with a curved arch entrance that looks like it's forced its way out of the ground. Trees bend around it and over it, a hard lattice of green and brown. Rocks are strewn around the entrance, moss-covered, as if the cave has only recently emerged in the landscape.

As soon as I'm inside the dark mouth I hear something. **Is that singing?** I ask.

'All the prophets from Athenas are here,' Aula says. 'Ashir . . . I reckon she and Ade must have planned this. They were waiting here. For us.'

What are they singing? I ask.

She glances at me. 'Peace,' she says. Together we cross the last few yards of forest floor and step inside.

It's dark, and my eyes take a little while to adjust; then I see the pale blue phosphorescence glimmering in the walls – the same as the passage to the door of Ariadnis and the tunnel that led to Lore's Cave.

The song grows louder as we move deeper. The walls narrow so that we're forced to move in single file.

'Look,' Taurus whispers.

There are paintings on the walls, daubed in faded paint. A splotchy circle that I recognise as the Old World, before the sea covered everything. A ball of bloody fire speeds towards it, the lines of its descent accentuated by fierce smudges.

'The comet,' Aula says.

My back presses into the opposing wall, though I don't have any reason to be scared.

'C'mon,' Etain says.

We walk slowly, watching the paintings tell the story of a world that was broken and a people who knew the end was near. A people who discovered magic, who built a boat and elevated it into the sky while the seas raised by the comet's impact destroyed everything they knew. Of their discovery of the island that was their saviour. There is nothing depicting a war or the Wise One.

'I guess these were done before they decided to tear each other apart over what kinda world to build,' Aula mutters, as if she can hear where my thoughts are going.

The passage stops suddenly, and we blink in the light of a fire. I put a hand to my mouth.

Aula

We're in this huge cavern, and standing in a circle, facing us, is what looks like nearly every prophet in Athenas, singing the Song of Peace. It's a sort of ceremonial hymn about letting wisdom in and calming bad impulses and Ashir sang it to me so often when I was a kid and had bad impulses that it must have made her throat sore. Course, my impulses en't exactly spot on now so at some point she must've given up. My throat seizes at the memory, but I ignore it.

I look for Ade, and find her standing next to Igra, her eyes closed, chanting along. Taurus comes to stand beside me. I wonder what he and Joomia think of this – what they thought of Ashir's funeral. Were they horrified? Or did they understand?

The song fades back into a hum, and it feels like I'm being held inside it, and I en't felt so safe since that moment, all those months ago, just before Ashir fell off my bed and screamed.

Then, her arm around Ade, Igra steps forward, beckoning us. I notice there's a book under Ade's arm. Where did she get a book from?

Joomia must notice too cos she gasps and says, **Where did you find it?**

'Took it,' Ade says to her. 'Come, come and see.'

'What is it?' I ask.

It's Lore's journal, says Joomia. **Taurus found it in Metis.**

'Technically,' says Taurus, slinging an arm around her, 'that was you.'

'Lore Sumati?' I ask. 'The one who went against Kreywar when he wanted to build . . . build Athenas?'

Igra nods.

'But it'll be blank now,' I say. 'All the books are blank.'

'They are,' Igra agrees. 'But Lore left something else.'

'What?' Etain asks. Her whole body is stiff and desperate not to look at me. 'A vision?'

'Memory,' Ade mumbles.

'You've seen it?' I ask.

Igra nods.

What was it? Joomia asks. **What did you see – can you show us?**

'Can't,' Ade says.

'Not by herself,' Igra puts in. 'But together . . .' She gestures to her fellow prophets.

'How did you get out?' I ask.

270

'We got ourselves out,' Igra says, sounding vaguely offended. 'We might not be as powerful as old Ashir, but we still see futures. We know which warnings to heed.' Of course they do. So why wouldn't Nadrik have guessed? Would it even occur to him that the prophets wouldn't tell him about *every* prophecy?

Ade hands the journal to Igra, who holds it out to Joomia. 'Take it,' she says. 'Hands on, all of you.'

We do as she says. Four hands on the cover.

Igra steps away. The humming of the prophets changes abruptly – like a current taking a sudden turn. The song swells down and then up, and a kind of fizzing starts in my hand and rushes up my arm and into my heart. I blink, and there's no cave any more.

Joomia

There's a black sky; tinged around the edges with an ember like the curling sides of burning paper. The ocean below me is black too, opaque as blood and calm as sleep. But there is movement on the water.

A boat, propelled by unknown forces, cuts across the rippling dark, and as I listen I hear voices inside it. As soon as that sound is a sensation, my perspective changes, and I am *inside* the boat, inside a cabin, where two people in a bed lie folded over each other, illuminated only by the gas lamps on the floor.

The man is thin and pale, his skin a faded yellow, his thick hair sticky and unwashed, his chin scuffed with stubble. But his eyes are bright and watchful, attending to the woman beside him. She looks tired and old and beautiful and dark. Her arched nose is pierced with a tiny jewelled flower, and her hair, sprawled over the pillow, is wrinkled and black as the ocean outside. Both of them have the faint, iridescent scars over their cheeks of untrained prophets.

'I had a vision of the island again,' the man is saying. 'There will be a war, when we get there.'

'Yes,' says the woman softly.

'I saw the war. I saw the cities that will be built in opposition,' he says. She presses her lips together and reaches for his hand. They hold on tightly to each other.

'All our plans for a new wisdom in the world,' she whispers. 'Everything we've been working towards. Meaningless. Useless.'

His eyes are wet as he kisses her fingers. 'But listen to me. I think I know how to end it. But it is not for us to do – it is for a future generation. We will never be able to stop the divide of our people. But perhaps, if we are careful, we can hold them to the promise of unity sometime in the future.'

She stills at his words. 'How?' she asks.

'We will give them a guardian to guide them. For every generation, that guardian will bring them to a greater wisdom, a greater purpose.'

She smiles sadly. 'And how will we get them to follow a guardian when we are gone? They barely follow us now as it is.'

He pauses, as if he is unsure how to phrase his next words. Then he says, 'Well, we give them a god who will tell them to.'

She stares at him, then she laughs. 'Dreams, Kreywar.'

'No, Lore. Think about it – their minds are shattered, our world is gone. If ever there was a time to convince anyone of a god, that time is now.'

She sits up, bristling. 'Even if by some miracle you manage that – why on Erthe would you create such a source of conflict in a people already covered in conflict? You and I both know the dangers of religion – you know how easily it can turn people against each other! War after war after war – even for people with gods who teach essentially the same thing!'

'But Lore, I'm not talking about many gods – I'm talking about one. One god, to teach them, bit by bit, the wisdom to go on. And then a guardian to unite them.'

She shakes her head. 'Mohammed, Moses, Jesus. All the guardians for one god. Or Buddha – the guardian *and* the god. You're not making any sense. We've both Seen what happens. They will divide. Whether that god is one or many, they will divide.'

He slams his fist on to the bed. 'Lore, you're not *listening*. I know nothing can unite them now. This is the future I am planning. This is the *one day*. You cannot heal a divide in one lifetime, of course not, but seven lifetimes? Or nine?'

Slowly she sits back down next to him and leans her forehead against his.

'I love you, Kreywar. I love that you will not give up.'

She does not say *but this will not work*, but he hears it. She lies down beside him, and closes her eyes. After a while, he does the same.

Lore stirs, a crease forming between her eyes. All at once, her scars come alight, bright as shining mineral.

And somehow, I'm seeing what she Sees . . .

Her vision shifts and smears and I see flashes of things I think I recognise, faces I think I know, but it passes too quickly for me to concentrate on. Then, something changes . . . the images solidify. I know this place. I *know* this vision. I'm in the passage next to the entrance to Ariadnis and the light is blinding. There are two children crying close by and when I look I see what is undoubtedly Taurus, still just a toddler, and Etain in a cradle next to him.

Next to me, two women – Ashir, who I recognise because of her children, and Ade, who is so, so young – her eyes blank and unfocused and red, her cheeks raw from tears. She is watching the sight before her in horror.

I saw Mathilde and Nadrik before, but then, in Ade's memory, the light was too blinding to see anything else. This time, in Lore's vision, I see what I missed.

A baby girl. She's lying between the two battling magi, wrapped in a blanket. Her eyes are closed, like she's sleeping. But she's not. She's dead.

She has a lot more hair than most babies I've seen: a kind of wispy brownish red. Her face is round and bruised as harvest fruit. I stare and stare, willing myself to understand.

And then, just like in Ade's memory, there is a snapping sound. Then both Nadrik and Mathilde are each holding a baby. Two babies, both screaming their heads off. Nadrik's baby has tufted hair – red. And the baby with Mathilde . . .

Lore sits up in bed with a shriek. Kreywar jumps, reaches under the bed and emerges with a scythe the size of his arm, his whole body tensed and ready, looking around for a sign of attack. He glances at Lore, the light of prophecy fading from her face.

He drops the scythe, and kneels on the bed. 'My love,' he whispers. 'What did you See?'

She is shaking. 'You were right. There will be a god,' she says. 'Although each city will treat the god differently. And there will be guardians ... Ch ... Chosen Ones. Ten individuals, but nine in total. I saw the last ones. They were the same person, but split in two. It will be them who unite us. And after it is done, there was a girl. I Saw the girl who would lead the people, and I Saw the boy who would be her compass.' She reaches, trembling, for his hands as her eyes begin to clear, and for several long moments they sit there, frozen with possibility.

'I know how to do it,' she says at last. 'How to get them to believe in the god, in the Chosen One.'

'How?' he asks.

'It's magic that neither of us have ever attempted, but Kreywar, I'm sure we could do it ...'

'*How?*' he breathes hoarsely.

'Rewrite their memories,' she says. 'Harvest the wisdom they have beneath all their prejudices. And put that wisdom in a book ...'

Lore's journal drops to the floor, and something slips up out of the pages. The ribbon of memory hovers like a breath in the air, and then it floats down. Every eye watches its descent. When it touches the journal's pages again, it disappears. Another prophet comes forward to fold the journal in a cloth and tuck it into a bag. Igra nods her approval.

I'm shaking like a leaf.

I can't look at anyone. Not Aula. Not Etain. Not even Taurus.

'Well,' says Igra, coming forward. 'Now you know.'

Is that the prophecy you and Ashir had before we were born? I ask Ade.

'Close enough,' Ade mutters.

You lied.

'Chosen One is Chosen Two. Etain leads. Taurus guides.'

YOU LIED TO ME.

Ade flinches. The people who can hear me take a step back.

'I tried,' Ade says quietly, and then she quotes herself: 'Two cities. Two Chosen Ones. Two. Always apart, always struggling. Not Wise God, not Wise Goddess. Wise *One*, Joomia. Wise *One*.'

That wasn't trying! I snap. **That was a riddle! What was I supposed to do with that?**

'Joomia—' Taurus says.

I round on him. **Did you know?**

'No! No, I swear I didn't! I'm just trying to say—'

What? What are you trying to say?

'What difference does it make?'

I can't believe my ears. **What *difference*? What difference it makes to someone if they're a twin or *half* a person?**

He winces. 'That isn't what I meant. I just mean – you're still *you*. And you were a baby when it happened. Some babies become twins when they're inside the womb. Why does it matter if it happened to you *just* after you were born?'

I open my mouth to answer him, and close it again. Why

276

does it matter to me? *Does* it matter? Isn't he right? I take a deep breath. I saw something that never occurred to me was possible, and it happened to *me* which makes it frightening. If I'm half a whole person, then doesn't that answer every little deficiency I've ever held against myself?

I realise, just as I reach boiling point, that I *do* have a choice here. I could hold those things against myself *now*, and in doing so take out all my feelings on everyone here in front of me.

Or I could breathe.

I take another deep breath.

You're right, I say at last, wishing it didn't feel like it cost me a vital organ to say it. **I'm sorry, I just . . .**

'Got scared,' Taurus supplies. 'I know, Joomia. Of course you're scared.'

I glance at Aula. She doesn't seem to have looked up from where the journal was lying. Etain makes a movement with her hand – like she's about to put it on Aula's shoulder, but stops at the last moment.

Taurus looks at Igra. 'So *it is* real, then?' he asks. 'The book and the tests? Even if the part where there's a god isn't?'

Igra says, 'Depends on your definition of god. No, there is no *Wise One*. But Lore and Kreywar created the cities, and Ariadnis, and the obstacles within it. And on top of that, they made everyone *believe* that the god existed. This god was their own creation, sprung from their own minds – and all of that required feats of magic that have never been seen since. If that is not god-like, what is?'

But if the Wise One doesn't exist, I protest, **how can any of**

277

it be true? How can there be a book to grant wisdom to one city or another? How can there be an Ariadnis to test them?

Taurus translates this to Igra, but it's Ade who answers me.

'It's real,' she says. 'Seen it. It's real.'

'She's the only Chosen One to survive the Wise One's test,' Igra reminds us.

'How?' Taurus asks. 'How come she survived it?'

'Her task was giving life,' Igra says.

But . . . how was that proving wisdom? I ask, turning to Ade.

Ade shakes her head. 'Not allowed. Not allowed to tell. I already paid.'

'Paid *what*?' Etain asks, but I think I already know.

Her mind, I say quietly.

Aula's still staring at the pile of dust on the cave floor, but she speaks then, quite calmly, as if she's coming out of a trance. 'I still don't understand the me and Joomia uniting everyone bit. How's it supposed to work? I reckon it en't just us holding hands and concentrating, is it?'

Ade's lips press tightly together, then she says, 'Don't know.'

I can see Aula's jaw set as she grits her teeth, echoing my frustration.

Then Etain clears her throat. 'You should go into Ariadnis tomorrow,' she says.

We all look at her.

'Tomorrow is nine days until your eighteenth, and the prophecy, but the previous Chosen Ones of Ariadnis want you to unite and go in *before*. It fits.'

Silence.

Igra begins to nod. 'That would be prudent.'

'*Just like that?*' Aula asks. 'Off you go, Aula and Joomia, and good luck with whatever the hell's in there.'

'That or Nadrik gets there first, or murders every citizen of Metis or finds a way to take everyone else's memory,' Etain counters. 'That or sit here and waste every sacrifice laid down for you. Or have you not done enough of that yet?'

Aula's face crumples. She takes a long, shivering breath, turns and staggers out of the cavern. I watch her go, feeling heavy and drawn out and like I'm not in my body.

'Don't *look* at me like that, Taurus,' Etain is snarling. 'Nadrik killed Ma, but *she* pointed him in the right direction.'

'Are you sure about that? What makes you so sure Ma didn't choose that fate for herself?'

'You didn't know her, Taurus.'

He looks stung, but says, 'I did. Well enough to know that she knew what she was doing!'

'If that's true then why are we *here*?' Etain roars. 'Why are we here debating whether or not the Chosen Ones will unite when we've been told all our lives that it *has* to happen? What was the point?' She kicks a stone and it clatters across the floor. 'What's the point of prophecies if you en't gonna listen to them?' There is silence.

'Etain,' Igra says. 'Go and rest. We brought food and water. Sit with your mother's sisters and let's all . . . breathe. All right?'

Etain trembles, then I see her bow like a branch. At Igra's beckoning, another prophet comes forward and leads

Etain to a corner of the cave.

Taurus looks at me, his eyes searching.

I think I should go and find Aula, I say, more to stop him from asking if I'm all right. Or why I'm looking at his sister like that.

'I'll . . . stay,' he says. 'I should talk to Etain.' He sighs, but he doesn't move. 'Nine, huh?' he says. 'Why is it always nine?'

'Because nine is the last number before infinity,' Igra says. 'All other numbers are made out of the first nine.'

'Except nought,' Taurus points out, I think trying for a smile.

Nought is a placeholder, I say, pushing him gently. **You never got maths, did you?**

On my way back towards the cavern entrance, I pause next to Ade and press my forehead to her shoulder. For a second, Ade's hand finds my hair and trails through it.

Aula

The moon is out. The breeze follows me as I run deep into the forest.

When I eventually stop, the sun has set, and the land before me is white and uneven, and it ends only a hundred yards away. After that, there is only a dark mass that stretches flat in every direction. Not land at all.

My hand in my mouth. The sea.

I limp blindly forward and find the word for what I'm walking on. Sand. *Walking on sand.*

I trudge down to the water. It's black as the stuff in Lore's vision but I know that when you see it in daylight it'll be blue and grey and white and other colours. It slithers towards me, ripples over my feet. It's cool. I squat down, offer my hands. The water runs between my fingers, frothing bubbles. I don't know how long I've been there when a hand appears on my shoulder.

'Shouldda known you'd find me,' I say.

I'm surprised I managed it, Joomia says. She sounds a little out of breath. She sits down next to me and stretches out her legs so the sea runs up them. It's so quiet. Away from the groans and clanks of engines, my ears feel like they're straining for another noise. **She doesn't mean it,** Joomia says. **Etain, I mean.**

'You don't know her,' I say. 'She's never getting over this. And why should she? She's right.' A wave washes a shell into my hand. I throw it back.

You didn't kill Ashir, Aula.

'Yeah, I did. She wouldn't have had to sacrifice anything if it weren't for me.'

Well, Joomia says, **she *did*. She chose to. Like Mathilde did for Metis, and Nadrik for Athenas. And Ade. You heard what she said – the task Ariadnis gave her was having us, and that's why she survived, where all the other Chosen Ones died. She would have had to choose between raising us herself or letting us get taken the way we did. And maybe she did the wise thing, and maybe she didn't. But I think we all have to make sacrifices sometimes. And maybe the reason Etain is so angry is because for her making those sacrifices never felt like a choice.**

I say, 'Do *you* feel like you've had choices?'

281

She takes a long time to answer me. **This doesn't feel like much of a choice: obey the prophecies, go into Ariadnis or something bad will happen. Do you think you have a choice?**

'Sometimes I do. I dunno . . . I think some choices belong to me more than others. Like Ashir . . . I gotta carry that one around with me for the rest of my life. It was my *choice* to tell Nadrik, Joomia. It was me.'

Without saying anything, she takes my hand. **Yes**, she says. **Yes, OK. But there are other choices you own too. Tell me about a good one.**

'Well. I slept with Taurus,' I say. It's out of my mouth before I remember who she is, and I freeze. She stares at me. And then a smile creeps right up over her face and, of course, she knows already, doesn't she? The next second we're both snorting with laughter.

Was that a momentous choice? she splutters.

I shake my head. 'I saw him at the Day of the Wise One celebrations and I just . . . I just wanted something that wasn't gonna be about me being a Chosen One. He called me Aula too, not the Chosen One. So I, um, chose him. And it was the first thing in ages I didn't regret. I wish *this* choice was more like that.'

You mean, something you can just say, *fuck it*, what the hell, I'll do it?

That has me smiling. 'Yeah. Exactly.'

I wish that too. We're quiet for a bit, just thinking. Then she says, **What are we going to do?**

I don't say anything.

Anything we do, we have to do together now, she goes on.

'But we never were alone, were we?' I say. 'Not like

we thought we were.'

She sighs. It answers a lot of questions. This . . . connection we have.

'How are we so different?' I wonder aloud. 'What made that happen?'

She shrugs. Maybe it is like Taurus says – like being twins or something. Or maybe if we'd been one girl instead of two, there would have been a bit of both of us in that one girl.

'Would that have been better?' I ask, my throat going tight. 'Would she have fucked up less?'

She squeezes my hand. I was wondering that myself. But I don't think so. Who *doesn't* make mistakes? How else are you supposed to grow, and be wise, like we're supposed to? Maybe that's why we're the last Chosen Ones. We've got twice the amount of experience. Maybe we're linked like this so that neither one of us can fulfil the prophecy alone. Neither one of us can walk away.

'Yeah?'

She puts her hand to her chest, and I know what she means. The ache. The emptiness. Even if we want to . . . *can* we live apart again?

It's been bad enough just being in different cities. If we walk away from each other, I don't know . . . I don't know if we'll survive.

'But *are* we gonna both survive?' I ask. It's the first time I've said anything like that before. 'Even if we pass the test, reach the book – who's to say we en't gonna just . . . die?'

We could run, she says. But run where? Even if we found somewhere on the island they couldn't touch us . . . even if we found more land somewhere out there.

'Maybe we should try it,' I say.

I expect her to say something doubtful, but she says, **Maybe. But there's nothing to say running won't kill us either. What if going to Ariadnis is something we just have to do? What if the magic in our blood that makes us the Chosen Ones just kills us the day our eighteenth birthday is up, whatever happens?**

'Please,' I say. 'Stop talking about dying.' She closes her mouth. We sit there, and watch the water. I put my head on her shoulder, and she leans her head against mine. 'It's not that I en't thought about it sometimes,' I say. 'But . . . I gotta be honest, Joomia, most of my life's been spent assuming I was gonna win.'

She laughs. **I don't seem like much of an opponent, do I?**

'Not cos I thought I was any wiser, but cos it would *kill* me if I let Nadrik down. Only then . . . then the previous Chosen Ones said last year that we had to unite, and I started thinking maybe, maybe there was another way. Not like I did anything about it, but—'

Joomia gives me a piercing look. **They expect a lot of us, so we expect a lot of us too. But there's no reward for being a hero. There's no reward for sticking your neck on the line. I've tried it most of my life, but I was never any good at it. Mostly I was just . . .**

'Afraid,' I finish for her, thinking of Ashir, thinking of what she said about how no one was gonna believe me if I said I was scared. She was right. But Joomia . . . Joomia *knows*. And just having her know that about me makes the choking panic of what I have to do ease a bit.

I think, she says, **if we were going to run, we would have run by now.**

284

I sit up, and the darkness makes me squint to look at her. I know she's right, and the second I know it I feel as if a wall has buckled inside me: a wall that was keeping me safe but blocking the way ahead.

We still have the night, she says. **Maybe some of tomorrow too.**

I realise that she means time to say goodbye. I close my eyes. 'Fuck it. Yeah. Let's do it.'

She laughs a little, and lets her head sink against my shoulder.

It's not over yet, Aula.

'If you say so,' I say.

9 Days

Aula

We fell asleep a little way back from the ocean, but the moon's still bright when I open my eyes. I wake Joomia and without saying anything we make our way back.

We've nearly reached the cave when Joomia stops short.

Nadrik is suddenly visible through a gap in the trees: head high, back straight. A line of mindless are filing into the cave ahead of him.

We run forward, abandoning caution, but he's already disappeared inside. Seconds later, we hear screams and yells. Once we get deeper, I see Igra trying to rally the prophets for a defence spell while the mindless try to wrestle them into submission. The strange part is – the spell seems to be working. Prophet magic is often sung – the rhythms of the music help concentrate the enchantment, or something like that. The prophets are all desperately trying to pick up a tune together; their panic is shaking them, but even so, I see the mindless falter. Their movements, so quick and supple in the forest, have become stiff and halting.

I wonder why Nadrik en't done anything, and I look for him just in time to see him throw Ade to the floor.

'STOP!' His hand makes a violent tugging gesture.

And the song of the prophets ends as the wind is sucked out of them. Everyone is instantly seized by one pair of mindless hands or another, and it makes me cold, how quick they are, how efficiently their hands and arms are positioned to cut off air.

'Where are they?' Nadrik's voice hisses across the cave, chilling the air like water snuffing out a fire. 'Where are my daughters?'

I hesitate.

My daughters.

And of course, while I'm being an idiot, Joomia strides right in behind him and says, **Here**.

Joomia

He gives me a bland smile. He gestures to the mindless, and I feel hands close over my wrists, shoving in my spine. They bring me to him, forcing me to my knees, pulling my head back by my hair to make me look at him.

'Where is Aula?' he asks.

I swallow and flick my eyes around the room – so it looks like I'm debating what to tell him. **We argued**, I say. **She ran off. I suppose you think I ought to have caught her.**

His smile widens.

I concentrate, trying to feel my way back to earlier, trying to feel how I felt when he was facing me last, and I made a branch appear out of a shelf.

I inch backwards. There is rock beneath me.

Rock—

Rock—

Nothing but rock—

But then, under my fingers, moss. Lichen.

Something's happened to me since back there in the forest. My power, now that I'm reaching for it, feels smoother, surer, as if releasing it the way I did has cured my fear. Maybe it's that I'm closer to Aula. Or maybe it's because I can't afford to be afraid any more.

Nadrik's not looking at me; he's glaring around at the women who used to be his prophets. Igra spits on the ground at his feet.

Small white flowers bloom between my toes.

'Treachery,' he says to his prophets, but he doesn't sound very surprised.

'Loyalty,' Igra mutters. 'Always to Ashir, the one we truly followed.'

Every prophet around the room draws herself upright. There is a fern, curling against my back now. I catch Nadrik looking towards Ade, like somehow she'll give him answers, and it's the most vulnerable look I've ever seen on his face. But then he turns to me and his blank stare is back, and he is offering me his hand.

'I will make this simple. I want the Book of Knowledge, and unless you want my mindless to decapitate your friends, you and Aula are going to get it for me.'

I stare at him.

'Did you hear me, girl?'

I nod.

'Then what is your answer?'

Slowly, I get my feet. There's a soft *crrshh* as the moss

291

twining itself to my tunic pulls away. But before I can speak, Aula steps forward from the shadows and plants her hands in his chest.

'Like hell,' she says. And the next second he is flying across the cave.

Aula

When he collides with the roof it explodes, showering rock, mineral and moss in every direction. Nadrik's shields scuff as he rolls down to the ground, but he regains his footing.

His lips barely move but the mindless react instantly, and there is a collective shriek as the prophets and Ade, Taurus and Etain all have their limbs wrenched.

'I warned you,' he says. 'Follow the prophecy, Aula. Do the *wise* thing, now.'

Several prophets let out moans of pain.

Igra bellows, 'Don't listen to him, Aula!'

'Joomia?' I whisper, offering my hand.

She nods, closes her fingers around mine and drops her other hand to the ground. I feel our powers click together, like pieces of a puzzle. There is a sound as large and impossible as a falling tree, and when she straightens, the mindless have become wood – frozen statues caught in violent acts.

Nadrik stares at us, eyes bright. I realise, then, he's not looking at Joomia. He's just looking at me.

'Ah, my girl,' he says.

Something inside me wobbles, and I turn my face away.

When I look back, he's gone. I take a long, deep breath.

Everyone is frozen, stuck in the grasping hands of the now immobile mindless.

Joomia looks around frowning. 'Aula, where is Ade?'

Joomia

While Aula frees everyone from the mindless's frozen grip, I go outside, where dawn is already rubbing the sky a few shades lighter.

I put a hand on a nearby tree to try to feel through its roots the way I would feel through the vines in Metis. There are thousands of trees – right across the island, each of them connected, all of them talking to each other.

I see Nadrik. He's walking, his head down, except when he checks over his shoulder every few seconds. Three mindless follow after him, pulling Ade with them. She's struggling, trying to haul them off balance, but they are strong and when she falls they just drag her.

'He knew he couldn't take you alone, so he's going to try something else,' Taurus says behind me. My heart has fallen into my gut, and every beat churns my stomach. *No time – no time – no time.* But talking with Aula last night has made me calmer. I don't know what's going to happen, and there's no time to guess. I think I just have to follow what seems right.

Try what? I ask.

'Ade's still Chosen,' Etain says as she emerges from the cave beside us. Behind her, Igra is directing all of the

293

prophets into the open. 'Could Ade get Nadrik into Ariadnis before you?'

I don't know. I don't know how it works.

'I don't reckon he'll like the thought of going against the prophecy,' Aula says. 'More likely he wants to use her as leverage against us. I'm guessing he's going to say *bring me the book or she gets it.*'

I feel myself going pale. **Would he do that? Would he kill her?**

'I dunno, Joomia,' Aula says.

'He would,' Etain says. 'He was in love with Ade. But she never was with him, not really. Ma told me that much.'

'I'll go after them,' Aula says wearily. 'Where did they go, Joomia?'

I close my eyes again, letting the roots guide me – I see Nadrik and Ade, but something else gets my attention. I make a fist against the trunk of the tree. Aula catches on to my expression.

'What?' she asks.

There are more mindless, I say. **In the foot of the passage that leads past Ariadnis to Metis. Waiting.**

Etain relays this to Igra as she approaches, and her whole body sags. 'So not only does he have Ade, if you refuse to give him the book, he can hold the whole city to ransom.'

Aula grits her teeth. '*Fuck.*'

'We have to warn the people of Metis,' Etain says. 'But how?'

'In the cave, Ade told me about times she'd come to the island. Outside of Metis. She said there were cliff pathways that lead to Low Tree, near where you found Lear, Joomia. If we can find those paths, we could take the prophets along them,' Taurus says, 'but it would be a long way, and even then, we could only *look* at what's happening from there. I don't know of any other way into the city except to climb, and there's no time.'

'No,' Etain says, her eyes narrowing. 'But . . . Joomia?'

I blink, still feeling the ghost of her hand on my arm. *Pathetic*.

'Could you make us a bridge from the cliff pathways to the lower branches?'

I hesitate. *Could I?*

Now? I ask faintly.

'No time like the present,' Igra growls.

I've never done anything like that before. It's so far . . .

Aula slips her hand through mine. 'You can do it,' she says.

I look at her, and she nods confidently. So I close my eyes, and put my hand on the ground. I picture the place Taurus has described. The earth is warm from the first morning light, but cold beneath the top soil, and it goes on and on. I'm expecting to struggle, but with Aula holding on to me, like a power source, it's almost easy. I follow the roots of hundreds of trees – right to the base of Low Tree in Metis and up. I follow branches, follow energy, and I feel the trees turning to me, like I've spoken and they're recognising my voice – speeding me along, taking me down to Low Tree.

It's like the vines and the branches galvanise, twist together, reaching out towards the cliff—

I blink and come out of it, gasping, and Aula hauls me to my feet.

'Did it work?' she asks, and I nod, expecting to feel tired, but it's as if I've been doused with cold water. The energy coursing through me – through my feet and into the roots and back again – is unbelievable.

I look at Etain. **You will need to go quickly. It is a long journey to the bridge. You'll see it when you come to it. Once you've got to Low Tree, ask for the Elders of Metis . . .** I sigh, knowing already how the Elders will react to this convoy from Athenas. **If you tell them what the mindless are, they'll believe you, especially if you tell them what you know about Nadrik and *how* you know it.**

'What about Mathilde?' Etain asks. 'Will she join us?'

Taurus twists his lip. 'We'll deal with her when we get there. And anyway, I think it's gotta be you that leads them, Etain.'

'The people of Metis will never listen to me,' Etain replies.

He smiles. 'I'll help you. That's what the prophecy says, right?'

'All the more reason to have prophets with you,' Igra says, drawing herself up. 'We're with you, Etain.'

The prophets nod, murmuring assent. The look they're giving Etain is unshakeable. It's real belief. Maybe it's because they believed in Ashir, but when I follow their eyes to Etain, I can't doubt it either. She looks scared, unsure, but still, there's something immovable about her. She glances at me, and my heart feels like it's in my stomach and throat and feet and head all at once.

'What will you do?' she asks.

I look at Aula.

'We need to rescue Ade, I guess,' she says.

I take my time in answering. **No. There's not enough time. Whatever happens, we're going to need to get to Ariadnis first. Ade is stronger than she seems,** I say, thinking of how much Ade has surprised me in the last few days.

'What about everyone's memories?' Aula asks. 'Can we help them.'

'That is a powerful spell,' Igra says. 'Nadrik will have anchored the memories to an object, something precious. Without severing that bond, we can do nothing to help those whose mind he has taken.'

I might know what the anchor is, I say, thinking of the memories in his study.

'What?' Taurus asks.

'His circlet!' Aula says, catching on. 'Of course—'

Etain cuts across. 'I know what you're thinking, Taurus, and I'm telling you not to. I need you with me.' She turns to look at me and glances briefly at Aula. 'If you two can go on and get into Ariadnis, we can warn Metis before Nadrik sends the mindless to round them up. We've bought ourselves some time – we can think on how to help the people then. It's enough.'

Aula looks like she wants to fight it, but she nods. 'OK. Let's go.'

Aula

I've got that fizzing nervousness when you're about to do something big and you're scared shitless to do it. I en't *worried* about myself any more – not with the stakes so high – but that doesn't stop my insides churning, my palms gumming with sweat.

It's pretty obvious we have to say goodbye. While Joomia convenes with Etain, Igra and her prophets, Taurus comes up close and takes my hand.

'You OK?' he says, leading me a little away from the others.

I wrinkle my nose. 'I've been better. You?'

'I don't understand how you can be so calm,' he says. 'You've been through so much. There's so much pressure on you . . . all of you. I'm just . . . I'm so frustrated I can't do anything about it. I'm not like you, or Joomia or Etain. There was never any prophecy made about me.'

'Well, forgive me for not showering you with sympathy about that one,' I say. 'Cos it's shit.'

He laughs. 'It's taken a long time for me to *get* how shit it is. I guess I should feel . . . free or something. But I'm still tied in. By my blood or not, Etain and Joomia are my sisters.' He sighs. 'If I'd been older, I'd have been able to take the Ritual of Acquisition – then at least I'd be able to *help*.'

'Who says you en't helping?'

He rolls his eyes.

I grab his face then. I don't mean to. It's instinct. 'Listen, you idiot. Just cos Joomia's the Chosen One, or Etain's

298

the future Leader or whatever the hell that means, doesn't mean they don't have to rely on anyone. It doesn't mean you're the pack horse – it means you're the hand stopping them from drowning! Didn't you hear what Lore said? You're the fucking *compass* when no one knows their arse from their tit. OK?'

He's looking at me. Right *into* me. 'Do you need a compass, Aula?'

I take a deep breath. *Look away*, I think. *Just look away.* 'I think it's a bit late for that now,' I say. 'But if I get out. If Joomia and me pass the Wise One's test . . .'

He's still looking at me. I check over his shoulder to see if anyone's looking and pull him behind the nearest tree and I kiss him – quickly, softly, three times.

'Are you crying?' I ask.

'Bit,' he mutters. He presses his forehead against mine. 'Go and talk to my sister, now.'

I try to shake my head. 'I don't even *want* her to forgive me. I'm surprised you can.'

'You might not want her to, but *she* wants to, even if she doesn't know it herself.'

We walk out from behind the tree, but no one's even noticed we left. Taurus goes to Joomia and I hear their *I love you*s whispered around each other's arms.

I don't remember making the decision to walk over to Etain, but then I'm in front of her. She looks right through me, as if I'm not there; but maybe the effort's too much cos then she meets my eyes.

'Etain,' I say. I don't have anything more than that.

'Aula,' she says. And her voice breaks.

And then we're in each other's arms.

We find that the rubble has been cleared from what was the tallest tower in Athenas and a clear pathway made from the beginning of the debris to its centre. I guess this is what the other mindless were doing while we were having our minds blown in the cave. I know it's saved us the trouble of clambering over all the wreckage but I would have preferred the time that clearing a space would have bought us, out in the waking sunlight and the warm air.

We take one last breath of clean air, and then we head to the enormous stump of the tree that is still wreathed in its metal case.

It's still alive, you know, Joomia says. **Even after all these years of being hollowed out and cased in metal. Even after it's fallen and broken . . . it's not dead yet.**

'Is that good for us?' I wonder, but not because I'm expecting her to answer.

We look down. There are no stairs now: no ladders. We see the last of them collapsed below: a fifteen-foot drop into the stone passage.

'Are the mindless still down there?' I ask.

Joomia puts her hand to the ground and closes her eyes.

Joomia

I follow the roots of Athenas down to the branches of Metis until I lock on to a familiar presence.

Mathilde is at the top of High Tree, staring at the passage

in the cliff that would take her to Ariadnis.

She takes a step. She takes another. What is she doing? There's this anxiousness about her, which I've never seen before. Does she suspect that Nadrik is coming? Does she know where I've gone? Is she plucking up the courage to go to Ariadnis herself? To help me? To stop me?

I will never find out.

There is a sound from somewhere further up the passage. Mathilde takes a step back. I frown, trying to identify what's coming. There are roots in the rock, but something is blocking me from feeling my way along them – perhaps Ariadnis itself.

Rolling, I think suddenly, as the reverberations come closer. *Something rolling down the passage.*

And I'm right. An orb the size of a human head rolls out of the passage and into the daylight. It stops just short of the first limb of the tree. Mathilde stares at it. It's glowing. Even in the midday sun, it's glowing.

There's time for her to take in a horrified breath.

And then the orb explodes.

I'm blown back into my body, blinking.

'What's happening?' Aula asks. I grab her hand for support, and force my consciousness back down into Metis, frantically hurtling down the connections between every root . . .

The air is clearing. Mindless are marching out of the passage. A hundred of them. And Nadrik is there already. Of course he is. But I don't see Ade.

He's walking forward, and he's bending over, and Mathilde is on her back.

301

'I've been waiting,' she says. She tries to sit up, but his hand is on her shoulder, pushing her back.

'I didn't mean to be late,' he says.

'You're here now,' she says. 'You and your army.'

'Ah, you noticed them. Would you like to tell them about how you destroyed their city with your rot?'

'Only if you tell them how you stole their minds.'

He laughs. 'Yes, it would all be rather difficult for them to process in their current state, wouldn't it?'

She tries to take a deep breath and I realise as I reach the branch she's lying on that there is a splinter the size of an arm buried in her stomach.

'You aren't going to win. Joomia's stronger than she thinks she is.'

He snorts. 'And if you lived, what then? You would be comfortable with her having the power? You hated what Ade did with her power. You hated that she squandered it. You hated that I got the child with the strength.'

'The child you ended up hating?' she murmurs.

He hesitates. And then he leans over her and whispers, 'I loved her. Just as much as Ade. When I took her, I swore I would protect her. Let her learn from me.'

'But then she grew up,' Mathilde whispers. She coughs. There must be blood in her mouth. 'And she was like her mother. I suppose nothing was worth the pain of Ade again?'

He grits his teeth.

She closes her eyes and opens them, like a child. 'I can't help feeling now that we've done it wrong, Nadrik,' she says. 'Perhaps there was another way, but we never saw it.'

'If there is,' he says quietly, 'we are too late.'

302

She smiles, then says, 'I am sorry for that.'

Her chest moves up to accommodate a breath. It does not move down. Nadrik rests his chin on his hand as he closes her eyes. Then he stands and walks back through the mindless streaming out of the passage.

Aula

I grab Joomia by the shoulders and shake her.

Tears start to brim in her eyes as she tells me what she saw.

'Don't,' I say. I cut off my feelings. I cut them off at the root like weeds. I stamp on them brutally. '*Don't*, Joomia. There's no time. We have to go!'

I swing myself down into the passage and catch Joomia as she follows.

For the most part the dust from the pillar's collapse has settled, and yet every step sends curling tongues of it rising into the dark. The need to keep putting one foot in front of the other grows so strong now I feel it throbbing in my gums. It's the same directionless *pull* of the ache. It en't optional.

We run the first part. It usually seems endless, but I guess there en't all those stairs to go down any more, so before too long I'm recognising the turns that means we're nearly there and I slow down. I reach out to the passage wall, and the minerals glow bright at my touch; moss and other cave plants spring boldly from the path of Joomia's fingers. Maybe it feels easy now cos this is it, we're here. I know it,

303

but I can't *feel* it.

And there's the archway; there's the half-circle of luminescent orbs. We stop.

There would have been a ceremony, if we had done this the way our cities wanted us to. But there en't. Joomia catches me looking at her.

What is it?

I don't want to be too mushy, but what the hell. 'I was just thinking . . . if you're literally the other half of me, I guess I can't be that bad.'

She nearly smiles. **What does that mean for me?**

I laugh, cos I reckon that's the first joke I've ever heard her crack, and it suits her.

Then we walk to the doorway and put our hands on the highest orbs.

The world whips sideways and smudges black.

And that's it.

We're inside.

The Chosen

We were not sleeping, precisely. A more honest comparison would be to say dozing. But the Chosen Ones are here, and so we wake.

While we wait for them to acclimatise, we turn our attention to the disturbances in Metis. The Elders have not long gathered for their meeting in the courtyard of Low Tree when their people come streaking in towards them along the branches, shouting over each other:

'We're under attack!'

'Athenas is here!'

'What do we do?'

Only Eros, Elder of Low Tree, hears them properly, and he feels his heartbeat slide to a trip.

Janaelle of Black Tree holds up an imperious hand. 'Calm yourselves. Take a breath and one of you try to exp—'

'We're under *attack*!' someone snaps. 'The Athenasians are here.'

'How many?' asks Albo of White Tree.

'*All of them.*'

Janaelle shakes her head. 'They are probably here to negotiate terms of the Chosen One's birthday next week. That is all.' She leans in. 'It is vital that they do not guess our Chosen One is gone.'

'They're *attacking*. They have weapons!'

307

Janaelle looks at Albo, who murmurs, 'Ceremonial weapons, perhaps?'

Eros raises peaceable hands to the crowd. 'We'll go out to meet them. We cannot assume hostility. Can someone find Mathilde?'

'She's dead,' says a new voice, winded and gasping. Lear's father, Ternos, limps into view, his face blank with shock. 'Eros, they have her on their shoulders. She's dead.'

A horrible silence.

Then, 'Summon the magi,' says Einar of Sap Tree. 'Get everyone down to Low Tree as fast as you can.'

Three citizens run off at once. Ternos only stays. 'How will they defend themselves?' he asks.

'Mathilde had the Chosen One make a stash of weapons some years ago,' says Janaelle, almost to herself.

Einar makes a scoffing sound. 'The Chosen One? Our powerless pretender?'

'Not Joomia,' Janaelle says. 'Ade. When she still had the Chosen One's gifts.'

Eros straightens his old back. 'She had no right to do that. We are *Metisians*. We are not people of war.'

'It doesn't matter now,' Janaelle says. 'She's dead, and we'll be dead too if someone doesn't stop them. I know where they are, Einar. Shall I get them?'

Einar nods, and she goes.

'No!' Eros shouts. 'No, Janaelle – wait. We are people of the Wise One. When do people of the Wise One ever strike without thinking?'

'The trouble is, Eros,' says Einar, 'they've struck *us*. And not just Mathilde – how many people have we lost now?

You and I both know the memory loss is their doing.'

'No more lost to that than we have,' calls a new voice.

Eros turns and sees a young woman climbing up into the courtyard. She's tall and solid, with old burns running up and down her bare arms and solid silver bangles around her neck and wrists. She has a level stare and an upright chin, her black hair splayed around her head like a mane. *Royal*, he thinks.

'An Athenasian messenger?' Einar snarls. 'Come to tell us to surrender?'

Etain glares, and despite himself, Einar drops his eyes. 'Not exactly,' she says. 'The army coming from the cliffs are your citizens too. Nadrik has taken their memories. They do as he bids.'

'Who are you?' Einar sneers.

Etain takes a deep breath. 'The daughter of the Head Prophet of Athenas.'

'Tsch,' Einar mutters. '*Prophet*, is it?'

'I think we should listen to her,' says Eros.

'Of course *you're* saying that,' Einar hisses. 'I never took you for a fool, Eros. They're coming *now*.'

Etain says, 'They are, and we won't be able to stop them.'

'So what?' Einar splutters. 'We surrender our city to *you* and no one gets hurt?'

'That's right,' says Taurus, striding forward. There's a smatter of shocked voices and shouts. 'This is my sister,' Taurus says to the Elders. 'You need to listen to her.'

Einar hesitates, registering dimly the resemblance between the siblings.

'They're coming,' says Eros, and indeed Metis's

309

remaining citizens are scurrying into the courtyard. 'Where are the magi?'

'They've gone to form a defensive circle,' someone answers.

The Elders turn automatically to Einar, but Etain cuts across them. 'Please. I have a plan that I think could save everyone's lives.'

There's a pause.

'You don't know this city,' Albo of White Tree points out.

'No,' says Taurus. 'But I do.'

There's muttering. Einar folds his arms. Etain sees through him. Sees his fear and doubt and anger. And so she reaches out and takes the old man's hand. 'Please,' she says. 'Will you listen?'

He holds her stare for as long as he can. And then his face softens. 'Let's hear it then,' he says.

Joomia

It's just dark at first. No sound of the other Chosen Ones. Nothing.

I can still feel Aula's hand. I can still hear the deep sound of her breath. For a while, I'm not paying much attention more than to that.

Aula?

'Yeah?'

Are we moving?

'Dunno,' she says. 'I can't feel my feet moving; it's like

310

there's a wind.'

As she says the last word, light blossoms in a strip before us, so bright I have to narrow my eyes against it. There is no noise, but I can imagine the sound of tearing starlight, as if this were the beginning of the universe. It's magnetic to look at, and the longer I stare the more I can see.

'Sorta like how the world was supposed to start, en't it?' Aula whispers. 'Darkness, darkness and then: light.'

Colours become visible, pale as clouds and too many to even name – swirling like the patterns on marbled paper. As I concentrate, I find I'm seeing darker colours too, shapes that are blurry at first before becoming clearer, bolder – as if they were shadow puppets that someone was trying to find the right spot for.

And then the shadows become the only thing I can see.

I get this horrible feeling—

'Joomia?' Aula says. Her voice sounds heavy, as if she's trying to wake herself up.

Yes?

'I don't think I can look away.'

I'm afraid to try.

There is a sound like a footstep and an echoing peal of silvery laughter.

TURN AROUND, CHOSEN ONES.

'On three,' Aula says; her voice is low now as she tries not to panic.

One. Two. Thr—

I take a deep breath and wrench my eyes from the moving shadows. Beside me, I feel Aula's hand tighten on mine as she does the same. We somehow end up staring

311

at each other instead, breathing hard. And that's when I realise why we can feel wind. We are falling. Slowly, for sure, but falling.

I blink and try to look around, to make sense of it, and this is what I see:

We are falling through the air of a cave the size of ten temples, and high above us is a light – not light like the one we were watching – but its true source. It's even more beautiful to look at directly, but instead of that magnetised feeling I get the sense of being repulsed, as if to keep looking at it will cost me something dear.

What is it? I whisper.

THE BEGINNING OF KNOWLEDGE.

The wind has picked up now.

Aula squints into the darkness below.

'There it is,' she whispers.

At first I don't see it because all I'm seeing is how the cave is really a mountain – the peak of it ends where the light begins, and from there the rock plunges downwards at a frighteningly steep angle. But then my eyes clear from the afterglow of the light, and I see the bluish veins of mineral . . .

Is this it? Ariadnis? I ask.

'I dunno if this is even *real*,' Aula says. 'How can there be a mountain *inside* the cliff?'

Perhaps it is pointless to ask questions at all, I think, given that we're also somehow falling through the air like it is water.

At which point, we begin to fall a lot faster. The breeze becomes a high wind; I'm suddenly flung head over feet, my hair whipped against my face. I shriek Aula's name as her hand is nearly ripped from me and she screams for me to hold on, bundling me against her with all her strength.

The ground looms—

We hit.

My head strikes rock, I tumble and I lose her hand.

Aula!

I'm rolling down, blinded. But I feel nothing. My skin is impenetrable. My skull is steel.

Then I stop.

I lie there for a long time. When I can't wait any more, I peel open my eyes.

I see the light first. It is far, far away now – as far as the moon. I'm looking up the mountain.

Aula?

'I'm here.'

I peer around, and find she's only feet away, her freckled face bleached even whiter by the strange light above us. I struggle to stand. There's nothing else around us for as far as I can see. I crane my neck to look at the light again, and still I have that sense of revulsion.

Well, at least it's pretty obvious what we have to do.

'Climbing?' Aula hisses. 'That's the big test?'

Aula

One thing I never expected to happen in Ariadnis was for me to be grumpy and sweaty.

This climb. It's going on for ever. I dunno what I was

expecting. Maybe that there'd be a ring to fight in; a collection of trite tasks based on wisdom quotes from one of those watery philosophy books Nadrik made me read; or that we'd have to turn ourselves inside out proving how wise we'd become or – honestly – I even sort of thought there'd be some kind of written test at some point.

But so far there's just the mountain, and the light, and us both struggling (on our hands and knees sometimes when the planes of the rock get too steep) upwards. We've been climbing for hours, and I swear the light en't getting any closer.

'I don't get it,' I say at last. 'This en't a test. This is torture.'

Joomia stops for a moment to put her head between her knees. **I'm not arguing**, she says.

I look towards the light again. It's more like moonlight than sunlight and it only seems to illuminate the area we're in; I can't see clearly further than six or seven feet in any direction. I spit on the ground. 'It's like those dreams where you're headed somewhere but you never seem to be making any progress. Like chasing a rainbow.'

Or running from a dragon, Joomia adds.

'How can it just be this? How is this about proving our wisdom?'

She sighs. **I don't know, Aula. All we had to go on was legends. Maybe they were all wrong. Maybe *test* was the wrong word. There are so many possibilities. But we do know that wherever *this* is, Lore and Kreywar created it, and that they wanted to stop conflict among their people. And so do we. So maybe we're not thinking about it the right way.**

314

'But it's not even like we're really using our powers,' I say.

You moved that boulder that was in our way before. And I used that knotgrass to make us handholds earlier.

'But that's what I mean – it's too easy! Knotgrass. Rocks. It's all just *here* for us to use. If this is a test about wisdom, why aren't we being forced to use our minds? You know, get cunning, having to think our way over a crevasse. Something like that.'

She rubs her forehead. **I get what you're saying but . . . do you *want* this to be hard?**

'I just want this to *mean* something. I want it to be worth all the time we've spent preparing for it. Our whole lives.'

Joomia grits her teeth as we come to another impossible rock face and gestures at knotgrass by her feet. She's been growing it up the mountain ever since we came to the first patch of it; the knotgrass begins to twine itself to the rock, growing thickly in the deepest cracks, striping itself up the rock until it comes to more traversable ground.

I wait for her to begin to climb before following her.

If we come out alive, Aula, then it will have been worth it. Even if it wasn't the challenge we expected.

I frown. It en't that I don't agree with her. It's just that, after everything we've done, I kind of thought it would feel a little bit more like an achievement.

The Chosen

The Chosen Ones climb.

315

Not understanding.

Not yet . . .

Beneath the rock of Ariadnis, Metis is silent as the mindless crawl in along its branches. They move like ants, acting on something like smell rather than sight.

In the courtyard of Low Tree, inside a dome of tightly woven vines, the remaining people of Metis are silent. They stand in concentric circles facing outward, and tightly packed. The magi stand at the edges, pouring power into their protection, listening, checking, holding.

In the next circle, Janaelle of Black Tree and Albo of White Tree hand out the weapons that Ade made long ago, when she was still a true citizen of Metis and her mother's influence could bend her to things she didn't want to do.

The Metisians are holding hands and silently repeating the plan that Etain has given them. They look to her occasionally, standing in the centre of them all and looking up to the newly domed ceiling in wonder. She can't see it, but judging by the richness of the light in the dome, she guesses the sun is moving into its afternoon slope.

The prophets around her have closed their eyes in concentration. All except Igra who sees Etain looking and winks.

Etain grabs her arm. 'Would Nadrik send them to attack? I thought this was all just leverage.'

Igra shakes her head. 'I've known Nadrik a long time – from a distance, perhaps – but enough. He is perhaps the cleverest man in nine generations but he is also very . . . child-like.'

Etain raises an eyebrow. '*Child-like?*'

'He loved Ade. More than he's dared to love anything before or since. I'm not defending him but—' She clears her throat, and begins to explain. 'Ade was the Chosen One of that generation – and there were different rules in place back then. Cos there weren't two Chosen Ones, Ade had to visit Athenas every now and then, bound as she was to the idea of making *both* cities wiser. On one of these visits, Ade met your mother, and on another, she met Nadrik. I en't gonna pretend I know the full story, but I reckon she fell in love with them both.' She sighs. 'Of course, one love proved the stronger. When she chose your mother over him . . . I cannot describe the anguish he felt – the *anger*. He brushed himself off and rose up through the political ranks, of course, but clearly he hasn't let go of his anger towards Metis and all it represented.'

'But Ashir was from Athenas,' Etain says. 'Metis isn't Nadrik's enemy.'

Igra sighs. 'But Ade was – *is* – from Metis. And Metis elected Mathilde – her mother – as their Elder.'

'But still he's attacking them? To feel avenged in front of a prophet who *clearly* isn't the woman he fell in love with any more?'

'As I said: child-like,' Igra says. 'He was always too coddled by the attitudes of Athenas: our brightest are always prized, venerated – spoiled, even.'

Etain sighs and scrubs her forehead with both hands.

'You're worried?' the old woman asks.

'I have no idea if this is going to work,' Etain says, so quietly it's barely a whisper.

Igra shrugs. 'That's the interesting part.'

'If you say so,' Etain says. 'I just want to go back to my forge and hammer. I never asked to be a leader.'

'All good heroes are reluctant ones,' Igra says patiently. 'Well, except us prophets. All too keen to be heroes, us.'

Etain smiles then, her eyes bright as she thinks of her mother.

'Beautiful, isn't it?' Igra says, nodding at the dome. 'I'm glad I saw it before I die.'

Etain gives her a fierce look. 'Die?'

'Yep.'

'You're going to die *today*? You Saw?'

Igra shrugs. 'I might. You never totally know with prophecies. If it is today, I can't complain. I've had a good innings. And it's a *really* good way to die.'

'But Igra, you could have left! We could have sent you out with the children and the—'

'Infirm,' Igra mutters, snorting. 'Nothing's set in stone, Etain. Nothing to worry about.'

'*Nothing?*'

'Some things happen and some things don't,' Igra says. 'If I decide *not* to die today, then maybe I won't. Same as you could walk away from all this right now if you wanted. Nothing's gonna stop you.'

'Nothing?'

'Of course. You really think the bottom would fall out of the world if you decide you're not up for it?'

Etain swallows, and we can see the truth is, she *had*. But even if someone frogmarched her out now, she'd fight her way back in.

'Thing about prophecy,' Igra says. 'It sort of *makes* you

318

who it says you're gonna be, most of the time. Maybe that's why they don't like it down here.'

One of the magi attracts their attention by waving his hand. *They're here*, he mouths.

Silhouetted between the vines and the sun behind it, a hundred mindless run towards the wall of defenders, silent as owls.

'Magi, ready!' yells an Elder.

'Metis, it's time!' bellows Janaelle across the hushed crowd.

Which is precisely the moment that Etain realises her brother has gone.

Joomia

The mountain begins to shake.

Aula and I hit the ground at the same time. I whisper to the knotgrass, until it grows in thick tufts around our hands and feet, rooting us where we crouch.

The ground beneath us is shuddering, quaking, but it doesn't feel real. There are no sudden rock slides – no showers of dust or loose shale. I squint to look at the cave around us – it's so easy to forget where we are – but the walls seem undisturbed.

It's not real, I say to Aula.

'It *feels* real,' she says back. 'It feels horrible.'

I can smell the grass – like minerals and damp earth and the rock like clean air. And I can feel both of those things under me, hard and sharp and sensory. But then I smell something more familiar, and I can feel it around me, and it suddenly casts the other sensations into doubt.

'What's that smell?' Aula asks me.

The trees, I say. **Mathilde's spell . . .**

'It's coming from all around us, Joomia. Can you smell it too?'

Yes, I say.

And because it's becoming natural to me, I follow the feeling deeper than my sense of touch or taste or smell can go. And I feel cocooned, safe, but something feels different. Inverted.

Somehow, there are roots above me, branches below me.

This is where we really are, I say to myself.

And the moment I think it, it's true.

The feeling of rock beneath me and grass holding me disappears.

I open my eyes.

We're in a cave.

Almost perfectly circular. Right in the centre, a huge stalagmite at least ten feet high. And resting on top of it, or hovering above it, I can't tell—

'The light,' Aula whispers. 'This doesn't make any sense. Did we get shrunk down, somehow? We thought we were climbing the mountain but we were actually climbing *that* thing?'

I don't think so, I say. **I think it was just an illusion.**

'But what for?'

I shrug. **Maybe the test was to realise it wasn't real. Maybe all this is to realise none of it was real.**

I take it all in. Beneath me, branches. I'm kneeling on

them. They criss-cross over each other in varying shades of green and brown and, where they meet the pillar, bursting into a spray of golden leaves – leaves that shouldn't be possible because there's no sun here, just that strange light.

They must have grown up through the cliff, I murmur, because they are unmistakeably vishaal branches.

Which means that the roots coming through the roof of the cave, and growing out of the wall, are from Athenas. I reach out to touch one that is curling down in a spiral. It feels rough and hairy, like the hide of some kind of animal.

We're right in the centre. Right between our cities.

'I can still smell something rotten,' Aula says, sniffing. 'It's everywhere.'

I laugh, a little disbelievingly, because it reminds me of an Old World play I read. *There is something rotten in the state of Denmark*. Wherever Denmark was. **What now?** I ask.

'I dunno, Joomia. I dunno what we're supposed to do,' Aula says.

And all at once, I'm furious. Long after they died, for nine generations, Lore and Kreywar have had us all playing out their little game. Did they foresee all this? Did they see us, here, in this cave, trying to solve a riddle we'd never been prepared for?

How did they expect two eighteen-year-olds to fix what nine generations of people couldn't? How did they think that would help? If they wanted to help their people why didn't they *do something* then and there – instead of bottling up their problems and burying them for someone else to deal with further down the line?

Aula looks at her hands. 'I dunno,' she repeats.

321

I squint up at the light at the top of the stalagmite, shading my eyes. **Fucking hell**, I say forcefully.

'Yeah,' she says.

We stand there, not looking at each other, for some time.

Finally Aula sits down on the ground, with a look on her face that says she deserves a break. 'Maybe . . . maybe it's the kind of thing that can only be solved further down the line, Joomia,' she says. Even to me it sounds like clutching at straws. I begin to circle the stalagmite, trying to think. She goes on, 'Maybe that's what all the Chosen Ones before us were supposed to do. Gain a bit of wisdom each time. Inch us forward, bit by bit.'

But if that were true, Aula, wouldn't it have been nice for them to share that wisdom, rather than leaving us cryptic clues: *unite or you're doomed, follow the path of wisdom*, blah blah blah.

She smiles. 'You're starting to sound like me. That's a good point, though: where *are* the other Chosen Ones? Isn't this where they bring us, every year, minus the light?'

I reach out to touch the stalagmite.

'Don't tell me we're not going to go for that light now that we're here,' she says.

Looks steep, though, I murmur.

'Not for you,' she says.

I look at her, and she's grinning at me. And I let go of my anger. Because I'm here, and she's here, and there's nothing else for us to do but go for it.

I start to climb.

The Chosen

As the Chosen Ones make their decision, Nadrik finally snaps. After what feels like hours of listening to her wails, he makes a savage movement with his hand and the air is momentarily sucked out of Ade's lungs.

She collapses on to her knees, winded, her eyes watery and red.

'Quiet,' he hisses savagely. 'Just *be quiet*.'

But she can't be quiet. She's heaving air back into her chest, rasping and coughing. He watches her with a horrible, sour look on his face.

'If you could have seen what you've become,' he says.

She meets his eyes, and in that second, she's all there. Furious, impetuous, knowing, loving Ade. And she hates him. She *hates* him.

He turns away, smoothing his hair back into its coil. 'I didn't want this, Ade. I didn't want it to be like this.'

'Well, that's reassuring,' says a new voice.

Nadrik swivels. He takes in the newcomer and laughs. Ashir's son, looking sweaty and skinny and distinctly unheroic.

'Here to seek a parley?'

'Memories,' Ade says, as the boy puts a protective hand on her shoulder.

But when Taurus looks at Nadrik, he doesn't feel fierce or powerful. 'Give them back,' he says. 'Please.'

'What makes you think I have them with me?'

Taurus's eyes flicker uncertainly to the circlet. Nadrik is impressed. 'All right. In what world would I just *give them back?'*

Taurus opens his mouth, to plead because he doesn't know any other way, but Ade gets there first. She leans in towards Nadrik, eyes steady. 'Ade can get you inside.'

Nadrik looks at the entrance to Ariadnis. Back at her. He shakes his head. 'Liar.'

She grunts and crosses the cavern to the doorway. Her hand finds a bulb of mineral, and the arch hums with energy. Taurus can feel it from where he's standing. She lets go quickly. 'Still works,' she says.

He stares at her. 'For the memories? That is your price?'

'Yep,' she says.

He considers, or pretends to.

'Ade . . .' Taurus says. He wants to warn her. Does she know what she's doing? But he can see in her face that she does.

She does not look at him, but says to Nadrik, 'To the boy.'

Carefully Nadrik lifts the crown from his brow, and without it his coil of grey-daubed hair falls over his shoulders. He offers the circlet to Taurus.

Taurus reaches for it.

But Nadrik pulls back. 'He will have it when I am sure you will keep your word,' he says. Ade begins to answer, but he cuts across her: 'You keep your promise,' he says, 'and I will keep mine.'

Ade sighs in apparent exhaustion. 'Hand,' she says, holding out hers.

Their fingers twine, and Ade reaches forward with her free arm – not for the bulbs, but the centre of the arch – and knocks.

Her eyes shut, her lips pressed together, she knocks again.

Taurus holds his breath.

Once more.

The archway begins to glow. It's like looking at the sun through the leaves – pleasant at first, until the wind or the sky shifts and suddenly the light is too bright.

Taurus flings his arms over his face.

There is a sound like a snare of fierce wind coming in through a canvas flap. The light cuts out.

When Taurus peers under the crook of his arm he sees the cavern empty, and is sure Nadrik has broken his word. But then there is a clatter of metal on stone. He lets his arms fall in time to see the circlet roll to a halt on the floor, the jewel blank and colourless.

Taurus stares at it and lets out a long curse. 'Now what?'

Below the cliff, the first mindless breaks through the protection of the vine dome with his hands and teeth and shoulders. Behind him are more, their voices silent but their mouths open and raw as wounds, as if they are gasping for air. The first rushes at the nearest group of Metisians, and Etain – eyes wide in horror – watches as Janaelle flings herself at the attacker, Ade's weapon clutched in her hand.

The weapons. Etain had barely glanced at them. They appeared to be no more than sticks or twigs that might just as well have been plucked from the paths or bridges. The only clue to how they might truly be used is the faint phosphorescence that gleams between the fibres of the wood, like veins under the skin.

It is only now that Etain sees their true use.

As Janaelle dives, brandishing her stick, vines come tearing out of it like spurting water, flicking up under the mindless's feet and wrapping swiftly and silently over his ankles, his torso, his face . . .

'Stop!' Etain yells. She doesn't know if Janaelle can't hear her or won't listen, but the vines go twisting on up the boy's face, down his throat . . . into his eye sockets.

'For Mathilde!' Janaelle screams.

'Igra!' Etain yells, panicking. This was *not* the plan. 'Now! *Now!*'

Igra draws herself up to her fullest height. 'Cassandrae!' she bellows, thrusting a finger into the air like a conductor.

And on her signal, the prophets begin to sing. At first just a hum: a baseline of voices warming the tune. Then come the complementary voices, filling the sound spaces with simple harmony, strengthening the song like a cross becoming a star, and then a web. It is not magic the way the magi practise it, or even the Chosen Ones. But as the harmony deepens, the song takes the strain of the magic being sewn along it.

Etain's plan is working.

Igra had been watching the young girl, hours earlier, as they'd marched side by side, negotiating the cliff paths to Metis. 'What are you thinking, Etain?' she asked.

Etain said, 'Did you know that the mindless would slow down while you were singing?'

Igra shrugged, indicating she had but hadn't thought much of it.

'If Nadrik hadn't silenced you, I don't reckon they'd've

been able to get to you.'

Igra scratched her nose. 'Prophet magic en't like other magic. It's raw. That's what makes it so corrosive to those who en't trained to harness it properly. A prophet's song is more powerful than other magic, even Nadrik's.'

Etain nodded, her eyes sparking like a forge. 'Could that be what spared us and the other citizens of Metis from Nadrik's memory spell, d'you think?'

'Well, that's an interesting idea,' said Igra. 'Raw magic's in all children of prophets. Right down in their blood.'

'Right,' said Etain.

'What are you thinking?' Igra asked again.

'I need a song,' Etain said. 'I know there's not much time, but I think this might be the only thing that will work. I need a song that will slow the mindless down until Aula and Joomia . . . well, to give us time.'

'Tall order,' Igra said, frowning to herself.

'But can it be done?'

'Leave it with me,' said Igra. 'I'll see what I can do.'

Now Etain watches, her tongue turning to rubber in her mouth as the song lifts the fine hairs on her spine. *Please work*, she thinks. *Please*.

The mindless slow, but not enough. Their movements are jerky and uneven, but they still reach their targets – and Nadrik has armed them well. Swords and daggers. Spears and arrows. Blood arcs through the air every few yards, and even with Ade's weapons, there are too many to hold back all at once. The number of mindless, Etain thinks, more than she could ever have imagined, must be what's stopping the Cassandrae's song from working.

Ma, help, Etain whispers. *I've killed them all.*

She feels a presence at her back, and swivels just in time for the arrow to thunk into her shoulder rather than through her chest. She sways and falls to her knees, her vision scattering. There is no pain yet, just blind panic. The same panic that breaks the song, that sets people running out of the encirclement of the dome.

I've failed.

Etain looks up, and now she can see the archer, his blank eyes aiming for her head. There's no time to dodge. There is just time for Igra, still roaring the song from somewhere deep in her chest, to run forward. Etain sees the old woman's body flinch as the arrow hits.

'No!'

She feels the pain then, as she scrambles to find Igra's fallen form in the chaos. 'Igra!'

Someone knocks against the shaft of the arrow in her shoulder and she screams in pain, but she knows not to pull it out, lest the arrowhead get left behind. She keeps going, shuffling forward on her knees to cradle the old prophet's head.

The arrow is lodged deep between Igra's bony ribs. The prophet sees Etain and smiles. 'Told you it was a good way to go. I nearly missed it. But here I am.' She hisses slightly, in pain. 'Listen to me. When the time comes, you must get everyone out of the city as fast as you can. You hear?'

'It's too late, Igra. There won't be anyone to get out of here because I've already failed. It's already over.'

Igra coughs. 'Nah, you en't begun yet,' she says. 'The prophets need a leader. These *people* need a leader.'

'I can't do it. I can't be anyone's leader.'

'Of course you can.'

'How?'

'You sing, my darling. I know you were listening when I was teaching it to them earlier. Sing.'

'I can't.'

'You're Ashir's daughter. You got her blood. Course you can.'

'But Ma's gone, Igra.'

'Yeah. But she was so proud of you. You think Ashir's pride could ever die?' She reaches up with one silky wrinkled hand and brushes Etain's coarse hair. 'Sing, my darling girl. Sing like yer heart's gonna come outta yer mouth.'

Etain gets shakily to her feet, remembering every single melody she ever heard living in the prophet house. Then she opens her mouth and joins the song.

It's hard to find the rhythm at first – the prophets who are still singing are having a hard time holding it together. But when they hear Etain's voice ringing like a bell over the noise, their voices grow stronger, and the ones who have lost the thread join them with renewed confidence.

Janaelle pauses her attack on a mindless whose movements have suddenly lengthened, as if they were moving through water. 'It's working!' she calls. 'It's working!'

Aula

There's light at first, but it pales and darkens. I feel a bit like I've been swallowed. We en't in the cave any more, but

329

where we are en't really describable. I can't really see anything.

There *is* a breeze coming from somewhere, and I breathe it in, tasting something like stale breath and rotting leaves and honey and really old wine. Or I could just be imagining it. Something is pressing against my skin – hard like the feel of a twig in your back, but brushing and soft, like feathers. I get the feeling I'm being searched. Not roughly, though. More like the feel of an old person's hand searching your face. A great looming consciousness, sizing us up, taking us in.

'Joomia?'

Aula? Where are we?

'I dunno. Maybe this is the real test.'

Perhaps we're supposed to show how worthy we are of the book or something. Maybe we show Ariadnis how um . . . wise we are?

I can feel us both wanting to laugh at that.

'Maybe we should start like how we usually do. You know . . . show the previous Chosen Ones what we've learned . . . all the stuff we've taken in and that.'

Worth a try.

So we open ourselves up, and we show them.

All our grief and chaos and unity and guilt and fear and love and loneliness. All of it.

Nadrik and Ashir; Etain and Taurus and Ade. Our hurts and our dreams and our hopes and our failures. They unfurl like millions of ribbons, some torn and some worn, some newer, some stronger.

Till we en't got anything left.

We're here now, for better or worse. We did what we could.

There's a quiet when we're finished.

Then:

YOU HAVE LEARNED WELL.

We wait for more, but the world is quiet.

'Was that it?' I say.

I don't know.

THE BOOK IS YOURS, IF YOU WISH.

Just like that? Joomia asks.

THE BOOK IS YOURS, IF YOU WISH, they repeat.

Talk about a loaded statement, Joomia mutters.

'What do you mean, if we wish?' I say indignantly. 'Of course we wish!'

WHAT WILL YOU DO WITH ALL THE KNOWLEDGE IN THE WORLD?

We are silent. 'This doesn't make any sense. That's such a dud question,' I say huffily.

I . . . Mathilde never talked about this, Joomia says. **What *are* we supposed to do with all the knowledge in the world?**

'Damned if I know,' I say. 'I never got that far in my head. I kind of assumed the book would come with some sort of instructions that would tell us what to do with it.' I pause.

Me too, she says.

There's a silence. Wise One, have we failed? What now? I feel like each second could be a century. I feel like I could have been here for ever, and everyone outside could have grown old and died and I just wouldn't know it. So I say, kind of in desperation, 'We're gonna try to be wise, like the Wise One, right? Is that the answer?'

IS THAT *YOUR* ANSWER? they ask.

'I dunno. I dunno how to be wise.'

Neither of us does, Joomia says. **We're not even eighteen yet. We're still learning.**

There's silence again. I sigh.

'I think I'll miss that,' I say. 'Learning, I mean. I en't exactly loved every moment I've fucked it up, but it makes life more interesting.' I laugh, thinking of Ashir teaching me songs when I was little and pretending not to wince at my voice. Taurus, spilling wine on my tunic, realising he saw something in me – for once, not in spite of me, but *because* of me. Etain teaching me how to hammer metal flat, bit by bit.

'It's funny, but if I'm honest I've never been sure how a book that makes you omniscient is gonna be any good for anyone, really,' I say. 'Cos, how can you teach – or be taught – by anyone who knows everything already? What's the point if you don't have to learn for yourself, make your own mistakes?'

Joomia

The change is immediate and more violent than I could possibly have anticipated. I feel my body jerking backwards like a puppet and into the cave again, as if I've been spat out like a pit in a choking throat. I feel a searing pain in my back as I hit the floor and there's a heavy thud as Aula lands next to me. There is a gentle dripping noise from somewhere far off, and something that sounds curiously like someone knocking on a door. I just lie there, spent.

'What happened?' Aula asks. 'Was that it?'

I don't know, I say, trying to remember what Aula could have said to upset the guardians.

'I didn't *mean* any of it,' Aula says, sounding panicked. She sits up. 'Oh shit, I was just thinking out loud!'

I close my eyes. *What's the point if you don't have to learn for yourself, make your own mistakes?* My gut wants to agree with her, but the worry that we've just ruined our chances at saving the island is choking most other thoughts.

Stop, I tell myself. *Think. Just think.*

Would having knowledge make our survival easier or would it ruin it?

No, I say slowly. **No, Aula, I think . . . I think you were right.**

'What? How do you know?'

Excitement from I don't know where bubbles in me as she asks the question.

The guardians said it themselves last time we were in Ariadnis. They said our cities had flouted wisdom and trusted power. Well, you know what power is, don't you?

'Er . . .'

It's *knowledge*, Aula. And knowledge is power, I say, remembering an old book on philosophy that Mathilde gave me. **They've been trying to tell us from the beginning. You were right. Knowledge . . . it's good to have it but it's not the same as wisdom. Knowledge is about certainty. Wisdom is . . . I don't know . . . it's about *living*.**

A smile spreads across her face.

We stay there, just thinking for a moment, I'm suddenly so tired. But there's that sound . . . that knocking . . . I have a sudden uneasy feeling that I'm not imagining it. I'm about to ask Aula if she hears it too when she says, 'Joomia. Look at the light.'

I turn my head. The light is twisting, writhing and splitting, as if it's being forced into a smaller shape. It expands, and then shrinks, getting smaller with every cycle. Then, with a sound like a muffled explosion, it goes out.

A wet, flapping noise follows, and then a slap as something lands on the floor of branches some feet away.

A book. Just like any other book. A little dusty. A little dog-eared.

But there is it is. Lying flat on the floor.

Waiting for one of us to walk forward and pick it up.

Aula

Before either of us can move, the walls begin to glow.

I stand bolt upright. 'What's happening?'

There's a sound like leaves underfoot, and an echo of a voice, and then two figures peel away from the wall, almost as if they'd been there the whole time.

There's a long pause, in which Ade struggles to her feet and leans against the wall, while Nadrik's eyes dart around the cave. He sees Joomia and then me and then he sees the book.

Before I can even get my mind around what the hell they're doing here, he moves.

Ade tries to catch hold of his robes, but they slip through her hands. Joomia is faster than me. She calls the branches

334

nearest to her, and they come: swift as rivers, pooling around the book and rising to form a cage around it, just in time for me to dive for him, knocking him sideways. He collapses under me, for once unprepared for my strength.

But he's not down for long; the edges of him shimmer, and he rolls backwards, flipping himself upright and aiming an orb of energy at my head in the same movement.

I twist in time to feel it clip my shoulder and thrust my heel into the wood beneath me. The shock wave ricochets outward, and Nadrik stumbles, his foot sinking into a gap between the lattice of branches, which close around his ankle.

Joomia's turn. She flattens herself on the ground, closes her eyes.

Nadrik's pulling himself free just as the ominous crack of falling wood resonates around us. He stares down at his toes and discovers they are now wooden, the grooves of bark tracing halfway up his calf. His mouth hardens. He gestures, the air hisses, and Joomia has to roll out from two of his attacks. The third one hits the roots covering the book and they burst open like rotten fruit.

I feel all of us take a breath.

Then Nadrik's diving, and I see Joomia pause, waiting for her moment. But I can't let her – despite everything, I can't let her destroy him. I'm running to meet him. For a moment we're airborne and then I'm throwing him with all my might.

He skids, then he's rolling like a boulder, and colliding with Ade. When he stops, he has her neck tight in the crook of his arm, his other hand out flat against the floor.

'*STOP!*' he demands.

All of us freeze, full of harsh breathing and flickering eyes.

'How,' I pant, 'did you get in here?'

Ade points to herself, wheezing.

Any point in asking why you brought *him*? Joomia asks, glaring at Nadrik.

He smiles. 'My passage here for the memories. Quite a desperate trade, even for her, but why don't we make a day of it?' He points. 'Her life for the book. *Give it to me.*'

Joomia turns to me with a hopeless expression.

'You know what,' I whisper. 'It would've been great if we'd been the ruthless kind of Chosen One who would've just let their mother die to get their hands on that thing.'

It would make things easier, wouldn't it? Joomia murmurs.

I stamp over to pick up the book from the ruin of the branches.

Ade is shaking her head. 'Listen, girls. I don't come back from this. Seen it. Doesn't matter.'

'Prophecies en't the same as facts,' I say.

'Doesn't matter.'

I throw the book at Nadrik's feet, shaking my head. 'Yeah, it does.'

'No!' Ade shouts. 'No! No!'

But Nadrik has released her and shoved her at Joomia and then the book is in his hands and he's feeling its spine, tracing its cover. He takes a breath, and looks up, as if he's heard the answer to a prayer.

His fingers fumble, perhaps with nerves, but he does it.

The pages peel apart, and the book lies open in his hands.

The Chosen

Beyond the cave walls, Taurus goes to sit further down the tunnel, trying to clear his mind. We watch him curiously. What now?

We can tell he doesn't want to try to break the crystal on Nadrik's circlet. Doesn't want the certainty of it being impossible. It occurred to him the second he picked it up that crystal is the one of the hardest materials on Erthe. He can almost see the memories hidden in the facets, imagines them squirming like tadpoles against their prison.

So *this* was what Aula was talking about. This is what it feels like when responsibility weighs down on you like rocks. The only thing more frightening than not doing anything is doing something and failing.

What do I do what do I do what do I do?

Without Joomia, without Etain, he's nothing.

He's not a magi, he's not a leader, he's not a prophet. He's certainly not a Chosen One. A hell of a lot of use a compass is when it doesn't know which way to turn. But he holds Aula's words in his head like a tallow in the dark. He sighs, suddenly angry at himself. *Sit up. Get up.* Do *something*.

He rubs his face, feeling stubble scratch against his palms; dirt and sweat crumble into his fingers. Then he crosses to the circlet where it lies on the ground and stamps down hard. He lifts his foot, not aware that he was holding his breath until it trails out of him in defeat. Because, of course, the crystal is still intact.

He tries the other foot.

He tries slamming the jewel against the wall of the cave

with the heel of his hand. He drags it back and forth across the rock of the floor. He uses the pommel of a knife strapped to his ankle. He even tries offering it to the arch of Ariadnis.

Finally he puts the circlet down next to him and lets out a shaky, despairing breath and tries to convince himself that there will be a way he hasn't thought of yet. But he is all alone, and all the people he cares about are either dead or far away.

It isn't until his tears have stopped that he has the memory of his mother, holding him against her when he was sick or sleepless or sad. She used to hum a song, and it always used to make him feel better. He thinks of Etain, how they'd sung together on the stairs just yesterday. He tries to remember Ashir's song now. How did it go?

He mumbles the tune under his breath, and for some reason, even that quiet sound comforts him. It comes back to him then, and he sings it, clear and true. It hurts his throat on the way out, but the longer he holds the notes for, the better he feels.

He's halfway through when he notices the crystal shaking on the floor.

He stops singing, and it stops trembling at the same moment.

Fumbling, he picks the song up again, focusing carefully on each note, trying to make it come out as pure as his tired lungs can manage.

The crystal trembles. And it trembles.

Keep singing, Taurus tells himself. *Keep singing*.

He does, and though his throat is cracked already from

lack of sleep and sadness and doubt, he sings the song, over and over and over.

There's a sound. He looks down. The crystal has cracked. Just a tiny hairline fracture, but as his voice continues the melody, it spreads further along the facets.

Good enough, he thinks. And he picks up the circlet and smashes it down once more.

The memories, when they pour from the broken shards, are as beautiful as fish and brighter than the mineral in the walls. He watches in awe as they spiral out in every direction, hundreds and hundreds of them – more than he would have dreamed. They are free now: floating in the air, flickering and darting around him. He expected them to take off immediately – perhaps sensing the minds they have been torn from by some instinct. But they remain clustered like grazing animals, lolling peaceably in the air, as if they had forgotten themselves, forgotten their purpose and where they are supposed to be.

Hesitantly Taurus gets to his feet and walks a little way down the tunnel towards Metis, wondering if he should herd them somehow. Wondering if it's possible.

He gets a shock when he turns and sees them following him, still lazily turning in the air. His heart gives a leap. He jogs backwards a few paces to see what will happen. The memories give a sudden burst of speed, stopping only when he stops. With a laugh, he turns and runs down the passage, faster and faster, careening on the loose bits of shale, throwing himself round corners, watching out of the corner of his eye to make sure they're following.

They are.

The compass, he thinks, and his heart is soaring.

Aula

At first, nothing happens, and I'm almost about to laugh, cos I'd like it to be that: the biggest anti-climax in history. But I'm wrong. I'm dead wrong.

I watch, horrified, as his eyes roll back in his head, as his fingers clench as if glued to the binding; as he lets out a scream and falls backwards.

He hits his head on the rock, but his scream goes on and on – his hands still clasping the pages. And then the lights come. They punch out of every crevice in the cliff and the cave around us – great torrents of light like tiny rivers all being sucked in, going on for ever. The cave begins to quake then, as hard as the pillar of Athenas shook before it fell.

My eyes stream against the brightness; my jaw is rattling. I reach for Ade and Joomia and wonder how the hell we're gonna get out of this one.

Nadrik writhes and jerks on the ground. My traitor heart twinges and before I can stop myself I'm saying, 'We gotta stop it! It's gonna kill him!'

I run to him, and try and take the book, but I'm thrown back before I've so much as laid a finger on it. Ade and Joomia help me up.

'Can't,' Ade says.

'Why not?'

'The book,' she says, and I can barely hear her over the thunder and lightning sounds of the cave collapsing. 'Book

340

meant for Chosen Ones. He . . . not Chosen.'

The rotten smell is overpowering now. I can taste it in the air.

'Nothing left to save,' Ade says, and I can see the scars around her eyes flashing white. 'Cities will crumble. Rot in mind and in matter.'

We've got to— Joomia stops talking as the streams of light begin to die out and the brightness is not so impossible. Nadrik's screaming lowers in pitch too; it becomes a gargle, and then it stops altogether, and all I can see is his eyes shut tight, and his chest heaving like a dog panting in the sun.

'Is he going to die?' I ask, but no one has time to answer me. Cos the next second his eyes are open and they're filled with a blinding light, and so is his mouth, and it's radiating out of him, and he's rising from the floor . . .

And, of course, that's the moment the roof of the cave begins to fall.

Joomia

Ade and I crouch beside Aula who shields us as best she can as the first shower of crumbling pebbles and dust and rotting root hits. I glance over at Nadrik, hoping that maybe he'll get hit by the debris – maybe that will stop the spell too – but the light, which seems to be coming even from under his skin now, appears to be protecting him.

What do we have to do? I ask. **What can we do to stop it?**

But I'm not expecting an answer. Not really. I reach for Aula's hand around Ade.

341

'This en't it!' Aula roars. 'It can't be! It en't over!'

Ade's hand pulls my head close. 'Listen, girl. Listen to me.'

I'm listening, I say, but distractedly.

'Unite,' she says. 'Unite.'

OK, Ade, I say, desperately wishing for something more than a word. I clench my teeth, straining to think. I look up at the ceiling of the cave as millennia of rock are shaken away. Ade moans beside me, covering her face with her hands. I close my eyes, and I see our two cities. Separate. And I hear Ade's voice again: *You were dead when you came out of me. Ashir knew you were dead, but she was trying to get you to breathe. You wouldn't.* Something slams open in my head like a trapdoor.

We're the same. We're the same person, I whisper.

Aula's head, which has been bowed in defeat, snaps up again. 'So?'

If you do not unite before your eighteenth birthday, I say. **Aula. Don't you see? The trees . . . and us . . .**

But I'm rambling, and she looks confused.

Shaking, I hold up two fingers, and twine them together. I watch it dawning on her – fear and confusion and hope all at once.

'We . . . we become one again?'

'Two cities. Two Chosen Ones. Uniting. One,' Ade says.

'But how?' Aula asks. There are tears on her face but I don't think she knows it.

There's no time. No time, no time, no time.

Ramon's face.

The trees, singing.

342

And the emptiness, pulling at the threads of me.

The Chosen

When Taurus reaches the battle, the memories disperse, shooting away towards the people to whom they belong. There's a brief flare of light as each memory connects with its owner then disappears without a trace.

The citizens of Athenas and Metis blink, shake themselves, stare at the scene around them. And then Taurus is among them. 'That way! That way! You need to get out of here! ETAIN!'

Etain turns. When she sees her brother, relief and exhaustion nearly take her feet out from under her. She stops singing at last and closes the last few feet between them.

'I thought . . .'

'I'm OK. Etain, your shoulder . . .'

She shakes her head, though her eyes are glazed in pain.

'We'll fix it. We need to get them out!' she says, voice raw. 'Get them across the bridge!'

Taurus nods, turning to yell and beckon the people in the right direction: but the prophets are already leading the way, and the citizens of both cities are following.

'Let's go,' he whispers.

Taurus and Etain are the last across the bridge. They hear the thunderous sound of rock breaking. They hear the branches of Metis stirring and the roots of Athenas waking. They look back.

There's one last moment of silence, and then everything explodes into motion.

Inside Ariadnis, the branches of Metis come to the Chosen Ones, shooting out of every crack in the floor; the roots of Athenas arch down, melding and twisting. And the cliff collapses. Rock cracks and tumbles, the metal casing the trunks of Athenas screaming as they split apart.

The world opens up below, and Joomia can see the familiar trees that make up her home growing towards her, twigs and leaves outstretched as if in welcome.

There are seconds for Aula and Joomia to hold on to their mother, and then they push her outwards and down: she tumbles along a branch, and then she's airborne, plummeting down to the ground.

The Chosen Ones call the branches to them, forming a protective knot around themselves and Nadrik. Everywhere is the sound of joining – of growing wood, of creaking boughs and slithering tendrils wrapping around each other.

And then the roof of the cliff splits too and sunlight comes pouring in, the most beautiful thing that either Aula or Joomia has ever seen.

Nadrik opens his eyes and sees the outlines of his daughters shiver. He blinks. Is he seeing this?

Athenas and Metis. They are joining.

Aula

The trees keep growing, together now, melded. And the sky

344

rushes towards us. I'm sure I could touch the clouds streaked across it.

I can see the sea, and the wind is in my face, in my hair. Out of the corner of my eye, I see my toes sink into the tree we're standing on, and wood grain forms on my feet. On Joomia's, next to mine. My hand is sweaty in hers, and I hold on to it, on to this last minute of feeling, of being me and alive. With our free hands we gesture left and right and the branches close in around us.

Nadrik stirs again, and the bluish light around him dims slightly as he turns his head. He looks at me. The light goes out.

'Aula?' His gaze flickers. 'And Joomia.'

He lifts one hand, and the book falls; the wind whips it out of our wooden cage and I hear its empty pages flapping like a bird's wing. All the wisdom is gone. It's in him now. He's still looking at us as Joomia calls the knotted branches around us to pull in tighter. I can only just make out the sunlight now through one of the gaps.

The vines slither over Nadrik, pressing him against the bark around us. He begins to transform instantly, starting from where Joomia changed his foot into wood, the grains sketching themselves fast against his legs. It's over his hands in seconds.

I begin to cry. 'I'm sorry,' I whisper. 'I'm sorry.'

Joomia

In the end, it turns out to be the emptiness – the ache – that

345

joins us. Surrender to it, open it wide, take away the door, and everything left just pours into one another, like removing a dam from a river.

I feel the moment our joined hands become one, just as bark traces itself over Nadrik's stunned face. His lips form a whorl, his eyes become hollows in the wood, his hair a mass of twigs. The tree has him then, and it's still growing, and he disappears inside.

It's just us left. But my left hand is gone. And my right. And I don't know whether that's my knee or her knee, my face or hers.

Our hair is whipped by the wind, red and brown—

The Chosen

For a moment, there is just one girl, standing on the tallest of the rapidly twining, growing trees.

She looks up and around at the world as though she has never seen it. The wood grain grows up her thighs, her chest turns to bark, and her face is frozen in an expression of boundless curiosity and wonder.

The cage of branches closes in around her.

And that's all, but it's enough.

63 Days After

The cliff, and Ariadnis, and the broken trees of Athenas are all gone, but so are the trees that were recognisable as Metis. There remain nine trees, as new and green and untouched by people as the original ones were when Lore and Kreywar first came to this island. But they are not like trees anyone has ever seen before. These trees wear the bark and the branches and the roots of another set of trees, like a web of connective tissue. They link them all: High, Low, Black, White, Wide, Bright, Wise, Sap and Knot, so that no tree can be differentiated from the other. Stronger together.

The biggest change, though, is this:

Sometimes, when the wind is up and the air tastes like the salt of the sea, the trees go silent.

Of course, all trees are quiet – but this is different. It's the quiet of someone listening. Of someone waiting for you to begin your tale, your adventure, your story. It's the quiet of patience and interest.

So the people of Athenas and Metis talk. They talk to the trees. And, after a pause, the trees – the leaves and the branches, the twigs and the bark – begin to talk back. Not with words, or with pictures or even actual messages – but somehow, after the people have asked the trees a question or told them a particularly interesting bit of news, a suggestion seems to bloom in their minds. Nothing fully formed, but a hint, a push in the direction they need to be pushed in. The trees offer their wisdom, and in return the people tell the trees their stories.

The people begin to ask specific questions:

'How should I plant this flower?'

'What should I teach my children?'

'When is it best to set off for the ocean?'

'What should I do? How do I lead them now?'

These last questions are Etain's, and she asks them now, over and over in her head, as the meeting goes on below her.

'Just say what it is you have to say, Einar,' Taurus is saying.

Einar sighs and rests his head on his clenched knuckles. 'We can't go on like this. We need to move back to the city.'

There are a number of them there, in a clearing high up on the island, a decent distance from the cave and the campsite where they've made shelters. Etain is sitting in the crook of a tree and staring out across the island at the place that used to be their home. Gathered around her are the Elders of Metis, minus Mathilde; the Prophets of Athenas, minus Ashir and Igra; and members of the Athenasian government, minus Nadrik.

Like the rest of the people that Etain and Taurus have saved, they are still in awe of the feat their new leader and her brother pulled off. Thanks to them, among the many who lost their minds to Nadrik: Lear can be a calming presence on Etain's council and Oriha can help with weaving shelters; a man from Athenas can sit in camp with his son, Sander, and wonder if he was right about that girl after all. But their wonder does not eclipse their frustrations at Etain's apparent need to make no decisions at all. Several of them are nodding and murmuring at Einar's suggestion, until Etain cuts them off.

'There en't any cities any more,' she says. 'They're gone.'

'Then, My Lady,' says Thetea, an Athenasian minister, 'we must begin to make our new home here.'

Etain looks scandalised. 'We en't *staying* here.'

'Then where?' snaps Janaelle. 'Where are we supposed to go? What are we supposed to do?'

These are the questions that have been on everyone's lips for weeks – and at the pronouncement of them, a furious storm of more questions, suggestions and accusations rise up out of them all like angry bees:

'The prophets tell us you were destined to lead us. We need you to *lead*.'

'Or if you don't *want* to lead, at least let us elect someone else—'

'Your ma wouldn't have liked this, Etain—'

'Never should have listened—'

'She's just too scared—'

'Arrogant, more like—'

'How are we supposed to keep going like this?'

'*I don't know!*' Etain barks. She cuts into the following hush by jumping out of the tree. 'I don't know, all right? I *told* you I wasn't sure if I should lead, but *you* all voted. You voted, and you chose me, and *here* I am and I'm telling you, I dunno yet. So either elect someone else or give me some *time* to think!' She sprints off through the crowd, knocking into shoulders and stumbling away into the trees.

Taurus glares around at them all before striding after her. He follows her down the cliff paths, down past the place where Joomia made the prophets a bridge to cross into Low Tree. It is not there now, but nothing about these trees is the same.

Etain waits for him before she steps off the cliff paths to the ground, and together they walk among the roots of what used to be their homes, craning their necks to look up, through the layers and layers of sun-dappled leaves.

For a while, they just walk in silence, but eventually Taurus asks, 'Why won't you bring us back here, Etain?'

'It just feels like the same mistake again,' she says.

'But it's our home,' he says.

'The *island* was our home, and we ended up getting trapped here by Lore and Kreywar when we couldn't stop fighting over what to do with it. I *want* to bring them back here, but what if there are arguments about how we should live again? I can't stop wars, Taurus, I can't. I'm just one person.'

'Aula believed in you,' he says.

'Aula is *gone!*' she shouts. 'Aula is gone and Joomia is gone and—' She stops and presses her fingers to her lips.

He takes a long breath. 'Yeah, I know,' he says, and his voice sounds swollen and raw.

Her thumb is gentle as she wipes a tear from his cheeks. She leans in and rests her forehead lightly on his shoulder. 'I'm sorry,' she says. 'You're the compass. Where is the compass pointing?'

'Here,' he says. 'Here, because we're not two sides any more. Here, because my *bones* are aching for this place. It will be different this time. The trees are listening. It—' But he stops.

350

She looks at him. 'What?'

He moves forward slowly, like a sleepwalker, like a *mindless*. She feels her palms grease with fear.

'Taurus, *what?*'

He points, his mouth slightly open. There is a book lying on the ground, just a few yards away. It's scattered with leaves, and the cover is warped and wrinkled black with mould.

Before she can stop him, he reaches out and flips it open. The pages are blank. They have already begun to decompose.

'He took it all inside him,' sings a familiar voice.

Ade. They've seen her once since the day this all happened, and she said only two words: *My fault.* Before they could ask her anything else, she had gone. Taurus supposes this is where she's been all this time. He thinks . . . he thinks there might be something different about her now. Though her hair is wild and her clothes are torn, she looks less bent over, less grey, somehow. *Because she belongs here*, he thinks, *and so do I*.

'He took it all inside him, all the wisdom, and they bound him inside the trees.'

'Nadrik,' Taurus says, in answer to Etain's questioning eyebrow.

Ade touches the tree trunk and strokes its rough bark. She bites her lip. 'And all that wisdom in him . . . is in the bark and the grain now.' She looks between them. Almost shyly. 'Something to show you,' she says. 'Will you come?'

'Of course,' says Taurus before Etain can utter some excuse.

351

She leads the siblings deeper into the trees, to the tallest of them all, and stops at a point around the base, where the trunk becomes the roots. She points at a huge knot in the bark, twisted in on itself. Taurus feels his heart thudding, though he can't understand why.

'Been getting bigger for days,' Ade says. 'Today, I think . . . I think it might be opening.'

They look at it for a long time; they touch it, probing.

At first, nothing happens, and then Etain grabs Taurus's arm, hard. 'Taurus. Look.'

They stand there, transfixed. As Ade said, the knot is opening.

They wait, without really knowing why. Hours pass, the light growing very dim. Slowly, and then not slowly at all, the knot untwists, becomes a hollow.

But it is not empty.

As it widens, Taurus sinks to his knees and Etain lets out a sob and Ade laughs, her eyes as bright as one who never saw the future.

Because there's a young woman there. Curled up like a child. She has tawny skin and reddish brown hair; she's freckled and naked as a nymph.

'My girl,' Ade says, as if this was eighteen years ago and she had just birthed her, squalling, into the world.

There's a pause, as long a heartbeat. As long as a lifetime.

And then the girl in the hollow of the tree stirs, and opens her eyes.

Acknowledgements

Thank you to:

My family: Mum and Dad, for a whole multitude of things but particularly for always letting me be myself and always saying *go for it*. Daile, who is always proud of me. Tilda and Phoebe for your wicked smiles and for all the love. Ferg for solidarity and listening when it counts.

Moll for always being my hero.

Granny, thank you for reading me Hans Christian Andersen picture books when I was little.

Rachel Faulkner, who edited *Ariadnis* with such an incredible understanding of who I was and what *it* was that I thought we might be sharing a brain. Silvia Molteni, who *loved it first* and spirited me so quickly into the hands of the Quercus Team. Thanks for your patience waiting for me to finish and for being so enthusiastic about all the subsequent drafts!

Lynda Nichols, The Best English Teacher in All the World and a very inspiring lady.

Helena Pielichaty, for showing an incredible belief in thirteen-year-old me and for genuinely setting me on this path.

The incredible Julia Green, and all the tutors at the Writing For Young People MA at Bath Spa. Particular thanks to Steve Voake for chatting to me on the drive home and for championing my story and being such a fantastic teacher. Lucy Christopher, you told me to start again with the characters and it *worked*. Thank you. My FANTASTIC Writing Group: Sharon, Chris, Mary, Cinders and Yael. You are such incredible writers, inspiring critique partners and (more importantly) wonderful people.

Hannah, Izzy and Aimee. Without you I would wilt and other gross over-simplifications.

Early Readers, particularly Becka, Yael, Jenny, Rosey, Doug and Cerise.

To all my Somerset pals and various adopted families, who supported and encouraged and asked me how it was going. My lovely London Family, and Ye Olde Brutonites, you are the best at parties and dancing and making me laugh.

P.S. Jess Appleton, you asked me in the library one time if you could be in the acknowledgements. CONSIDER THIS ME FOLLOWING THROUGH.

After it is done, there was a girl.
I Saw the girl who would lead the people,
and I Saw the boy who would be her compass.

ANASSA

COMING 2018